YOU WON'T SEE ME COMING

YOU WON'T SEE ME COMING

KRISTEN ORLANDO

Swoon Reads | NEW YORK

A Swoon Reads Book
An Imprint of Feiwel and Friends and Macmillan Publishing Group, LLC
175 Fifth Avenue, New York, NY 10010

Our books may be purchased in bulk for promotional, educational, or business use. Please
contact your local bookseller or the Macmillan Corporate and Premium Sales Department at
(800) 221-7945 ext. 5442 or by email at MacmillanSpecialMarkets@macmillan.com.

Library of Congress Control Number: 2018945048

ISBN 9781250123633 (hardcover) / ISBN 9781250123640 (ebook)

Book design by Vikki Sheatsley and Eileen Savage

First edition, 2019

1 3 5 7 9 10 8 6 4 2

swoonreads.com

To Dad:
Thank you for reading every single
word I've ever written. I'm so grateful.

YOU
WON'T
SEE
ME
COMING

ONE

I'VE COME TO HATE MY HANDS. I USED TO JUST THINK they were ugly. My palms, too big. My fingers, too short. My skin, too wrinkly. Freak hands, I used to joke. I don't make jokes about my hands now. When I stare down at them, I still see his blood. Blazing red ovals with tiny tails on my fingernails, knuckles, and wrists. The rational side of me knows it's gone. Washed away in a tiny bathroom sink at thirty thousand feet, Santino Torres's DNA circling the drain somewhere over the Indian Ocean. Still, if the light is right, I see it, freckling my skin.

The bell at the front door of the bookshop jingles, breaking my zombie-like trance. I shake my head, clearing my mind, and my hands begin to move again, searching for a book Bird Lady asked us to order. She has a name: Dorothy. But she has one singular passion in life: birds. She loves birds so much that she wears broaches with pictures of her pet birds on them. Her purse is covered in colorfully stitched birds. Her winter scarf, again: birds. I've been living here for only a few weeks, but in a town as small as Manchester,

1

Vermont, you get to know the locals pretty fast. I'm told Manchester is packed with New Yorkers and Bostonians with vacation houses in the summer and tourists for the leaves in the autumn. But come winter, as the temperatures dip and snow begins to fall, the volume of visitors fades and we're left alone with the bitter cold and the townsfolk.

"Olivia, did you find it yet?" Bird Lady's coarse voice asks from behind me. My shoulders tense, still uneasy with the sound of my new name.

I've been a dozen different Reagans. Reagan Bailey. Reagan Schultz. Reagan MacMillan. But with Fernando searching for me, eager to put a bullet in my skull, the Black Angels said keeping my first name was no longer an option. Staying any version of my former self was far too dangerous. Before, I would have kicked and screamed over losing my name. But now, I just don't care. With each new identity and cover story, I used to keep pieces of Reagan Elizabeth Hillis behind the pretender mask. I weaved my true self into the girl I was instructed to become. But not now. The girl I was before is disappearing. And I doubt she's ever coming back.

"Just about," I answer and clear my throat. I lift the lid of one more box and flip through all our recent orders. Finally, I find it. I pull out the latest edition of the *Field Guide to North American Birds* and turn back around to face Bird Lady.

"I certainly hope the shop didn't give my copy away," Bird Lady says playfully, her wrinkles deepening around her mouth.

"Of course not, Dorothy," I reply with a small smile and hand her the book. "We didn't even put it out on the shelves. We saved it especially for you."

"Well, it's not really for me," she answers and pulls open her wallet. It has birds all over it. Of course. "It's for my youngest grand-daughter for Christmas. She's ten. I hope she'll like it."

"I'm sure she'll just love it," I reply as sweetly as possible and plaster a fake smile on my face (my cheeks ache at the end of a shift from all the forced glee) as I scan the book and begin to ring her up. "That will be twenty-three dollars and forty-nine cents."

"Here you go, dear." Bird Lady hands me her credit card, which I swipe and hand back to her. The printer whines and spits out a receipt.

"I hope you have a great evening," I say and hand her a plastic green-and-white Manchester Book Loft bag with the present for her granddaughter tucked inside.

"You too," Bird Lady replies and wags her bony finger at me. "Now don't work too hard."

"I'll try," I answer with an artificial laugh and watch as Bird Lady slowly walks across the store, out the front door, and into the snowy, dark night.

I glance down at my mother's watch ticking away on my wrist: 9:57. Nearly closing time. I scan the lower floor of the bookstore. It's empty. "O Tannenbaum" from *A Charlie Brown Christmas* plays over the speakers; each cheerful strike of the piano keys makes my heart heavier, my mood darker. Christmas used to be my favorite time of year. Not just because of the carols and presents and lights, the general merriness that comes with the holiday season. I used to love Christmas because it meant my parents were home. With their seniority, they were able to request the days around Christmas off and, unless it was a true emergency, they were almost never called away.

We had our little traditions for that week. We'd make Christmas cookies using twenty-year-old cookie cutters, and Dad would make fun of the crooked candy canes and the blobs that were supposed to be Santa Claus. Then Mom would yell at him for licking red and green dyed icing off of his fingers before touching other cookies, spreading his germs everywhere. Aunt Sam would come over to try to put together gingerbread houses, but they were always disasters, falling down or having the candy picked off of cookie rooftops within the first twenty-four hours of construction. Mom would make us string popcorn for the Christmas tree and I'd always whine and say we should just buy strings of little gold beads and call it a day. "You'll miss these moments when you're grown up," my mother used to say. I'd roll my eyes when she'd turn her back and think *yeah right.* But I'd do just about anything to have those moments back. This will be my second Christmas without my mother. My first without Dad. He's still so angry with me, I doubt I'll even get a phone call. Even if he wasn't so irate with me, the Black Angels would never allow him to visit me for the holiday. I must stay hidden. I must remain a ghost.

I clear my throat, lost memories stinging at my eyes. I try to push back the sorrow that's crept out of its little box, flooding my bloodstream and leaving my layered body cold. I shove my hands into the pockets of my jeans and dig my fingers into my hipbones, redirecting the ache. The threatening gloom retreats, tucking itself back where it belongs. I don't deserve to feel sad.

I did this myself.

"Olivia, you ready to go?" my manager, Adam, calls to me as he emerges from behind a row of cookbooks. He's twenty-six with a law degree from Columbia but opted out of taking the bar exam. He gave up an almost guaranteed partnership at his dad's prestigious Manhattan law firm to move to Vermont and start a very different life. I feel like there's a lot of that up here. People who leave behind lives of privilege to make cheese or blow glass or something. Smaller paychecks but a simpler, happy life. And with its sweeping mountain views and postcard-worthy quaintness, I can see why so many give up everything for peace in the Green Mountain State.

"Yeah, let me just close out," I say and punch a few buttons into the register, locking it with a key for the night.

"Ben's waiting for you," Adam says, and my shoulders flinch beneath my thick sweater once again. I'll never get used to his new name either.

"Okay. Your key, good sir," I say and hand over the key to the downstairs register. For being in a small town, the Manchester Book Loft is quite expansive, with two floors, a large café that serves delicious goodies, and lots of quirky nooks where customers can hide out and get lost in a good book.

"Let's get out of here before the snow really starts coming down," Adam says, flipping off the light behind me. With a curly mop of blond hair and an easy smile, Adam looks like a cherub. I'm kind of surprised he doesn't have wings coming out of his flannel button-down shirts. That baby face is the current catch of Manchester that every single girl (and divorced cougar) has her eye on.

I follow Adam through the store, turning out lights one by one.

When I reach the Young Adult section, I catch my distorted reflection, the light inside creating an imperfect mirror against the dark window. It takes all my energy to repress the shiver crawling up my vertebrae. I barely recognize myself. My long dark hair has been chopped into a bob and dyed honey blond. I'm a horrible-looking blond, and I hate maintaining this modern Barbie hairstyle. The worst part is bleaching my dark eyebrows, trying to make this new me look somewhat natural. I avoid mirrors. The acid in my stomach roils every time I see myself. Just another reminder of why I'm here. What I've lost.

What I've done.

"Liv," Adam's voice calls out to me from the last dark room.

"Coming," I say and flip off the light. My ghostly reflection disappears.

I walk past the magazine display, past a pair of comfy, worn couches, and up three small steps that lead into the café.

"Hello, love," a voice says once I reach the top. I look up to see the new version of Luke smiling at me. His beautiful blond hair has been trimmed short and dyed a dark brown (lots of hair dye under our bathroom sink). He's even started wearing colored contacts, turning his two pools of cornflower blue a muddy brown. The only pieces that remain of the Ohio boy I fell for are his dimples.

"Hi, babe," I reply and lean in for a quick kiss, the scruff of his threatening five o'clock shadow (which he has to shave daily since it's so much lighter than his hair) scratching my face. "You make out okay?"

"Sold out of all my apple crumb bars," he responds sweetly and pulls my body in for a side hug. I wrap my arms around his waist and take in his scent. He smells like coffee and powdered sugar from a twelve-hour shift working in the bakery and café section of the bookstore. I never learned to cook. I thought I'd never need to. I was supposed to be a Black Angel: my days spent rescuing hostages, taking down terrorists, and arresting drug kingpins. But Luke is a master in the kitchen. His mother is an amazing baker. He spent hours with her, melting chocolate for triple-chocolate-chip cookies and kneading dough for pies. So when it came to finding a real job, he was easy. But I didn't have much to offer the real world. I mean, if someone needs a swift kick to the face or a quick and clean execution, I'm your girl. But starting a hit man business while trying to hide out is probably not the best-laid plan in the world.

"Here, let me help you with your coat," Luke says as I slip my arms through my camel-colored peacoat.

"Ben, you guys working tomorrow?" asks Imogene as she throws on her blue puffy winter jacket. She pulls her long, dark hair out of the neck of her coat and zips it up over her petite frame. She's one of the baristas in the Book Loft café and makes one hell of a cappuccino, complete with decorative foam hearts or leaves or flowers.

"Yeah, we're both on for tomorrow," Luke responds and pulls me into his body again, giving me a kiss on the forehead as the four of us walk out of the warm bookstore and into a chilly December night.

"You two have a great evening," Adam says as he locks the front door of the now dark Manchester Book Loft. "Shit, I forgot to turn off the Christmas music."

"That's okay. The books love *A Charlie Brown Christmas*," Imogene says with a throaty laugh.

"Screw it," Adam says and puts the key in his pocket. "See you guys tomorrow."

"Have a good one," Luke says cheerfully as he takes my gloved hand into his own. We walk in silence to our car, parked two blocks away, and I relish these quiet minutes. Fat snowflakes cascade down from a black sky, like falling stars, filling the dark trees and carpeting the sidewalk with their brightness. The spruce trees near the bookstore are wrapped in old-fashioned Christmas lights. Bright bulbs blink red, yellow, green, and blue. Garland is wrapped around store windows and a wreath hangs on nearly every door. Twinkle lights hug thin parkway trees and thick felt red ribbons are tied into perfect bows on every light post. It's like walking onto the set of a Hallmark Christmas movie, but without the hollow buildings and paper snow.

We approach Charlie's, a popular bar with the locals, and my stomach begins to knot with what's next. Our turn is coming up. In ten seconds, we'll be out of sight of Imogene and Adam.

In ten seconds, the show's over.

I breathe in the cold night air and it stings against the delicate flesh of my lungs like a warning. We pass by Charlie's front door. It opens and the sound of clinking glasses and AC/DC's "Thunderstruck" fills the quiet. We turn the corner, off the main street, and like clockwork, Luke drops my hand. No, doesn't drop. More like heaves it back to me. The boy from the bookstore disappears, his smile replaced by a scowl. His eyes angry, lips tight, and dimples gone until the next day when he has to throw a phony smile my way while we work. Pretend we're a couple. Make believe that we're happy.

I look up at him with wounded eyes, missing his hand in mine. Even if it's all for show. He can feel my eyes on him. I know it. He shoves his hands into the pockets of his heavy coat and stares straight ahead, his face far icier than Vermont's below freezing temperatures. I thread my rejected fingers through my other hand, filling the space where his palm used to be. I take in a bottomless breath, preparing myself for another evening of tense silence. And I deserve it. I deserve his anger, his borderline-hatred. Because I didn't ruin just one life. I've ruined two. Without consideration. And without his permission.

I lie in bed at night, trying to come up with things to say to him. I run through apologies, scenarios where I beg for his forgiveness. But I have yet to say those words out loud. I'm too afraid of what he'll say. Because I know what I've done is unforgivable.

The Reagan I was before may be fading, evaporating into the air, piece by broken piece. But the beautiful boy I fell for is truly gone.

For good.

TWO

THE LIGHTS OF OUR SUV POINT DOWN THE TWISTING
road that leads to our small house in the woods. Luke doesn't speak
to me during our fifteen-minute drive from downtown Manchester
to our two-bedroom cottage in Rupert, a city that makes Manchester
look like a thriving metropolis. The only true "businesses" in Rupert
are a general store, a one-room post office, and a dairy farm with an
honor system payment policy for its milk, homemade ice cream,
and fresh cheese. More people are probably buried in the cemetery, a
five-minute walk from our driveway, than living in the blink-and-
you'll-miss-it village. But it's safe. Or at least safer than being back in
DC with the Black Angels. Not that we had much choice in the
matter.

After our frantic escape from Indonesia, we were flown to a top
secret Black Angels base just outside of Portland, Maine, where we
were ordered to change our appearance while senior leaders back
at CORE figured out what to do with their two rebel trainees. I
pleaded with the leaders over a video conference call not to punish

Luke. Told them he didn't want to go rogue. That he was just trying to keep me alive. I begged them to let him back into Qualifiers. To give him a chance at making the training academy and becoming a Black Angel. But it was too late. His face was captured on the security camera in Torres's SUV at the warehouse. His name was already burned into Fernando's brain. He didn't execute one of the drug world's most vicious leaders. I did. But it didn't matter. Luke was standing beside me while I pulled the trigger. And now he was just as wanted, just as hunted, as me.

Some of the senior leaders voted to kick us out completely. Give us new identities and let us fend for ourselves. They argued I'd been given chance after chance, yet continually spit in the face of their Directives and procedures. Some said I didn't deserve protective custody. But at the end of the day, I'm still Jonathan Hillis's daughter. And as pissed as my father was (and still very much is), he pulled every string he could to keep us safe, to get us into the Shadow Program, the Black Angels' version of Witness Protection.

After cutting and dyeing our hair, putting in our colored contacts, and changing our appearance as much as possible, we boarded one more Black Angels jet and were handed two manila envelopes with our new lives sealed inside. Olivia Cooperman. Benjamin Zeligs. High school sweethearts from Philadelphia who decided to take a gap year before attending college. Take a breath in Vermont before life really began. They gave us new driver's licenses, birth certificates, social security numbers, passports, and detailed cover stories that they told us to memorize. We were shuffled off the jet and into a blacked-out van at a private airport near Manchester. A Black Angel watcher I'd never met before escorted us to our safe house in Rupert.

It was stocked with food and money and weapons. Untraceable satellite phones and firewalled computers. A small panic room in the old stone cellar.

"Call Sam for further orders," the Black Angel watcher instructed, handing me a burner cell phone. "Good luck."

And he was gone. We were left alone in the shadow of the Vermont mountains without watchers or the security team I'd grown accustomed to. We'd lost the privilege of round-the-clock protection. I never thought I'd ever describe armed men stalking my every move as a privilege. But as I wait to feel the blade of a knife on my neck or the barrel of a gun at my back, I realize they were exactly that.

Sam instructed us to get jobs in town. Make a couple of friends but to not be overly friendly. To keep up our new appearances. Call CORE only during emergencies. And watch our backs.

"So, we can't even talk anymore?" I said into the burner cell phone on our first night in Rupert, tears tightening my vocal cords as I sat in the kitchen, a gun on the table and snow falling outside.

"No," she answered with a sigh. "At least not often. You should have thought about all this, Reagan."

"I know," I whispered. They were the only words I could force out before hanging up. I couldn't bring myself to say *thank you* or *I'm sorry* or even *good-bye*. I haven't spoken to Sam since.

Luke turns the SUV into our driveway, the gravel crunching beneath its tires, filling the car with its first sounds during our ride. I look over at him as he eases the car into our garage. I glance at him often on these drives, during our forced togetherness, because I know I'll lose him once we get into the house.

My eyes are always desperate, pleading for him to speak to me about something. Anything. Luke only talks to me out of necessity. *We're almost out of toilet paper. Pick up bananas at the store if they look good. Adam said he needs you to close tonight.* These are the little gems I cling to. I answer him eagerly, hungry for more words. But he gives me only what he needs to. Instructions, never conversation.

As he turns off the car, I tear my eyes away from him and reach for the door handle.

"Wait," he reminds me, his hand grabbing at my arm. I look down, staring at his fingers, realizing it's the first time he's touched me when it's not an act. But as he pulls his hand away, I know it's not out of love but rather an unconscious protective habit.

Luke lowers the garage door and watches it close behind us in the rearview mirror before grabbing his gun out of its hiding spot beneath the driver's seat.

"Okay," he instructs and hops out of his side of the car. I do the same. "I think you have a false sense of security living in the middle of nowhere, Reagan. But Fernando could still find us up here. No thanks to you."

His last declaration is wrapped in barbed wire and hurled over his shoulder, catching and tearing at my skin as I follow him into our dimly lit house. It's probably the closest we've come to true dialogue since Indonesia.

And even if every word is painful, I don't want this to stop.

"I know," I answer as I throw my purse on the kitchen table.

"And please stop putting your stuff wherever you feel like it," Luke says, pointing at my purse. "This house is a mess."

"Who are you, my father?" I ask, the words escaping my mouth before my tongue can wrangle them in.

"I'm being far kinder to you than your father would be if he was here right now," Luke answers curtly, walking around the counter and to the fridge in the corner of our small kitchen. He pushes aside cans of Dr Pepper and juice before grabbing a bottle of water.

"I get it. I get how angry you are," I say as he turns around. "But is this how it's going to be for the rest of our lives? I mean, who knows how long we have to hide out up here."

"Not long, I hope," Luke says and takes a swig of water, droplets falling down his chin. He wipes them away with the collar of his navy long-sleeved T-shirt.

"What's that supposed to mean?"

"It means I can't wait to get away from here."

"You mean away from me?"

"I didn't say that," Luke offers unconvincingly.

"You don't have to. It's written all over your face," I say, my chin nodding in his direction. "Look, I can't go back and undo what I've done."

"I don't think you would if you could," Luke responds, brushing past me and walking down the hall. I follow him into our tiny living room.

"You don't think I'd take back killing Torres?" I say, my fingers digging into the center of my chest. "After seeing what it's done to you? Done to us?"

"No, I really don't think you would," Luke answers, shaking his head as he turns on the lamp next to our lumpy gray couch, the

14

luxurious furnishings of Black Angel–sanctioned safe houses long gone. "I think you'd make the exact same choice."

"Luke, how can you say that?"

"How can I not?" Luke says, his eyes narrowed. He looks me up and down, shaking his head. "I begged you to stay in that camp in Indonesia. I pleaded with you on that car ride to apprehend him. I did everything I could to get you to see reason and not to kill Torres. I *knew* what would happen if you shot him and so did you. But you did it anyway. You didn't give a crap about the consequences. Your mission was singular and selfish: kill Torres. That's what it was for a year. You had time to think about it and change your mind. But you *chose* this. You chose to kill him. So don't tell me that you'd take it back if you could. Because I know you. You wouldn't change it. Not for me. Not for anyone."

Luke's words suck out every trace of air in my chest. His words aren't just mean. They're true. I am selfish. It's the unfortunate adjective used to describe me the most. Not brave. Not loyal. Not fearless. Selfish. I only see what's in front of me. What I want. What I need. What I think is right. I ignore everyone trying to turn my head from side to side. I push away their anxious attempts to get me to see the bigger picture, the wide and expansive world beyond my narrow one. It's easy to blame Torres or my mother's death on my selfish behavior. But as I finally suck oxygen into my aching chest I realize, I've always been this way. Even when I thought I was doing good, the end always somehow benefited me.

"I don't know what you want me to say," I reply quietly, holding out my hands in surrender.

"It'd be nice to start with I'm sorry," Luke answers, running his fingers through his dark hair, his muscle memory forgetting just how short he was forced to cut it.

"I'm sure I've said I'm sorry," I say and chew at the inside of my lip.

"No. Not really," Luke says and shakes his head. "I've been waiting for it. But three weeks later and still no sorry."

I stare down at the floor and know he's right. I haven't said it out loud. Only to the Luke in my head. Because sorry has never felt close to good enough. So I've said nothing.

I clear my throat, keep my eyes on the ground, and say, "Of course I'm sorry. But how do you say you're sorry for something like this?"

I feel Luke staring at me. I glance up, still half expecting to be met with his kind blue eyes. But they're just as dark as his mood. My Luke is not in this room. He hasn't changed. I've changed him.

"Listen to other people, Reagan," Luke finally replies softly and turns his back on me. "Then you'll never have to say you're sorry."

"Luke, please don't walk out on me," I call out to him as he climbs up the steep stairs that lead to our two small bedrooms. "Please, stay and talk to me. Let's try to work on this."

"There's nothing to work on," he throws over his shoulder. "I'll pretend to be your boyfriend when we're out in the world for our cover. I'll keep you safe. That's all I can do."

"But Luke . . ." I call after him but he answers me by slamming his bedroom door.

You did this to yourself, Reagan. You did this to yourself.

I lower my body onto our couch, still fully dressed in my coat, hat, and gloves. My body begins to shake even though my blood is burgeoning on searing. The floorboards of our old house creak above my head. I look up and listen as he opens and closes his dresser drawers, changes into his pajamas, the old bed whining beneath him as he climbs under the covers.

"Oh God," I whisper, grasping at my knees, rocking my body back and forth. "What have I done?"

THREE

"LIV, I THOUGHT YOU'D LIKE A SNACK," LUKE SAYS, placing a white dish on the counter next to a stack of books I'm supposed to put away. I carefully move the plate closer to me, trying not to elbow the wobbly tower of discarded holiday gifts customers decide not to purchase once they made it to the register.

"Thank you," I reply and look up at him. He smiles at me for the first time in twenty-four hours. But it's only because Adam is standing a few feet away sorting through store receipts and inventory slips.

"I made extra. I know they're your favorite," Luke adds as I look down at the oversized triple-chocolate-chip cookie. He's right. They are my favorite. I can tell the cookie is still warm without even touching it, its semisweet chocolate chips glistening and melting onto the plate. Perhaps this is more than a cookie. Maybe it's an *I'm sorry*.

"Thanks, babe," I say with a hopeful smile and lean across the countertop to give him a kiss. The moment his cold lips meet mine, my optimism evaporates. It's still a stage kiss. Without feelings or heat or emotion. Purely for show. So I guess the cookie is too. Just another prop in our little play.

"You guys are so cute, I want to puke," Adam jokes beside me, inciting a forced laugh from this show's leading man and leading lady.

"Better get back," Luke says, dusting the flour and powdered sugar off of his green-and-white-striped apron. "Enjoy the cookie."

"I will," I answer with a stage smile and take a bite, the warm chocolate coating my tongue. I watch Luke as he walks away from me. He doesn't look back. He never looks back.

"You guys are obnoxiously adorable," Adam says, eyeing my fake smile as I watch Luke leave. It's early afternoon and the Book Loft is momentarily slow. But soon school will let out and students will fill up the café in search of snacks, hot chocolate, and coffee. The day's gossip will bounce off the walls, ruining the quiet for the retirees who come here to relax and read. "How'd you two meet?"

"Biology class," I answer, sticking to the carefully scripted cover we were told to memorize on the plane. "We were assigned to be lab partners."

"Fell in love while dissecting frogs?" Adam asks, raising an eyebrow.

"Yes," I answer with a genuine laugh. "Nothing says 'let's make out' like the smell of formaldehyde."

Adam chuckles and turns back to his stack of invoices, marking each one with his signature. "You guys are really lucky to have found each other."

"Oh, what are you talking about?" I say and take another bite of my cookie. "You're like Manchester's most eligible bachelor. I bet if we raffled off dates with you we could raise some serious money."

"Ha, maybe," Adam says, looking up from his stack of paperwork, his easy smile sinking. He opens his mouth to say something then closes it.

"What?"

"It's just hard to find something that lasts past Saturday night."

"Those are words to a song from the forties, you know," I say, licking chocolate off of my thumb. "Ever hear of 'Sunday Kind of Love'?"

"I don't think so," Adam says. "Sing it."

"You don't want to hear me sing," I answer awkwardly, a large chunk of cookie in my mouth. I cover my lips with my hand as I swallow it down. "My grandma used to sing it when I was a kid. It's an old jazz standard tune. It goes 'I want a Sunday kind of love / A love to last past Saturday night.'"

"Exactly," Adam says, pointing a finger at me. "The newness is exciting but it'd be nice to have something that's . . . you know . . . comfortable."

"Sweatpants kind of love?" I ask.

"Sweatpants, holey T-shirt, and morning breath kind of love," Adam answers. "They should really add that into the lyrics."

"I don't think 'Morning Breath Kind of Love' would have sold as many records."

"Yeah. Maybe you're right."

Adam smiles at me before looking back down at his paperwork, his grin quickly fading, and his face suddenly sullen and serious.

I study him, lean my elbows against the countertop, and say, "I had you all wrong."

"What do you mean?" Adam asks.

"I don't know," I answer with a shrug. "I guess I thought you'd be more interested in having fun and dating every girl in town than having a girlfriend."

"I'm an old soul, I guess," Adam answers, still shuffling through papers, busying his hands with staples and signatures. "Besides, if I wanted to hook up every weekend, I'd have taken the bar, bought a bunch of two-thousand-dollar suits, and stayed in New York. Believe me, Liv. I'll take what you two have any day."

Adam closes his folder and walks toward his cramped office in the back of the store, leaving me alone with my lies. But for me, I'm not acting. I'm not faking my feelings for Luke. Sometimes, I lose myself in the illusion of our manufactured bliss. I scold myself for forgetting that he's really pretending. He's just trying to stay alive.

The irony is not lost on me. This is exactly the life I dreamed of back in Ohio. The quiet, white picket-fence life my mother told me I wasn't supposed to have. She said I wasn't meant to be happy. I was meant to change the world. Over a year after that last fight in our New Albany living room, I'm so very far from either one.

I catch Luke across the store in the café, pulling out a tray of cookies, getting ready for the afternoon rush. His hand moves across his face, pushing away hair that's no longer there, cut off onto a bathroom floor in Maine. Some tics just don't die.

I miss him. I miss his blond hair and blue eyes. I miss his dimples. The way his cheeks folded almost in half when I made him laugh. I miss the sound of my name on his tongue. My real name.

21

The way he used to touch me on the small of my back. Like I was something precious. Something to care for. Something to love.

Luke turns around, smiling at Imogene, and my blood chills, my heart slows. My body returns to its default state of numb.

———•◦•———

At the end of every shift, fifteen minutes before closing time, my stomach predictably tightens into an uneasy knot. There's an old clock with a bell tower at the Presbyterian church down the street. Its bells sing out the Westminster Chimes at the top of each hour, and clang once, twice, and three times to mark each quarter hour.

At 9:44, my skin begins to ache, like I know the three bells and a night of icy silence are coming. But tonight, my skin pricks ten minutes earlier than normal. Those imaginary pins penetrate my spine, an unconscious warning. At first, I wait to hear the clangs. But when the bells don't come, I slowly turn around and see a pair of dark eyes watching me from across the store. When my eyes lock with his, I expect him to look away. He doesn't. He's standing near the magazines, a copy of *GQ* open in his hands. But he's still staring. I examine his face, categorizing each feature. A paranoid twitch from my Black Angel upbringing. Five foot ten. Dark hair. Dark eyes. Fair skin. Strong jaw. Mid-twenties. Even as I look him up and down, his eyes don't leave mine.

One Mississippi. Two Mississippi. Three Mississippi.

"Liv," a voice says from behind me, startling me to the point that I nearly drop the biographies I'm re-shelving. I turn around. Luke.

"Jesus," I whisper and pull a quivering hand to my chest.

"What's wrong with you?" Luke asks, cocking his head.

"Nothing, I just..." I turn back around but the stranger is gone. I crane my neck, looking for him in the rows of books or up in the café. But he's disappeared.

"Liv," Luke says again.

"Sorry," I answer, turning around and shaking my head. "You just scared me. That's all."

"I'm going out with Imogene and Adam after closing," he says, tossing me the keys to the SUV.

"You're not coming home with me?" I ask, staring down at the keys in my hand, each word slow to escape my throat.

"No," he says and puts his hands into the pocket of his jeans. "I'll get a ride from Adam later."

"Oh...o...kay," I stammer and look down at the keys, my fingers pressing hard into the metal.

"What is it?" Luke asks, narrowing his color-corrected dark eyes at me.

I close my fist around the silver heart key chain I bought at a knick-knacky store a couple blocks away and consider asking him to walk me to the car after our shift. But I don't want to alarm him. Or make him angry. Or remind him of the danger we're in. The danger I put him in.

It was nothing. It was nothing.

"Nothing," I answer quietly and turn toward the bookshelf. Luke stands there, studying me for a second longer, and I wait for him to push. He's the one person in my life who always knows when something is wrong and never lets me get away with hiding it. I shelve a biography on George Washington and another on David Foster

Wallace. I pretend to concentrate and hold in an anxious breath, anticipating his questioning. But he says nothing. He just stares at me for one long beat before turning on his heel and disappearing beyond the high shelves.

———— •◆• ————

By the time I get home, my lungs ache from holding my breath on and off during the drive. I had to force myself every two minutes to take in new air. On the walk alone to the car, I had my hand in the pocket of my oversized tote, my finger wrapped around the trigger of my loaded Glock 22. I could feel my heart beating faster with each step, blood rushing to every muscle. A vital physical side effect of fear. Fight or flight. Ready to kill. Ready to run.

My body was blazing beneath my peacoat in spite of it being barely twenty degrees outside. The combination of extreme temperatures caused my skin to burn and the bottom of my feet to itch in my leather boots.

As I turned the corner past Charlie's, my legs picked up the pace. I waited to hear the crunch of someone's feet behind me in the snow. I could almost feel the pressure of a gun barrel at my back and taste a dirty hand on my freezing mouth. The daymares played out behind my eyes. But the footsteps and gun barrel and the silencing hand never came. As I sat in the car with the doors locked, my breath still visible despite the blast of manufactured hot air, I leaned forward, resting my forehead against the top of the steering wheel, the stitches in the cold leather digging into my skin. Perhaps I'm just

24

paranoid, looking for monsters in the shadows. Imagining things that aren't really there.

Without Luke at home, the stillness of our house freaks me out. We live in near silence, but I find comfort in hearing the floor creak or the water run while he brushes his teeth. There's life in this house. Even if that life wants very little to do with me.

I sit at our crappy, plastic kitchen table, still dressed in my winter coat. I don't even have the energy to untie my scarf. It's wool. I hate wool. It itches the skin on my neck, but I leave it be. I stare at my ghostly reflection in our dark window, my heart pounding anxious beats against my breastbone, still waiting for the stranger's face to appear, pressed up against the glass.

No one is safe. Torres's voice rattles against my brain. I see him, tied up to a metal pipe with the belts of his dead guards, promising to kill the people I loved. I've tried to forget about those final words. Excuse them away as the last desperate lie of a manipulative man. But there's a wariness that has been growing in my gut. And after seeing the stranger, it's inflated, pressing against my organs and making me sick.

There's a mole in the Black Angels.

I'm sure of it. How would Santino Torres know about Harper? How could he name all of the people I was close to at CORE? And until I can figure out who has been feeding the Torres syndicate information, we will never ever be safe.

The skin around my neck flares and I finally force my hands to move and unwrap my scarf. I take off my coat too, throwing it over the extra chair. I grab my computer off the kitchen countertop and begin my nightly check on Harper. After years of not being allowed to be on social media, I've created several fake accounts to keep tabs on her.

I log onto Twitter first and read through her latest tweets.

Whose idea was it to schedule 9am classes on Fridays? I want to strangle pre-college Harper.

Sick of all the tourists who have invaded NYC for Christmas. If I have to walk around one more person taking a selfie in the park . . .

My lips crinkle at the typical Harper snark. But a third tweet catches my eye.

Smitten is all it says. If it had a heart-eyes emoji next to those words, I'd seriously think someone had hacked into her account. I click into the replies to get more info. There are only two replies.

With a face like that, who wouldn't be?

New boy? Drinks tonight. Time to spill.

New boy? I caught up on all her posts from the last year a couple of weeks ago. She rarely mentions guys or relationships. Most of our evenings at the Dead End Diner revolved around fries, milkshakes, and her disdain for relationships and boyfriend/girlfriend oversharers. Just . . . doesn't seem like Harper.

Pictures. Pictures. I need pictures.

I switch over to Instagram. Since my last check, Harper has posted three new photos. I flip through them. A picture of Harper and her roommate eating big slices of pepperoni pizza. A photo of Harper on the street wearing a Yankees cap and a leather jacket; her wavy hair flying and her tongue sticking out playfully for the camera. The last photo is a screenshot from a FaceTime call. Harper is smiling in a tiny square in the corner. A guy with dark hair and high cheekbones smiles back at her. His long eyelashes outline his almond-shaped eyes, and a five o'clock shadow makes him even sexier. I see what has Harper so smitten. But as I stare into his face, acid begins to sear my stomach lining.

I read the caption of the photo. *My favorite time of day.* The photo has over one hundred likes and a few comments.

Damn, Harper.

Lucky boy. Lucky girl.

Mateo! Wow.

Your prince! I hope you get to meet him soon.

Shit. She hasn't met him in person yet?

The bile spins, the tenuous tissue at my core burning. A physical reaction to the uneasy words on repeat in my mind: *Something's not right. Something's not right.*

My hands move quickly as I open up my email and shoot a note to Cam. Our electronics are completely untraceable and secure. Even so, I'm not really supposed to be talking to Cam. But we've been secretly touching base with the occasional email or late-night phone call.

Hey. Can you call me tonight? Need your help.

I hit send and close out the email. I stare back at Harper's photo of Mateo. She looks so happy. I bite down hard on my lip, hoping the panic ballooning inside of me is misguided.

The satellite phone rings on the kitchen counter, making me jump. I stand up and rush to it.

"Hello?"

"Everything okay?" Cam's strained voice asks on the other end.

"Yeah, I'm fine," I answer and sit back down at the kitchen table. "That was fast. You didn't need to call right away."

"I worry about you," Cam replies quietly into the phone. "I saw your email, grabbed my phone, and ran down to one of the conference rooms."

"We're okay," I say and rest my forehead in my open palm. "I mean we're safe. We're not okay, of course."

"He still not really talking to you?" Cam asks with a sigh.

"Only when he has to," I say, tapping my fingers on the table. "We got into it last night. Everything just kind of came out. I knew he was angry. I don't think I realized just how much he hated me."

"He doesn't hate you," Cam says.

"He does," I interrupt. "I mean, who can blame him? If I had this amazing life in front of me and someone just threw a grenade on it, I'd hate them too."

"He's just upset," Cam replies. "He'll come around. He loves you, Reagan."

"Not anymore," I say quietly.

"So what's going on?" Cam asks on the other end, rescuing me from falling into a sinkhole of self-pity.

"I told you about the threats Torres made before he died. That he'd still come after the people in my life. So I've been checking in on Harper's social media and all has seemed okay but . . . she's talking to this guy now. And they haven't met yet in person and the timing just feels weird and fishy. I guess I'm just worried about her."

"You worried it's one of Torres's guys?" Cam asks.

"Maybe," I answer slowly. "I don't want to be so paranoid but something is just . . . off."

"Let me look into it," Cam answers. "Just email me all of her social media handles and I'll do some digging."

"Okay, I will," I say. "And Cam . . . just . . . don't tell anyone."

"Of course," Cam answers. "I'm not supposed to be talking to you anyway."

"Right," I say. But that's not why I want him to stay silent.

I've been running through my list of mole suspects for the last couple weeks. Lex. Anusha. The senior leaders. Even Sam has been someone I've considered. But for me, Cam is out. His mother and father were nearly killed a couple months ago at the hand of Torres's men. There's no way he could be involved. My circle of trust is getting smaller and smaller.

Cam clears his throat. "I better run. It's almost lights out."

I glance over at the clock on the oven: 11:56.

"I kind of miss having a bedtime," I reply.

My throat thickens with the sentiment I hate the most. Regret. The phone falls silent as I try to push the growing lump in my throat back down.

"Thanks for checking on her," I finally say, my throat clear from emotional obstructions.

"Of course," Cam answers. "We miss you, Reagan. A lot."

And with that, Cam hangs up. I keep the phone pressed to my ear, listening to the hollowness of a dead line.

"Miss you more," I whisper into the receiver. To no one. To nothing.

FOUR

CONDENSATION ENCIRCLES MY GLASS, FOGGING IT
with dew. I watch as water droplets run down its elegant curve, creating clear rivers that allow me to peer inside. My eyes are stuck staring at one droplet high on the glass, getting ready to run. Finally, it
breaks free, picking up other droplets, greedily growing in size as it
makes its way down to the circular base. It joins the other fallen droplets, soaking into a thick Bud Light coaster.

"Olivia, you sure you don't want anything besides a Coke?" Adam
asks and touches my hand, finally pulling me out of my stare. "The
bartender never checks IDs."

"You would know," Imogene replies, reaching for a fry in the
plastic red basket at the center of our table.

"What does that mean?" Adam says, dipping his own fry into
ketchup.

"Oh, don't pretend like you didn't take every college girl with a
summer house to Charlie's this July," Imogene replies, her thin lips
parting into a playful smile.

Adam shrugs, a sheepish grin tickling the corners of his lips. "Lots of hot girls up here over break. What am I supposed to do?"

"Control yourself," Imogene replies and rolls her eyes. "This kid caused so much drama this summer. There was literally a catfight that broke out in the Book Loft over him. Like scratching, hair pulling, the works."

"Are you serious?" Luke says with a laugh, dunking his fries into a cup of ranch, giving away his midwesternness.

"Yeah, it was a kind of a cluster," Adam answers, taking a long sip of beer. "How was I supposed to know they were sisters?"

"They had the same last name, you idiot," Imogene replies, her eyes narrowing into slits.

"I didn't know their last names," Adam counters, draining his last gulp of beer. "And on that note, time for another round. You guys want anything?"

"No, I'm good," I answer.

"Get an order of pickle chips," Luke replies as he shoves the last of the French fries into his mouth.

"I'll come with you," Imogene says, grabbing her wallet off the table and hopping off her high-back bar stool.

The two of them weave their way around the tables, half of them occupied by local couples, friends and co-workers I recognize from the downtown shops, restaurants, and cafés. Charlie's has been around for fifty-five years and it has both the wear and character to prove it. The dark-wood bar top is chipped and scuffed, with people's names and initials carved everywhere. Dollar bills have been pinned to the low ceilings, a tradition that lives on for first-time patrons. High-end liquor bottles (the expensive stuff is for the tourists; they keep the cheap stuff out of view for the locals in the know) line the back of the bar, glowing from the bottom and reflected in the large mirror, calling out to drinkers to have just one more round.

The old-fashioned jukebox in the corner blares a new song. I recognize the first few measures of the piano before Michael McDonald's voice picks up the lyrics.

"You don't know me but I'm your brother. I was raised here in this living hell," his deep voice sings to me. The Doobie Brothers' "Takin' It to the Streets."

The last time I heard this song, I was with Luke in the Weixels' bonus room, singing along with the record player, feeling happier than I ever had in my entire life. It was the night before my Templeton visit. Less than twenty-four hours before my first kiss with Luke. That was the night Luke told me to stop trying to live my life for someone else. It was the first and last time I allowed myself to think that my life could actually belong to me and not the Black Angels.

"I know what you're thinking about," Luke says, his eyes fixed on the empty basket of fries. His fingers pick at the checkered paper, damp with grease.

"You do?" I ask, wondering if he recognizes the song. If he's reliving the moment, wishing he could go back in time, like I am.

"Yes," he answers and finally looks up at me. "The song. The records."

"I wasn't sure if you'd remember," I reply, cradling my glass in my hands, condensation wetting my chapped skin.

"I remember everything," Luke answers before turning his attention back to the empty basket. And from his monotone voice, I can't tell if that's a good or bad thing.

"Okay, pickle chips are coming," Adam says, setting down a fresh beer, its frothy head spilling over the glass's edge as he climbs onto the chair next to me.

I scan the room for Imogene, and that's when I see him. The muscles in my neck compress as my eyes lock with the stranger in the corner. He's cradling a tumbler full of ice and a dark brown liquor. He stares at me for a moment, then knocks back his drink, stands up, and puts on his leather jacket. Dread swells at my center, pushing down on my lungs, as I watch him place a bill on the counter and hurry toward the front door.

Where is he going? What is he doing?

He pushes past a couple making their way into the bar, knocking the girl's shoulder before slipping into the darkness.

Without thinking, I jump up, yanking my peacoat off the chair. The chair wobbles and nearly tips over.

"Liv, what is it?" Luke asks next to me, his eyes wide and suddenly concerned.

"Nothing," I reply, shaking my head and thinking fast. "I just have a headache and think I left some Tylenol in the car. I'll be right back."

My legs carry me through the dark bar before Luke can ask me another question. I swing open the door, a gust of wind biting at my skin, warm with synthetic heat. I throw on my coat as I scan the sidewalk, searching for his dark jacket in the white snow.

I spot him a block away, heading back toward the Book Loft. My body moves slowly up the sidewalk. I reach inside my bag, searching for my gun.

Where is it? Where is it?

It's not in its usual spot. I look down at the bag and dig a little deeper. Finally, I feel the weight of the pistol in my hand. The cool steel against my exposed hands makes my stomach twist, fear tingling up my fingertips like razor blades until it reaches my arms, my shoulders, my neck. I cling to the shadow of the buildings, trying to stay out of the glare of the streetlights wrapped in evergreen and red ribbons. Even in the darkness, he'd spot me.

The man pauses, looking down at something in his hand. His phone? A gun? My legs freeze midstep and my breath vacates my body.

Don't turn around. Don't turn around.

He doesn't. My legs pick up speed as he reaches the parking lot and unlocks a blue car. My Black Angel mind immediately takes in its features, memorizing every characteristic I can see.

Blue. Four-door. Toyota. Massachusetts license plate.

I sneak up closer, trying to read the plate's letters and numbers. *G-D-B . . .*

"What are you doing?" a voice asks behind me and I spin around. Luke.

"Jesus Christ, Luke," I hiss, my hand pulled over my frantic heartbeat.

"You know, for a trained spy," Luke begins. "You don't really know how to exit a room with a graceful excuse."

I turn back around toward the parking lot, my neck craning, eyes searching for the car to get the rest of the license plate. But it's gone. He's gone. Again.

"Why did you follow me?" I ask, spinning back toward Luke.

"Because I knew something was wrong and I wanted to make

sure you were okay," he answers, shoving his ungloved hands into the pockets of his thick black coat.

"I didn't think you'd care if I was," I say, crossing my arms over my chest for warmth.

"Don't be dramatic," Luke answers, rolling his dark eyes. "Of course I care. And don't pout and act like I don't have a right to be mad at you."

"I know," I answer quietly and take a breath. "You do."

I need to give him that. I shouldn't sulk and think *that* will magically get him to forgive me. I did this. And while we'll never get things back to the way they used to be, maybe if I give him enough space and time, one day we'll be okay. Not great, but okay. Friends again. That, I know, is the best I can hope for.

"So what's going on?" Luke says, his neck turning from side to side, searching the empty sidewalk for the reason I bolted out of the bar.

"There was just a guy in the bar staring at me weird," I answer and look down, my boots kicking at the fresh layer of snow. "I saw him in the bookstore yesterday too. I haven't seen him in town before. He's not a local. He just . . . has me worried. That's all."

"Not every person who looks at you for a second too long is out to get you," Luke says and we turn to walk back toward the bar.

But someone wants to kill us. Someone will always be after us, my mind screams, the silent declaration, like a needle at the center of my chest.

"I know," I lie, staring at each new footprint in the white. I don't want to freak Luke out. Poison him with my own anxiety and fears.

35

"We're supposed to be safe here," Luke says quietly. "The Black Angels wouldn't put us somewhere they didn't think was safe."

"But what about the mole?" I reply, looking back up into Luke's eyes. "We don't know who it is and they might know where we are."

"I'm not entirely convinced there is a mole," Luke says, leaning against the brick wall outside of Charlie's. The door swings open and Fleetwood Mac's "The Chain" pours out into the snow.

"Running in the shadows. Damn your love. Damn your lies."

The drumbeat in the song is nearly in sync with my heart.

"What?" my exasperated voice pushes out, my eyebrows cinching together. "There has to be a mole. How would Santino know about Cam or Anusha? About Harper?"

"Look," Luke says with a sigh, his hands up in the air in half protest and half surrender. "Let's just go back inside and conspiracy theory this later. This is a very long time to search for Tylenol. They're going to wonder what happened to us."

"Fine," I answer, my voice defeated.

"We're safe here, Reagan," Luke says, touching me on the left shoulder and staring into my eyes. After a moment of holding my body and my gaze, he lets go and opens the door for me. As I walk into the dark bar, I wonder if Luke even believes his own declaration. And if those words will ever be true.

———◦◆◦———

A basket of pickle chips later, we're back at the house. Luke is asleep upstairs while I check my email, hoping for a follow-up report from Cam. I click into my inbox. Empty.

Perhaps it's nothing, my mind whispers as I close my eyes and take in a clearing breath, hoping fresh oxygen will push out the anxiety that clings to each organ, like barnacles taking over the bottom of a boat. I put my fingers up to my temples, rubbing them counterclockwise as I repeat over and over again, *It's nothing. It's nothing. It's nothing.*

I open my eyes again and stare at the empty inbox. I hit refresh every few seconds and finally give up, opening a new window and logging onto Twitter to read Harper's latest tweets.

Last exam taken! Last paper in! So this is what freedom feels like?

In a post-all-nighter haze. Could someone come to my dorm and just pour coffee into my mouth?

Tomorrow, please come. I can't wait another day.

What does that mean? I click into the replies.

Finally!! I cannot wait to hear about him.

Mateo Day! I demand a full report over lunch.

"Shit, shit, shit," I whisper to no one, my heart straining, unable to get out a full beat. I open up my email, my hands furiously typing out a note to Cam.

Dude! What did you find out? Harper just posted on Twitter all giddy about meeting Mateo tomorrow. I'm starting to FREAK OUT over here.

My fingers hit send. My legs bounce up and down involuntarily beneath the table as I stare at my empty inbox, willing for a quick, "I checked. He's real. You have nothing to worry about, you psychopath" response from Cam. Sixty seconds later, the satellite phone rings.

"Please say you have good news," I say.

"I'm sorry," Cam answers, slightly out of breath. "I have no news."

"What?" I say loudly, my free hand slamming down onto the table.

"Reagan, chill. I'm sorry, things are crazy here," he answers with a sigh. "We've been in training all day. I haven't had a moment to check. I've got his details. I'm going to do it right now. Just go to bed, I'm sure you have nothing to worry about."

"How can I go to bed?" I ask, standing up from my seat at the table and pacing around our tiny kitchen.

"It may take me some time," Cam says. "What do you think us hackers do? Just like pound out a little code and boom, we've got a full profile with the headline 'Bad Guy' on it?"

"No," I say. *Yes*, I think.

"Look, give me a couple hours," Cam says and I can hear him tapping away on his keyboard. "I promise you. The second I figure out if this guy's a liar or not, I'll call you, okay?"

"Fine," I answer, and the restlessness that started in my legs climbs up to my torso and down my arms, forcing me to cradle the phone in between my cheek and shoulder to shake out the crippling nerves.

"Get some sleep."

Highly unlikely, I think as I hear Cam click off on the other side.

I pick at my chapped lips as I stare at the digital green numbers of my clock. I taste metal on the tip of my tongue, a sure sign that I'm bleeding, as the clock switches from 2:41 to 2:42 a.m. It's been over two hours since I hung up with Cam and I have yet to fall asleep. Not that I thought I would.

I roll onto my back and stare at the shadows on the ceiling. I close my eyes and force my hands away from my bleeding lips. I fold my hands across my chest and repeat my selfish prayer.

Please be nothing. Please be nothing. Please God, be nothing.

More than anything, I want Harper to be safe. But it's more than that. I want her to be happy too. She got so screwed over by the last guy she dated at New Albany. Chad. Ugh. He was a senior when we were juniors. He treated her like a princess. Or so we thought. A few months into their fairy-tale relationship (complete with lovey-dovey texts, sweet romantic dinners, and even the occasional bouquet of flowers), Malika caught wind he was banging half the lacrosse team. Sure enough, Harper showed up unexpectedly at his house and caught him with his pants down (literally) with the team's captain. She cried every day for a week. Malika and I took turns supplying her with cookie dough ice cream and reruns of *Friends*. Ever since, she's been so guarded. She said she'd never be made a fool out of again. Even if Mateo is everything he claims to be, I'll freaking cut him if he hurts my girl.

The high-pitch shrill of the phone fills my room and I lunge for it on the nightstand.

"What did you find out?" I say and sit up straight in the bed.

"You were right," Cam says, his voice breathy with panic. "He's claiming to be a junior at the University of Pennsylvania but he's not. I hacked into school records; he's not listed as a student there. And his IP address isn't in Philadelphia. It's in Colombia."

"Shit," I say and jump out of the bed, sheets and blankets still tangled around my body, causing me to fall forward. My free hand braces me against the cold wood floor. "I knew it. What else do you have? Think it's one of Torres's guys?"

"I think so," Cam answers. "It took me a long time to break through. They have his computer firewalled pretty well. But he's *definitely* not the international studies major he claims to be."

"When are they meeting?" I ask as I flip on my light and start running around my room, furiously tearing off my pajama bottoms, and throwing on a pair of jeans.

"Tomorrow morning at eight thirty for breakfast at some café in Greenwich Village," Cam says. "You've got to figure out a way to warn her before morning."

"I know, but her phone is probably tapped," I reply, cradling the sat phone in my ear as I pull on a pair of mismatched socks, my heart beating so loudly in my ears I can barely make out my own words. "I can't call and warn her. They'll hear the call and then figure out some other way to snatch her earlier."

"And they'll find you too," Cam says, his voice weighty with worry in my ear. "What are you going to do?"

"What choice do I have?" I ask, throwing my sheet and blanket off the floor and back onto my bed as I search for the sweatshirt I had on earlier. "I've got to get down to New York and stop her."

"But your cover," Cam says. "This could expose you."

"Well, I don't have a lot of options here," I snap, opening up a black backpack and sprinting around the room, picking up a pair of jeans, a few T-shirts, underwear, pajama pants, and socks, and throwing them inside. "You're the only one who knows about the Torres threats. The Black Angels are done with me. There's no way they're going to pull together some type of middle-of-the-night operation for a friend I haven't seen in over a year. Who I'm not supposed to even be in contact with anymore."

"Maybe if I explained——" Cam begins.

"No way. I don't trust them," I cut him off, my shaking hands searching the bottom of my closet for a baseball cap. "Someone on the inside was working with Torres before he died."

"What? How do you know?"

"Because he practically told me before I killed him," I say and take in a sharp breath. "Look, I don't have time to explain. But if the mole finds out, they'll just tip off Fernando, and Harper could get taken *now*. We can't risk it."

"You really think so?"

"Absolutely. There is no one in that bunker I trust except for my father and you. I've got weapons. I've got a car. I've got to do this on my own."

"At least bring Luke with you," Cam insists. "You cannot take on a team of assassins by yourself. Unless you want both you and Harper to die."

He's right. Someone needs to grab Harper while the other stands by as the getaway driver. This is a two-person job. I don't want to force Luke to go rogue again. And I certainly don't want to put him in danger. But I can't do this alone.

"He's going to be pissed," I say quietly.

"Not as pissed as he'd be if he woke up to some note saying you were gone," Cam says.

"Fine," I answer, getting down on my knees and pushing down

on one of the old floorboards in my room. The plank moves with ease, revealing an envelope filled with one hundred twenty-dollar bills. I hope we can make this quick and clean. Grab Harper and get her to safety. But if we're spotted, if Torres's team intercepts us, we might have to run. And we'll need cash. "Will you get me all the details about Harper? Where she lives, where she's staying tonight?"

"On it," Cam says. "You need to get on the road now. If you don't leave soon, you'll never make it."

I pull back my curtain. Shit. It's snowing. Even on a clear day, it's at least a four-hour drive to New York City.

"Okay. Talk to you soon," I say and hang up. I throw the phone on my bed and walk across the hallway. I open Luke's door without knocking and flip on his lights. His eyes, groggy with sleep, squint up at me as I hover over his bed.

"Get dressed," I say, tossing him a sweatshirt off the floor. "We're going to New York."

FIVE

SWISH. SWISH. SWISH. SWISH.

The windshield wipers of our SUV are on full speed, pushing fast-falling snow out of the way as Luke steers the car off the treacherously icy Vermont back roads and onto Interstate 87 south as we race toward Manhattan.

Well . . . as fast as you *can* race in a snowstorm.

I look over at Luke as he grips the steering wheel, his knuckles white, and his mouth pressed into a straight line. He hasn't said a word since we left the house. I gave him a three-minute briefing. Told him about Mateo. That Harper was being targeted by Fernando. That she was heading into a trap in the morning and we had to stop her before she left her dorm. He listened, nodding intently. I braced my body for an argument. But there was none. Harper and Luke have been close friends since the Weixels moved to New Albany in middle school. There's a long history that predates my move next door to Luke on Landon Lane: splashing together at pool parties and sharing a freezing bleacher seat at football games, long talks, and winding walks on neighborhood paths.

"Let's go get our girl," he said as he climbed out of his bed and began quickly packing his bag. We loaded weapons cases, a computer, and two satellite phones into the car and were gone in under five minutes.

Despite finally being on a highway, we still face snow-covered roads. At four a.m., there's almost no one on the roads. We don't even have tire tracks to follow.

Luke gently pushes down on the car's accelerator but the car fishtails, spinning to the right.

My left hand automatically grips the center console.

"Shit, shit, shit," Luke whispers harshly under his breath. He spins the wheel, trying to correct the car's dangerous maneuver. He pulls us out of the spin and lifts his foot off the accelerator, decreasing our speed. I take a breath but feel little relief when I look at the clock: 4:14. God, I hope we make it to her apartment before eight.

"The things I get you involved in, right?" I say, filling the car with some of the first words of our drive.

"It's like you can read my mind," Luke says, shaking his head, his eyes fixed on the road. I stare at him, waiting for him to tell me he's just kidding. He doesn't. Because he's not.

Finally, I turn away and begin counting the large lights that line this stretch of highway.

One. Two. Three. Four.

"I wish you all had never met me," I say softly as I stare out the window.

Five. Six. Seven. Eight.

Luke clears his throat and shifts awkwardly in his seat, unsure of what to say. But his silence says it all.

He wishes he'd never met me either. And I don't blame him one bit.

I grip my tongue between my teeth to stop the tears that threaten to rise from the base of my throat. Since Indonesia, so many conversations I've had with Luke have left me teetering on the edge of tears. I hate it. It makes me feel so weak. But more than feeling guilty over all I've done, I'm just . . . so sad. There's really no other way to say it. Luke used to be the hand that pulled me out of the darkness. But now, he's the hand that pushes me down.

"I wish you'd gone to AP bio that day," I continue, still staring out the window.

"What are you talking about?" Luke asks.

"The Monday after I kissed that soccer player at Mark Ricardi's party," I answer and close my eyes, picturing a sullen Luke walking toward me on a windy New Albany High School quad. "I skipped AP bio to avoid you. But you skipped too. You found me sitting outside. And then we heard the scream. We saw someone trying to take that girl. And I raced home knowing my parents were next. I think about that day a lot."

"I'd never skipped a class before," Luke answers quietly.

"I know. And think about how different your life would be. If you were in class that day, you wouldn't have seen that happen so you'd never have followed me home. You wouldn't know who I really was or about the Black Angels. You wouldn't have followed me down to Colombia or to Qualifiers or to that warehouse in Indonesia. You'd be at West Point. You'd be living the life you were supposed to."

45

"But I'd never know what happened to you," Luke answers, glancing over at my side of the car. "You'd have just disappeared on me."

"But maybe that would have been best."

I look over at Luke. He pushes his full lips to one side, a pensive quirk of his. "Maybe," he finally admits. "It's funny how one choice that seems so insignificant in the moment can change just . . . everything."

"The butterfly effect."

"The Reagan effect."

I turn away, staring back out the window, unsure of what that means but unwilling to ask. All I know for certain is if Luke and Harper had never met me, their lives would be better. Their names would never have been on Santino Torres's lips.

They would be safe.

<hr />

I cannot stop my knees from bouncing. I look at the clock for what must be the hundredth time in the last ten minutes: 7:53. Knowing Harper, she'll leave her dorm early to be sure she makes it to her 8:30 date on time. We only have a matter of minutes to get to her dorm and run interference before she walks right into Fernando's perilous setup. I know these people. She'll be kidnapped at best. Killed at worst. Used as a pawn to pull us out of hiding. And as I think about Harper dotting her lips with pink gloss, getting excited about her date, having no idea she's in danger, I've never hated myself more.

My fingernails dig into the skin of my palms, trying to draw pain. Stop me from feeling sorry for myself. There's no time to wish for another life when the most important thing right now is saving Harper's. No amount of self-pity can undo all I've already done.

I glance at the clock again: 7:54. I pick at my lip until I taste that metallic rush of blood on my tongue once again. I force myself to stop looking at the clock and stare outside.

We pass by low-rise buildings, different-colored bricks breaking them apart. Deep red, then cream, then gray. Air-conditioning units stick out of random windows and metal fire escapes climb up the sides. My Black Angel mind has always been trained to be observant, but an architecture class taught by Victoria Browning, a senior leader at CORE and the one in charge of all of us trainees, must have really seeped into my subconscious. Because now when I look at buildings, I look at the materials and details that tell the story of each structure, but I also look for the escape routes and potential hazards.

Please get there. Please get there. Please get there, my mind repeats its silent prayer as we pass by more apartment buildings with delis and bodegas and dry cleaners in the commercial spaces below.

I pull down on my Columbus Blue Jackets baseball cap and look at the car's navigation. Four minutes until we're in front of Harper's dorm on Eleventh Street and Third Avenue.

"I have never been so happy for a snowy Saturday in my life," Luke says as he pulls down Second Avenue with an ease I wouldn't expect to find in Manhattan. There are still cars and cabs on the road, of course, but not as many as I thought there'd be. Most New Yorkers must have looked out the window and opted to stay in bed, wait out the snowy morning under the covers before heading out to brunch or last minute Christmas shopping.

The phone rings.

I grab it before it can even finish its first ring, answering it on speaker. "So what's the word?"

"Okay, you're not going to like this one," Cam says as Luke slows the SUV at a stoplight, still four blocks away. "There are two entrances to this dorm. One on Eleventh Street and one on Twelfth Street."

"God damn it," I reply and slap my hand against my jittering knee. "So how are we going to know which entrance to park in front of?"

"A coin flip?" Cam suggests.

"You're right," I answer with extra bite in my voice. "Life-or-death decisions should be decided on a coin flip."

"Hang on. I'm pulling up some satellite images from the building," Cam says and I can hear him typing on the other end of the phone. "Okay . . . looks like the Eleventh Street exit is a lot more popular."

"But which way is the café?" I ask and hear Cam on his keyboard again.

"It's near Washington Square Park," Cam answers. "So she's going to have to walk south and west. So, logically, she's going to leave out of the most southwest exit."

"Unless her dorm room is closer to the Twelfth Street exit," Luke interjects as the light turns from red to green.

"Thanks, Cam," I say. "We're almost there. We'll figure it out."

"Coin flip," Cam says again. "Call me after you grab her."

"Will do. Thanks, Cam," I reply and hang up the phone.

"What do you want to do?" Luke asks, stopping at another stoplight. We're just two blocks away now. I bite down on my ragged thumbnail and look out the window just as a gust of wind opens an old woman's long winter coat.

"Eleventh Street," I finally answer as I watch the woman struggle to pull her coat back together. "Harper is a total baby when it comes to the cold. Even if her room is closer to the Twelfth Street exit, she'll walk to the Eleventh Street one just to skip a block in the snow."

"I sure hope you're right," Luke answers with an annoyed sigh as I eye the clock: 7:58.

"Me too, Luke," I reply quietly as we pass by Twelfth Street, now one block away. "Me too."

I stare out the window as we pass a small movie theater, a bodega, and a sushi restaurant before Luke turns right onto Eleventh Street. My hands immediately begin to tingle. I vigorously shake them out before the anxiety can crawl any further up my body, crippling me and stealing my strength. I lean forward in my seat, feeling beneath the metal and leather until I find my loaded Glock 22, ready for a gunfight. I pull out the magazine, quickly scanning the fifteen bullets before reloading. We're expecting Fernando's people to lure Harper into a car closer to the café, but these guys are crazy. It's not like they haven't shot at civilians in broad daylight before.

"Let's go over the game plan again," Luke says as he pulls up to a loading zone near the dorm's exit. "She hasn't heard from you in over a year. I'm still afraid it won't be as easy as just, 'Hey, remember me? Your long-lost best friend who disappeared off the face of the earth? Just happened to be strolling by your dorm. Want to get into my car with this guy who looks a little bit like Luke Weixel? Oh wait . . . it is Luke Weixel?'"

"I know her. She'll be so excited to see me she won't care," I answer and stare at the double doors of the residence hall, waiting for Harper's face to appear. "Harper trusts me. If I tell her she needs to get into the car, she will. *She* is the least of my worries right now."

I look in the mirrors of our car, searching for signs of Fernando's people. There's a white van parked across the street. I search for a driver or passenger. There's none. A dark four-door car is parked half a block away, a guy dressed in a suit in the driver's seat. He's reading the paper and smoking a cigarette, completely ignoring us. Looks like just a driver, waiting to pick up a passenger. At least I hope.

"You see the van?" Luke asks, looking in his mirror before opening up the center console and checking for his own weapon.

"I do. There's no one inside," I answer, studying it closer. I see a white and orange piece of paper tucked beneath its windshield wiper. It lifts and flaps, pushed up by a gust of wind. "They've got a ticket. Looks like it was parked there overnight. You'll have to watch it when I get out of the car to get Harper, okay? Make sure there's no movement. I'm sure Fernando's people are waiting closer to the café but there could definitely be a second team ready to take her on this block."

"I know," Luke says, his face falling at the reminder of just how dangerous this morning could get. His chest rises beneath his puffy coat and I suddenly wish we still had access to CORE's walk-in closet of bulletproof vests. The Black Angels didn't leave us any. Probably

50

because they thought we'd just need guns to defend ourselves. The plan was to keep us hidden, not have us go on missions in the middle of Manhattan.

I glance at the clock as the digital numbers change to 8:02. I check my mirror again, my lips pressing together between my teeth.

"Someone's coming," Luke says and I look back up at the double doors as a figure walks away from the elevators. As it gets closer, I see long, wavy blond hair. And as she circles the front desk, I see her fair skin and can almost make out her hazel eyes. Harper.

"It's her. Let's do this. And fast," I command, pulling down on my baseball cap and shoving the gun into my pocket. I pop open the passenger door and step out onto the snowy sidewalk. "Keep all the doors unlocked."

I slam the SUV door before Luke can reply to my instructions and look up and down the block. It's empty. I look through the glass doors as Harper stops in the lobby to zip up her puffy red jacket and pull down on the strings of her knitted white hat. Just the sight of her warms me for a moment at my freezing core. God, I've missed her so much.

Harper runs her gloved fingers through her hair before pushing open the door and bounding out into the cold.

"Harper," I say cautiously as I walk closer to her on the sidewalk. Her face turns toward mine, her eyes flashing with confusion then recognition then pure joy.

"Holy shit. Reagan?" Harper squeals and runs toward me. She all but jumps into my arms, her hair flying and getting caught in my mouth. She pulls away, cupping my cheeks in her hands. "Oh my God. What are you doing here? Where have you been? And what the hell have you done to your hair?"

Bang. Bang. Bang.

Bullets whiz past our heads, shattering the glass door behind us. Harper lets out a piercing scream, her hands clinging to my arms as she instinctively tries to pull us down to the ground.

"No, stop," I yell and yank her body up, pushing her hard toward the SUV. "Harper, get in."

"What is happening?" Harper screams as I frantically pull open the back door.

"Get in," I shout, shoving a still shrieking and struggling Harper into the backseat.

Bang. Bang. Bang.

Shit. I can hear the unmistakable buzz of a bullet flying centimeters away from my face as I climb into the front seat and slam the door.

"Go, Luke, go," I say, pounding on the front dashboard as Luke peels down the street.

"Luke?" Harper yells, her mouth hanging open as her head swivels between her two nearly unrecognizable friends. "Reagan? What. The actual. Fuck?"

Bang.

A bullet hits the back of the car, causing Harper to scream and dive down onto the backseat.

My head whips around and behind us is the once passengerless white van barreling down Eleventh Street, a guy with a gun hanging out the window, ready to shoot again.

SIX

"THE VAN. DAMN IT, I SHOULD HAVE KNOWN," I YELL as Luke floors it down Eleventh Street. "They're reloading."

"Oh my God," Harper shrieks, her voice muffled by the leather seat her entire face is pushed against.

Luke blows through the red light and makes a wild left-hand turn, driving south onto Third Avenue, the white van practically on our bumper. A cabbie leans on his horn as he's forced to slam on his brakes, his yellow cab skidding on the slick roads in the middle of the intersection, just feet away from a collision.

"Jesus Christ," Harper screams, still curled up in the fetal position in the backseat, both hands covering her head. "What the hell is happening? Where are we going?"

"Harper, just stay down," I yell, turning around in my seat to get another look at the shooter. He's wearing a baseball cap but still, I can tell he's young. Maybe even our age. My eyes tear away from his face and watch as he reloads his pistol, just waiting for the chance to shoot again.

"Luke, you've got to lose them," I say, my voice exploding as I turn back toward him.

"What do you think I'm trying to do?" he hollers back at me, his foot pushing down on the accelerator as our car races down the lightly trafficked Manhattan street. The lights are green at the intersections of Tenth and Ninth Streets, but I can see a few cars and yellow cabs stopped at a red light ahead. Despite the halt in traffic, Luke continues speeding toward the red light at the Eighth Street intersection.

Please turn green. Please turn green.

I spin my head around in my seat; the van is still half a car length behind us. When I turn back around, the light remains bloodred. The traffic, unmoved. And so is Luke's speed.

"Luke, Luke, Luke," I say as I clutch the bottom of my seat with both hands.

"Hang on," his mouth pushes out as the SUV jumps the sidewalk, forcing a woman carrying a tray of coffees to jump out of the way, brown liquid pouring down her coat.

"What are you doing?" I shriek, my nails digging into the leather seat.

"Hold on," he yells, barreling the car off Third Avenue and down Eighth Street. Cars immediately begin honking their horns, drivers wildly waving their arms or turning their wheels to get out of our way. We're going the wrong way down a freaking one-way street.

"Luke . . ." I begin.

"I know, I know," he says, checking his mirrors as I check mine. They're still behind us.

"Shit," I say under my breath as the engine revs and Luke pushes the car faster and faster down Eighth Street. I turn around in my seat. The gun is reloaded and in the passenger's hand, poised for a chance to take another shot.

"Oh no," Luke says, whipping my body back around. A big truck has turned off of the next street, our grilles barreling toward each other.

"Oh Jesus," Harper cries out, lifting her head from its crouched position to see what all the fuss is about. The truck flashes its lights and blares its horn one, two, three times. The driver's face contorts down at us in shock. But still, he drives toward us.

"Hold on, hold on," Luke instructs through clenched teeth before swinging the car toward the right and jumping a high curb, steering the SUV back onto the sidewalk. Without a seat belt on, my body slams against the door and my head knocks against the thick glass window; my skull and shoulder both immediately radiate with pain.

The truck's horn is still blaring as Luke pulls around it, skidding on a patch of ice as he steers the car back onto Eighth Street. Still going the wrong way.

"God damn it. They're still there," I yell as I look back at the white van.

Without saying a word, Luke makes a wild left-hand turn onto Broadway, forcing my hands up to the SUV's ceiling to stop my body from slamming into the side of the car again. Luke's foot pushes down on the pedal, weaving us in and out of traffic, dodging trucks and cars and cabbies, all doing their best to drive at a reasonable speed in the snow. We must look completely insane. I'm shocked we haven't heard the sounds of police sirens behind us yet. Someone must have called the cops by now.

No matter the lane we switch to, the van stays right on our tail.

Horns are honking at us with nearly every maneuver, and Harper's unbelted body slides along the backseat, ping-ponging between the two doors.

The skin around my chest hums as my heart alternates between clenching fear and pounding adrenaline. My feet dig into the floor, instinctively bracing my body as we race down Broadway, passing Fifth and Sixth Streets, blowing through red lights and giving very little respect to traffic laws. I look back at Harper only to realize she's watching me from her hunkered down position in the backseat. When our eyes lock, she lifts her head a few inches off the seat.

"Are we going to die today?" she asks, her voice quiet. Her eyes are so wide, I can see the whites all the way around her hazel irises.

"No," I answer and grab for her hand. "I won't let you die today."

Just as the words escape my lips, a bullet strikes the back window, cracking the glass.

"Oh my God, oh my God, oh my God," Harper screams, pulling her hand out of my grasp and bringing her arms toward her head.

"Hold on," Luke says, making a sharp right turn onto Bleecker. Again, going the wrong way down a one-way street.

"Again!" I yell at Luke as cars lean on their horns, flash their lights, or skid to a stop.

"Got any better ideas?" he asks as he jumps the sidewalk, nearly sideswiping a woman with a stroller.

"Yes," I say, grabbing for the gun in my pocket. The sidewalk is completely clear in front of us. Now is as good a time as any. "Hold the car steady. Harper, stay down."

I turn around in my seat, roll down the window, and lean out of the car as far as I can. I point my pistol, but I don't aim for their windows. I aim for their tires.

Boom! Boom!

One tire blows, then another, and the driver loses control. I watch his face as he spins the wheel, furiously trying to keep the van moving forward. But it's no use. Sparks fly as the van spins on the sidewalk before slamming into the red brick wall of an apartment building.

"Got him," I yell as the van grows smaller and smaller in our nearly shattered back window.

"We've got to get out of this city," Luke says as he guides the car back onto Bleecker and then turns (going the correct way, thank you God) onto Thompson Street.

"The Holland Tunnel will get us to New Jersey," I say and plug it into the navigation built into our dashboard. I studied the maps on the drive down to Manhattan and talked Luke through every potential escape route off of this concrete island. The satellite makes quick work of finding what I want and where we are. "We're only a mile away."

"Are we safe?" Harper asks meekly as she slowly pushes her body up from the backseat.

"We are," I answer, turning around to face her. "For now."

"Great," she answers, pulling her white knit cap off her head and throwing it on the floor. Her big eyes narrow into slits as she crosses her arms over her chest and leans back in her seat. "So . . . let's catch up. You first. Just who the hell are you, Reagan MacMillan?"

SEVEN

"SO . . . YOU'RE LIKE A NINJA?"

"You lied to me every single day for a year? Are you sure you aren't a sociopath?"

"A drug lord? Like a guy from *Breaking Bad*?"

"Holy shit."

"I think I'm going to throw up."

"Is that why your hair looks so horrible?"

"No seriously, if we weren't in a tunnel and running away from men with guns, I'd make you pull over so I could puke."

These are just a handful of the responses from Harper as I explained to her who I really am. About the Black Angels. The failed mission in Colombia. How Luke got dragged into all of this. Qualifiers at CORE. Killing Torres in Indonesia. Fernando. Mateo. And why someone is now trying to kill all three of us.

"So, your mom," Harper says quietly in the backseat. "She really is gone? That part is true?"

"Yes," I reply as our car finally emerges on the other side of the

Holland Tunnel in New Jersey, the light in the car transitioning from black to bright.

She really is gone, my mind repeats.

My chest tightens before the nightmare of memories floods my body. I see Mom's terrified face. The smell of gunpowder fills my nose. Then the sensation of blood, sticky and warm, coats my hands. I shake my head, trying to erase the horrific scene that still plays on a daily loop behind my eyes.

"She died," I continue. "Just not in a car accident like I told you in my last email to you."

"And the same people who killed her now want to kill me?" Harper says, two fingers pointing into the center of her chest. "This is bat-shit crazy. I don't understand why they want to kill me. What the hell did I do?"

"You didn't do anything," I say. "My parents killed Santino Torres's son. I killed his brother. Even though Santino is dead, he promised me this wasn't over. Before he died, he said he'd find a way to kill me. Hurt the people I love."

"This is all so, so insane," Harper says, taking in a shaky breath and pulling off her fitted black gloves with her teeth. "I just . . . why didn't you try to warn me before someone tried to shoot me in the middle of New York City?"

"What was I supposed to do?" I say, checking the mirrors to make sure no one is following us. "Call you up and explain I've been training to be a spy my whole life and by the way, people might try to kill you, so be careful? I didn't even know it was true. I thought Santino might be bluffing. Saying anything to stay alive. But when he brought you up . . . I just don't know how he knew about you.

Knew where to find you. I mean Luke and my friends at CORE, I could understand. But you . . . it's just proof there's a mole in the Black Angels feeding them information."

"Who do you think it is?" Luke asks as he drives west on Interstate 78 and as far away from Manhattan as we can get.

"I don't know," I say and shake my head, flipping through a mental list of everyone I know at CORE. "It's obviously not my father. Or Cam. I mean, he wouldn't have his own parents targeted. But besides those two, it could literally be anybody else. My no list is much shorter than my suspect list right now."

"You suspect even Anusha?" Luke asks, his voice surprised. "She's one of your closest friends. And she didn't even grow up as a Black Angel."

"Exactly," I answer, pointing my finger at him. "We don't really know anything about her. We've never met her family. We know nothing about her life before the Black Angels except what she's told us. She could be a plant. She's smart enough."

"I can't see it," Luke says, emphatically shaking his head. "She wouldn't get so close to you and then do this to you."

"That's exactly what a good double agent would do, Luke," I answer quietly, the thought of Anusha actually being the mole twisting at my gut.

"Well, I don't know how it could be Sam," Luke says, changing lanes and checking his mirror, using Black Angel—taught maneuvers to see if we're being followed by any of the other cars on the road. "*I'd* even trust her with my life, and I don't know her like you do."

"I don't trust anyone right now," I answer, turning my face away from Luke and his questions. "All I know is someone I'd die for could be trying to kill us."

Luke opens his mouth, perhaps to protest, perhaps to bring up another name, but pulls his lips together and stares straight ahead down the highway.

The interstate is beginning to fill up, even with the snow. It's falling faster now, the big, thick flakes lingering on the hoods of cars and collecting on the edge of windows, begging to come inside before sliding off or being pushed away by the wind. The frosty white makes it difficult to see the white lines of the highway, forcing traffic to slow, and I suddenly miss the egg-yolk yellow lines of the two-lane country roads.

"You don't think it's safe to go back to Vermont?" Luke asks after a stretch of silence.

"No," I say and shake my head. "Now that they know what we look like, they could do facial recognition with surveillance cameras and track us down there."

"You really think Fernando's people have that kind of technology?" Luke says, glancing at me, then turning his eyes back to the snowy highway.

"I don't know but I'm not willing to take that kind of risk," I say and point at our cracked but not shattered (thank you, Black Angels, for the bulletproof glass) back window. "Are you?"

"I guess not," Luke answers, biting down on the inside of his cheek.

"They're still going to be looking for us," I say, turning back toward the window. "We need to get off the highway soon and call Cam. Figure out a way to switch cars and keep driving west."

I press my head against the glass as we pass the fenced-in back-yards of a New Jersey neighborhood that I'm sure has some cute name for real estate marketing purposes. All of these people went to bed with muddy flower beds and dead leaves and forgotten dog droppings in the grass. This morning, they wake up with the ugliness of everyday life gone, blanketed by several inches of white. It's not exactly the snow of fairy tales, but it's still dazzling as it falls. Snow, especially around Christmas, is nothing short of magical. Even when there's dog shit hiding a few inches below.

"God, I'm so stupid," Harper says, her voice thin in the backseat. I turn around to see her studying her hands, wringing them together, pulling at her fingers.

"Why do you say that?" I ask her.

"I thought he was really nice," Harper says, still staring down at her hands.

"Who? Mateo?" I ask.

"Yeah. I feel stupid for liking him so much," Harper says, her eyes clouding as she continues to try to put all the pieces of this screwed-up puzzle together. "So he was just . . . it was all just . . ."

"It was all fake," I confirm as Harper watches the snow out the window. I touch her on her knee, startling her out of her stare. "A setup. A way to get at you. Probably to flush us out."

"So, what happens now?" Harper asks, looking back and forth between us. "Can you guys just drop me off in Ohio or something?"

Luke shoots me a look, his eyebrows raised in my direction.

Shit. My hands immediately rise to my cheeks as my mind races. For the last six hours, all I could think about was getting to Harper and fleeing Manhattan. All I wanted was to keep my best friend alive. The fallout from all this, she's not ready for. And quite frankly, neither am I.

God, what have I done?

My tongue swells in my mouth. I bite down on it to stop it from thickening, blocking the very hard truth that must tumble out of my mouth.

I turn back around to face Harper, the frown that's already on her face falling even deeper as she reads the concern sketched across my own.

"What?" she asks, pushing her hands against her thighs and locking her elbows.

"You can't go home," I say and shake my head. "It's way too dangerous. If Fernando's people knew where your dorm was, they absolutely know where you live in New Albany. They'll find you and take you. You're not safe there."

"But it's holiday break," Harper says, leaning back in her seat and crossing her arms over her chest, her voice and stance growing more and more defensive. "I was supposed to fly home tomorrow. I've got a plane ticket. My parents are expecting me."

"I know," I answer and take a breath, trying to find some relief from the rancid remorse at the pit of my stomach. But air doesn't help. "We'll work with CORE to come up with some kind of cover story. To make sure your parents know you're okay. But you cannot call them without our permission. And you absolutely cannot tell them what's going on or then they'll be at risk too."

"We should probably tell Cam that they need a guard on their house," Luke says, and I nod.

"What? A guard? For my family?" Harper says, getting louder with each word.

"They won't know anyone is even there," I assure her. "They'll be out of view. It's just a precaution."

"I'll die if something happens to my parents," Harper says, her fingers now shaking and digging into her stomach. "Please. You cannot let anything happen to them, Reagan."

"I promise you," I say, trying to take her trembling hand into my own. "I will make sure they are safe."

"Just like you made sure I was safe?" Harper says, her voice growing angry. She yanks her hand away from mine.

"Harper, look, just calm down and . . ." I begin, but she cuts me off.

"How am I supposed to calm down?" Harper snaps, bringing her hands to her head and pulling at her hair, her eyes now filling with tears. "Unless you have Valium on you, I am going to freak out. I've got someone trying to kill me. I'm not allowed to go home. My family is in danger. I'm driving who knows where and can't be with the people I love for Christmas."

"Neither can I," I say quietly, immediately regretting my horrible attempt at empathy as soon as the words leave my mouth.

"Yeah, but you chose this crazy, dangerous life, Reagan," Harper says, narrowing her eyes at me. "I didn't. But somehow along the way, it looks like you cursed me with it too."

You obliterate everything you touch.

The last words of Santino Torres come back to me, the memory causing my body to sway. He was right. All I do is hurt.

My jaw slacks as I search for the right words. But they don't come. And they probably never will. Because how do you even begin to apologize for destroying so many lives?

I turn back around in my seat and stare at the growing snow-storm, my lips clenched between my teeth. Besides the windshield wipers, the car is silent. My brain repeats the daily affirmation that began the morning after my mother's murder.

You should have died. You should have died. You should have died.

EIGHT

"WILL THAT BE CREDIT CARD OR CASH?" ASKS THE petite motel clerk with mousey brown hair and meek voice. I'm standing on beige linoleum floors meant to look like tile. But the glue has worn off in the corners and they're starting to peel back. The wobbly front desk is wrapped in seventies knotted wood paneling and looks like it could tip over with one good push. Large black water spots dot the tiled ceiling panels and the buzz of the cheap fluorescent lights burrows into my ear canal.

"Cash," I answer quickly and reach into my wallet to pull out the forty-five dollars that is advertised on the sign out front.

After calling Cam, we were able to change out our damaged SUV for a black Jeep from a Black Angel watcher in Cranford, New Jersey. From there, we were instructed to stay on back roads (fewer security cameras at off-the-grid diners and motels) and keep driving west through Pennsylvania. We've been getting instructions directly from Cam and Sam (she was brought in against my initial protest). I was told my father was busy with a mission back at CORE and would "deal with me later." Yeah. Can't wait. Every time the phone rings, I want to throw myself out of the car. While it's moving.

"You'll be staying in room one forty-one," she says, handing me a real key. I haven't seen a real key at a hotel in ... well ... maybe ever. "Checkout is at noon."

"Thanks," I say, gripping the green plastic key chain. "Is there a restaurant or fast food or anything near here?"

"There's an Arby's about five miles away," she says, looking over my shoulder at the whirling snowstorm. "But I wouldn't go out if I were you. Tow trucks can take hours to get out here. Vending machine's a few doors down from your room if you're hungry."

"Okay," I say with a nod. A dinner of Cheetos and Twizzlers it is.

"I hope you enjoy your stay," the clerk calls after me as I walk back out into the dark December night. The wind immediately rips open my coat and my hair is covered in thick white flakes in a matter of seconds. I move quickly toward the waiting Jeep and hop back in the front seat, welcoming the blast of artificial heat.

"Room one forty-one. Closest food place is several miles down the street," I answer and search for the direction of our room. "Looks like it's a vending machine kind of night."

"Aw, man," Harper says, squirming in the backseat. "I'm starving. We've barely eaten anything today."

The watcher brought us gas station hot dogs (that tasted like they had been cooking on one of those little rolly machines for five days) and bottled water when we switched out cars so we didn't have to stop and get caught anywhere on camera.

"I know," I answer and point Luke in the direction of room 141

67

on the opposite side of the L-shaped motel. "I'm hungry too. But these back roads are completely covered. And it's not like we can call AAA if we skid off the road. We can stop at the Arby's on the way out of town tomorrow."

"Oh my God. It's an Arby's?" Harper says before slapping her hands on the leather seats in frustration. "I'd seriously strangle an ugly cat for a roast beef and cheddar sandwich right now. I'd strangle a really cute one for a large curly fry."

"You're crazy," Luke says with a little laugh as he backs out of his spot near the motel lobby. "But yeah, it's better we stay put. I'll get us some vending machine goodies."

"There better be Doritos in that vending machine," Harper replies as Luke carefully guides the car through the slick parking lot toward our room. "Or don't even bother coming back."

———✦———

Click. Click. Click. Click.

Harper is sitting on one of the two double beds in our motel room, turning the knob on the brass reading light next to the bed on and off. On and off. She sits on the bedspread, a hideous beige, brown, and rust flower pattern, still in her puffy jacket, staring blankly at the boxy TV that has probably been bolted down onto the dresser since 1993.

I unbutton my jacket and throw it onto one of the two rust-colored chairs that anchor a small wood table.

Click. Click. Click. Click.

This room, like most of our drive today, is tense and silent. Except for the clicking. That's new.

"Do you want to watch TV or something?" I ask and cross the room to pick up the remote.

"I wouldn't touch that if I were you," Harper says, shaking her head. "I read that TV remotes are *the* most disgusting things in a hotel room. Even fancy places. So imagine how many germs are on a remote in a place like this."

"This place is not *that* bad," I reply, skipping the remote and sitting down on the opposite double bed.

"Are you kidding me?" Harper asks, raising her eyebrows, still fiddling with the light switch. "This motel is where prostitutes come to die."

"I know you're used to five star, but this is not the coke-and-hooker den you think it is. It's just a rundown motel."

"Are you kidding me?" Harper says, scrunching up her face. "I don't even want to take off my coat."

The door behind me swings open, crashing violently against the wall, causing both Harper and me to jump. I spin around, my nerves firing, ready to attack.

"Jesus," I say, my tense shoulders falling as I see Luke standing in the doorway, struggling to carry two armfuls of vending machine goodies.

"Sorry, I'm juggling like half the contents of that vending machine," Luke replies, a gust of wind picking up the snow on the pavement outside our room, the snowflakes swirling around Luke's legs. He steps inside the room, slamming the door with his foot, before dumping thousands of calories worth of snacks on the bed next to me.

"Ladies, a feast," he says, taking off his coat and throwing it with mine on the chair. "And there were Doritos. I got the kind you like, Harper."

"Cool Ranch?" she asks, her eyes comically wide with hope.

"Cool Ranch," he responds, tossing her the blue bag.

"God, I love you," she says, shaking her head and tearing open the cellophane. "And I missed the shit out of you, Luke. Well, missed the shit out of both of you this last year."

"We missed you too," I reply, an unexpected rush of emotion tightening my vocal cords. Harper catches the change in my voice and looks up at me, her face softening for the first time all day. She'll never really understand just how much I missed her. How I used to lie awake in the safe house in Virginia and try to imagine an alternate life back with her and Malika in New Albany. How I've gone on spring break and to prom and to graduation parties with her, all in my own mind. And that these manufactured memories kept me breathing when all I wanted was to follow my mother into the black.

"It was hard when you guys didn't come back to school," Harper says, her mouth crunching down on chips. "I thought it was weird that it happened at the same time, but the excuses made sense."

"What cover story did CORE come up with for you, Luke?" I ask, realizing I never had.

"That I got accepted into a JROTC program that would help my chances of getting into West Point," he says, taking a seat next to me on the bed and opening up a bag of pizza-flavored Combos.

"It was believable," Harper says, licking remnants of Cool Ranch flavoring off her fingers. "And then of course getting your email, Reagan, I was so devastated for you. I emailed you a million times. Called your cell phone over and over again. Finally, I think I got a message saying your phone had been disconnected and I stopped calling. I was just so . . . confused. And sad."

"I'm really sorry," I say, my nails picking at the pilled fabric of the chair. "I wasn't allowed to reach out to you. I had to beg them to even let me write you that email to say good-bye."

"I'm glad I know that now," Harper says, glancing up at me for a moment and then back down at her bag of chips. "I just didn't understand why you wouldn't want to talk to me anymore. Why I couldn't come to your mother's funeral or visit you. I was pissed to be honest. But I sort of thought maybe your past reminded you of your mother and that's why you cut me out of your life. Couldn't have predicted it was because you two were training to be secret government operatives or whatever the hell you are."

The satellite phone begins ringing and my muscles immediately clench, knowing who will be on the other end.

I don't want to deal with you. I don't want to deal with you.

Luke glances at the phone behind us on the table and then back at me, knowing it's most likely my father.

Ring. Ring. Ring.

"I know you don't want to talk to him," he says, reading my mind. "But you've got to answer it or they're going to think something is wrong."

He's right. I rise from my spot on the bed and pick up the satellite phone.

"Hello," I say into the mouthpiece.

71

"Reagan Elizabeth, just what the hell were you thinking?" My father's gruff voice fills my ear. I look up to see Harper and Luke trying to occupy themselves with their bags of snacks but clearly able to hear my father on the other end.

"Nice to hear your voice too, Dad," I say and lean my body against the wood table.

"Answer me, Reagan," he pushes.

"I was doing what you trained me to do," I say with a sigh.

"What I trained you to do was follow orders and yet you've managed to constantly screw that up, which is how you got yourself into this mess in the first place. You don't understand the shit I had to do to get you into the Shadow Program. The strings I pulled and favors I called in to put you somewhere safe. And you couldn't even last up in Vermont for one month without going rogue. If it wasn't for me, you and Luke would have been handed new IDs before being dropped off at some bus station with a few hundred dollars in your pockets."

"Dad, look . . . I'm very grateful . . ." I begin but he keeps talking.

"Do you know just how badly Fernando wants to kill you and Luke?" he asks, his voice swelling with fury. "Do you get it? Do you even understand what you did in Indonesia? By killing Santino Torres, you have taken away the leader of one of the most powerful drug cartels in the world. You have weakened their business and the leaders that are left want your head on a stake."

"Of course I understood the risk of leaving Vermont," I reply, cradling the satellite phone between my ear and shoulder as I throw on my peacoat. "But what was I supposed to do, Dad? Let Harper get kidnapped? Let her die? Because God forbid I screw up your position at CORE or make you look bad for pulling strings to get us into the Shadow Program."

"Reagan, do not minimize all I've done for you," my father says, his voice growing harsher by the second. I open the door and step outside into the winter storm, away from the prying eyes and ears of my friends. "I still can barely get my head around what you did in Indonesia. Not to mention the fact that you *lied* to me for a year."

"I never lied to you, Dad," I reply, a burst of freezing wind striking my cheek. I hug my arms to my chest, trying to conserve the little warmth I have, and suddenly I wish I was back at our house in New Albany, fighting over a boy or bad grades or sneaking out at night. Something normal fathers and daughters fight about. Not this.

"Yes, you did," he answers. "I thought you were becoming a Black Angel because you wanted to help people. I believed you were in Qualifiers for the right reasons. We cut other promising trainees who really wanted to be there. All so you could kill Santino. All so you could get your revenge."

My entire body is trembling and I can't tell if it's from the cold or this long-awaited confrontation or both. I shake out my free arm, trying to stop the quivering, but it doesn't help.

"I killed the man who killed my mother," I hiss. "Your wife. Remember?"

My legs take several large steps down the open motel corridor until I reach the door for the vending machine and ice. I slip inside the semi-warm space, my eyes quickly scanning the room for cameras.

"Do not patronize me," my father answers, his voice cracking with wrath. "Your mother was my world. Of course I wanted Santino dead. But there is a right way and a wrong way to do things. And Reagan, you chose the wrong way. You could have stayed with the Black Angels and helped us catch him down the road and still go on to change the world. But you wanted to do it your way. So you lied and manipulated me. You've betrayed me. And you've betrayed your mother."

His words knock me back. I force my body up against the cinderblock wall of the tiny, enclosed space just to stay upright.

Selfish girl. Selfish girl. Selfish girl.

"I . . . I'm . . ." my voice stammers as tears scratch at my throat, stealing the words on my tongue. I picture my father pacing in front of the desk at his small office in CORE, his neck red from both his rage and the tie he's worn all day.

After several seconds of silence, I clear my throat and push my voice to speak. "I'm sorry, Dad. I'm really sorry. For everything."

Dad takes in a deep breath on the other end of the phone and I picture him shaking his head, his thumb and middle fingers rubbing at opposite, pulsing temples.

"I'm just really disappointed in you, Reagan," my father says. "I never thought I'd say that. You used to make me so proud."

Disappointed. One of the worst words a parent could say. Angry, yes. Annoyed, irritated, pissed off. Those emotions come and go. But disappointment cuts. It lingers.

"So, what are we going to do about Harper?" I ask, anxious to change the subject. There's nothing more I can say. Nothing I can do to make him forgive me.

My body finally gives in and slides down the slick cinder-block wall until it settles on the cold tile beneath my feet. "Have you been able to reach her parents?"

"We got a message to them," my dad replies, his voice deepening, changing from father to Black Angel senior leader. "They think she's going to be working on a movie as a production assistant in NYC over the holiday break. They asked if they could come and visit her on set, but we told her she was going to be too busy. Once we're off the phone, you need to give her a sat phone and have her call them. Make sure she tells them how excited she is but reiterate again how busy she'll be. Also make sure she tells them she lost her phone in a taxi and won't be able to call or text much until her new phone arrives. That should hold them off from getting too worried for a few days. We'll instruct you when she can call them. But do not allow her to call on her own, got it?"

"Got it," I answer. "We made her throw her cell phone out the window back in Manhattan."

"Well, at least that's one smart move, Reagan," Dad answers, making little effort to hide his exasperation with me even as the conversation moves into mission mode. "We're still searching for Fernando and his people. We know they are obviously in the country, and we're doing our best to locate them, but between several terror threats in Europe and a high-profile kidnapping, some of our guys have been taken off the hunt. But we're looking."

"Thanks, Dad," I say, my throat tightening, making it hard to swallow. "So . . . what are we supposed to do now?"

"You've got an army of assassins looking for the three of you," Dad says, his voice teetering between annoyance and worry. "So there's really only one thing you can do."

"And what's that?"

"Run."

NINE

RUN. RUN. RUN.

Dad's words have been playing on a loop in my head for hours, rattling against my skull like a drumbeat.

Run. Run. Run.

My knees bounce to the steady, imaginary sound as I sit in the rust-colored chair, my Glock 22 on my lap, and stare out the window. It's after three a.m. and I said I'd take the first watch even though I haven't slept in nearly forty-eight hours. But my brain has yet to reach that delirious state of exhaustion. I'm wired and edgy, my muscles twitching below my sweatshirt, just waiting for Fernando's people to hunt us down.

Luke and Harper are asleep in opposite beds. They didn't want to go to sleep but I said they had to. That they wouldn't be able to function the next day without rest. They both were reluctantly lulled to sleep by a late-night episode of *Forensic Files.'* I don't know what it is about that narrator's voice. Even though he's talking about blood splatter and bullet wounds, *Forensic Files* is strangely (and maybe sadistically) calming and can put anyone out for the night.

A pair of headlights invades our dark space. The curtains are strategically half closed so I can stay hidden yet see out without having to move the fabric, alerting anyone to our whereabouts. Harper is sleeping in the bed closest to me. The light hits her peaceful face, stirring her out of a dream. Once the car is parked and the light is gone, I pull back the curtain an inch with my fingertip and peer outside, clutching my gun, my finger poised near the trigger.

"What is it?" Harper whispers nervously next to me. "Is it them?"

"I don't know," I whisper back and squint my eyes at the tan pickup truck parked two spots over from our car. A young couple finally steps out from the truck, a sleeping toddler wrapped in the woman's arms. The family makes their way to a room a few doors down and slams the door shut behind them.

"Well?" Harper whispers harshly.

"It was nothing," I reply, closing the curtain and returning the gun to my lap. "Just a family probably wanting to get some rest and get out of the snowstorm. Go back to sleep."

"I wasn't really sleeping," Harper says, propping herself up on her elbow. "My brain won't stop. I don't know how you ever sleep."

"I don't really," I answer and settle my body back in my lumpy, uncomfortable chair. "Occupational hazard. Even before everything with my mom and living at CORE and stuff . . . I didn't really sleep. My brain was always going."

I was a hard sleeper as a kid. At least until I found out what my parents really did for a living. Before I even realized just how dangerous their jobs really were, every sound, every movement would wake me. My parents' footsteps in the hallway. Tree branches hitting my window during a storm. Pipes knocking while someone brushed their teeth. The sounds of ordinary life would rouse me from my half dream, my eyes wide, my muscles tight, ready to fight or flee. I realize now that I've never felt safe. I've always been poised for death and disaster. I've spent my life waiting for something bad to happen.

Something like this.

Even in the dark, I can see Harper's eyes studying me, her eyebrows cinching closer together.

"What?" I finally ask.

"Nothing, it's just . . ." Harper says, looking down as her hands smooth out the comforter. She then lifts her head up, her eyes focused on me. "How did you keep all the lies straight?"

"I don't know," I say and tuck a strand of my hair behind my ear. "It's what I was trained to do my entire life. I've had a lot of cover stories. So I've told a lot of lies."

Harper glances down again as her fingers pick at the blanket's tiny balls of fading yellow fabric. She rubs the pilling pieces between her thumb and index finger, easing them free. After a few moments, she looks back up at me, pain and betrayal written in her eyes, and before she even opens her mouth, I know what she's going to say.

"So, how often did you lie to me?" she asks, her voice scratchy with tempered emotions. "Even after you ghosted me, when I talked about you, I still referred to you as my best friend. But . . . I didn't really know you at all. Did I?"

I lick my lips as I think about the question. A stinging, nagging guilt always lingered beneath the surface of my skin when it came to Harper and Malika. Because they thought they knew me so well. They thought they knew all my secrets. My biggest fears and hopes and dreams. Some of it was manufactured, lies from the pretender to fit in, go unnoticed. But part of it was me. At least, I think it was. Sometimes I didn't know where the pretender ended and the real Reagan began. I think maybe I still don't.

"Some things I said because they were part of my cover," I finally answer. "Some things were really me."

"So, were Malika and I just part of your cover?" Harper asks, her chest rising and voice giving way to the wounds she's been trying to hide. "Was our friendship just all bullshit? A lie? Did you become friends with us just to fit into whatever new identity you were trying to spin?"

The aching knot in my stomach tightens because the truth will hurt her. Yes, I did target Malika and Harper as friends when I first got to New Albany High School. They were the "fringers." Invited to the big parties but never the exclusive birthday dinners or sleepovers with all the popular girls. They were known around school but never the center of attention. They were the small and uncomplicated group of friends I immediately knew I needed to infiltrate so I could blend into high school life quickly. It pains me to admit that my motivation to become friends with Harper and Malika was part of my training because I grew to love everything about them.

"The truth?" I ask, nervous that telling Harper she was part of my never-stand-out strategy might wreck her. But I'm just so tired of the lies. "At first, I thought you guys were the perfect friends to make so I could blend in quickly. But honestly, you really did become my best friends. And I loved you. I never had friends like you and

Malika before. Becoming your best friend made me envision a totally different life for myself. One where I walked away from the Black Angels and just lived as ... well ... me."

"Really?" Harper asks, her eyes widening.

"Absolutely. Girls like me don't often find friends like you. I missed you every single day after I left. I had this alternate universe in my head that I'd escape to where we were still best friends. I used to imagine that we'd write each other emails about college. That you'd tell me about all your film classes and how much you loved New York and how you were never coming back to Ohio. And I'd imagine Malika would write about Georgia and all the hot guys down there and how she wanted to rush a sorority, and we'd make fun of her."

"She does want to rush in the spring and you bet your ass I make so much fun of her," Harper says, rubbing her button nose with the back of her hand and stifling a laugh. "I can't believe she wants to be a sorority girl."

"Oh, I totally can," I answer, picturing Malika at that last Mark Ricardi party. Colorful dress, drink in hand, holding court with the entire Australian travel soccer team. "Think about it. She was always the first girl up on the coffee table at parties. She was ridiculously good at beer pong. She wanted every party to have some sort of theme. Even her sleepovers had themes. Totally prepping herself for sorority life."

"Oh my God, you're right," Harper says, laying her body back down in the bed. "She *was* a sorority girl in training. I missed that about her and we've been friends forever."

"Again. Occupational hazard. I analyze."

"Even your friends?"

"I guess so."

"So analyze me, Dr. MacMillan," Harper says, her smile growing wider before hitting her hand to her forehead. "Crap. I mean Hillis or whatever the hell your name really is."

"It's Hillis," I answer and cock my head to one side. "So . . . you really want my analysis of you?"

"Absolutely," Harper says, pushing her body into a sitting position.

"Well, you're one of the most self-assured people I've ever met," I begin, shifting my body so I can look at Harper while still watching out the window. "You don't really care what everyone else is doing or what everyone else thinks. You do your own thing and have a lot of confidence in the decisions you make. And all of this makes you effortlessly cool. You are funny and sarcastic and quick-witted, yes, but you are mush on the inside. Your heart is both the softest and strongest thing about you. You'd do pretty much anything for the people you love."

Harper's eyes shine, even in the pale light, and I can tell she's biting at the inside of her cheek to stop herself from crying.

"My world was lonely without you in it," I say quietly, causing that shine in her eyes to turn into tears. One breaks free and falls down her cheek. She sniffs and quickly wipes it away. Harper was my color, my joy. I didn't realize how drab and gray everything was without her there. But I hate the reason that we're now back together.

"Mine too," she finally says, pushing her wavy hair over her shoulder. "I'm sorry I've been so mean to you today. This is just all . . .

it's just a lot. You don't deserve for me to get so angry with you. Thank you for saving me and..."

"Do not apologize to me," I cut her off, waving my hand at her. "There's nothing for you to apologize for. I'm the one who is sorry you're in danger."

"You didn't do it," Harper says, shaking her head, a wavy curl brushing against her cheek.

"I know I'm not the bad guy here," I answer, pushing out my chest and stretching my sore back. "But you know how some people have the golden touch? I have the poison touch. Everything I do turns bad."

"That's not true."

"Yes, it is."

Harper looks around our rundown motel room. It's hard for anyone to argue with me on that one. Dead mother? Check. Lunatic looking for me for over a year? Check. Army of assassins now after all of us? Check.

She opens her mouth but clamps her jaw shut.

"What?" I push.

Harper lays her body back down on the bed and laces her fingers together, settling them on top of her stomach. She stares at the ceiling and sucks in a slow and steady breath through her pursed lips. "What's going to happen, Reagan? I mean, am I ever going to be allowed to go back to school? Will I see my family again?"

My shoulders seize up, the tendons collecting into tight lumps. I've been asking myself those very same questions all day. I don't have the answers, and I'm just as terrified to know the truth as she is.

"I don't know," I finally answer and shake my head. "I don't know what's going to happen."

Logic tells me there's no way Harper will be back at NYU for second semester. That the chances of her living a normal life again are slim. That her dreams of becoming a film director are over. Because if someone wants you dead, the last thing you need is your name in the pages of *Variety* or your face on *E! News*.

Harper sighs and closes her eyes, rolling her body onto her side toward me. She settles her face into the thin pillow. After sixty seconds of silence, her breath deepens and I think she's fallen asleep until she whispers, "Reagan?"

"Yes?"

"I'm scared."

I reach out and touch her hand. She keeps her eyes closed but threads her fingers through mine. I trace the lines of her high cheekbones, the arch of her thick eyebrows, her collection of long eyelashes. I want so desperately to tell her, *Don't worry. It will be okay. There's nothing to be scared about.* But I'm all out of lies.

"Me too," I whisper back. She squeezes my hand hard one time and then lets go.

I return my empty hand to the loaded pistol on my lap. As I watch her fall asleep, a visceral fear floods my bloodstream, pushing against my veins and tightening my chest. I dig my fingers into my center, rubbing at my flesh and trying to relax this vital muscle, but it constricts even more. I look back out the window and into the dark night as my heart pounds its anxious commands.

Run. Run. Run.

TEN

"IF YOU HAVE A RUDOLPH NOSE AND ANTLERS ON your car, I kind of know everything I need to know about you," Harper says as we pass a car brimming with Christmas cheer. I watch Harper in my rearview mirror as she takes a gulp of her coffee. Her face cringes before she coughs into her gloved hand. "And in other news, this coffee is horrible."

"Bad coffee is better than no coffee," I reply, taking a sip of my own gas station coffee. It's bitter and maybe even a little gritty, but it's the only cure for my fuzzy head. Two hours of sleep in two days, and I'm the one driving this leg of our little road trip (trying to forget about the assassins who want to slit our throats and thinking of this as a road trip subdues my desire to slam the Jeep into a concrete barrier or break down into hysterical tears).

"I'm sure it tastes at least half decent to you with all of the sugar and cream you put in it," Luke says in the seat next to me. I take another sip.

"Yeah, yours is like sugar water with a little coffee flavoring," Harper adds.

"Well, who would ever think that taking your coffee black at a gas station would be a good idea," I reply as I put my coffee back into the cup holder and steer the Jeep up the ramp onto Interstate 76. I know the Black Angels said to stay on as many back roads as possible, but the country roads are still covered in snow, and we need to move. We can't stay in the same place for longer than a day. We've always got to be one step ahead of Fernando and his assassins.

"When did you start taking your coffee black anyways, Harper?" Luke asks, turning around to look at her. "You've always taken cream and sugar. And don't get me started on the sugary Frappuccinos you drank every single day sophomore and junior year. What did you do, go to NYU and suddenly decide that milk and sweetener were only for people in flyover states?"

"Oh, stop it," Harper says. I look in my rearview mirror and see her smiling. "I'm not an NYU elitist."

"Not yet," Luke answers, which makes Harper laugh and punch him in the shoulder. Hard. Luke immediately grabs at the bruising flesh beneath his coat. "Ow! Okay, okay, I'm just kidding. Stop hitting me. Seriously though, how are you liking NYU?"

"Love everything about it," Harper answers, her voice growing quieter with each word. I glance back in the mirror as the smile on her face vanishes. She catches my eyes for a moment before turning her head and staring out the window, her face dulling at the sight of our cold, gray morning. Luke takes a gulp of his coffee, probably wishing he had never asked. No good can come from reminding

Harper of the life she had twenty-four hours ago. The one she'll now likely lose. Because of us. Because of me.

The car falls quiet as we travel down the plowed highway, snow piled high on each of the interstate's shoulders, the white graying and splattered with mud. The snow has stopped, the *swish, swish, swish* of the windshield wipers is gone. Silence expands in the car, making the air heavier and harder to breathe, and I long for noise.

I turn on the radio, scanning until we find a station. The crystal-clear voice of Karen Carpenter singing "Ave Maria" fills the car and that hollow spot inside me begins to moan.

The Carpenters' Christmas album was Mom's favorite. Mine too. "Ave Maria" was even a favorite of my father's, who never did get into the spirit of the season. We weren't a particularly religious family. We didn't go to church or read the Bible or pray before family dinner. But one night, just a few days before Christmas, Mom and I sat in our dark family room, tree lit and fireplace on, listening to Karen Carpenter sing in Latin about the Blessed Mother.

"She must have been really scared," my mother had said to me as she sipped the cup of herbal tea she always drank before bed to help her sleep.

"Who?" I had asked.

"Mary," she said, her lips gathering into a pondering pout. "Finding herself pregnant and on this long journey. Knowing she has to raise this very important child. That her son will one day change the world."

I had pulled the blanket higher up on my chest and rested my face against the couch's cool leather as I looked over at my mother. We never really talked about religion or beliefs or faith. I knew the basic stories of the Bible. The headlines. Jesus. The crucifixion. Moses. The parting of the Red Sea. Noah and the flood. But that was all. It wasn't a subject that we avoided. It just wasn't a topic of conversation. Still, I was curious and asked, "Do you think Jesus was really the Son of God?"

I had watched my mother as her eyes studied the bright lights and colorful ornaments on the tree. After a few moments, she slowly turned her head toward me. "I don't know," she had answered with a gentle shrug. "I guess I'd like to think so. And if it is all true, what an amazing woman Mary was, right? What a responsibility to shoulder."

"Reagan," Luke's voice pulls me out of my own head. "The same car has been following us ever since we got on the highway."

Shit. What am I doing? I should be paying attention.

"Which one?" I ask and look into my rearview mirror, surveying the vehicles behind us. There's a red SUV in the left lane directly behind us. A white four-door car in the middle lane. A gray pickup truck behind them and a black SUV in the far right lane.

"The pickup," Luke replies, turning around slightly in his seat to get a better look.

"Where?" Harper asks and begins to turn around to look out the back window.

"Don't, Harper," I say, my voice a little too harsh. She turns her body back around. "If it is Fernando's people, we don't want them to know they've been spotted."

"What the hell, you guys?" Harper says, sinking her body lower into her seat. "We switched cars. I ditched my cell phone. How could they find us? I thought we were safe."

We're never safe, my mind laments. But I can't tell Harper that or she'll freak out.

"We've taken every precaution to keep us safe," I answer and want to roll my eyes at my sterile, stereotypical Black Angel reply.

"It may not even be anything," Luke says, now facing forward and watching the truck in his side mirror. "Can you get a visual on the passenger and driver?"

"No, I can't," I answer, easing up on the accelerator, hoping to bring the truck a little closer to us so I can see inside the cab. But as I decelerate, the truck eases up on the gas as well. The red SUV is now on my ass, the driver throwing his hands up in the air, visibly agitated by my slowing pace. I turn on my blinker and move the car into the middle lane. As the SUV zooms past me, the driver and passenger both shoot me a scowl like I was going thirty miles per hour instead of seventy.

"Chill out, assholes!" Harper yells, reacting to the duo of dirty looks.

I ease up on the gas again, trying to pull the truck closer to us in traffic. But they don't take the bait.

"I still can't see them," I say and shake my head. I look in my rearview mirror one more time but can only make out two lumpy figures in the passenger and driver's seats. "They keep slowing down when we slow down."

"On purpose?" Harper says, her voice tightening.

"I don't know," I say and shake my head.

"It's them, it's them, it's them, it's them," Harper groans, wringing her hands together and trying to look over her shoulder again.

"Harper, stop," I command, whipping her head back around with the sternness in my voice. "It may be nothing. It could just be a family on the road. But you have to stay calm."

I feel immediately bad for demanding calmness out of someone whose biggest problem forty-eight hours ago was getting through a three-hour History of Film exam. How can I expect Harper to be calm when she went from never seeing a gun in real life to having assassins *shoot* at her? I'm lucky she hasn't had a complete breakdown yet. Still, she obeys, taking in a deep breath before sinking further into her seat.

"I can't see them either, Reagan," Luke says, narrowing his eyes and staring at the truck in the passenger-side mirror. "See what happens if you speed up."

I put on my blinker, change lanes, and hit the gas. I don't want to tip them off by going too fast, but as I reach eighty miles an hour, I look in my rearview to see the truck changing lanes and speeding up behind me.

"Keep up the speed," Luke instructs. "Either they're just trying to get around that car or they're following us."

I push the Jeep's speed to eighty-five, the tires crunching against freshly laid salt. The truck stays far enough back that I still cannot make out their faces or even genders, but it keeps up with our increasing pace.

"Come on," I say to the rearview mirror. "Who are you?"

I move the Jeep back into the middle lane, my heart pounding against my sternum, and take my foot off the accelerator. I wait for the truck to maintain their fast speed, move closer to us. But they hang back, their speed still parallel with mine.

"Damn it," Luke says as he watches, rubbing his anxious hands against his jeans.

It's them, it's them, it's them. My brain repeats Harper's whimper as the nerves in my fingers begin to tingle, quickly spreading to my hands, forearms, and biceps. I roll back my shoulders, trying to stop the debilitating buzz from spreading as I glance in the rearview mirror at the truck, my breath held in my throbbing chest. I hit the accelerator once again and this time, the truck stays back. Perhaps it's nothing. Or perhaps my constant change in speed has tipped them off.

"I'm going to get off here and see what happens," I say, more to myself than to Harper or Luke. I pull the car into the right-hand lane and make my way toward the next exit to some forgettable town with one motel, three fast food restaurants, and two gas stations making up the local economy.

I watch in my rearview mirror as the truck changes lanes. I finally take in a breath, the air entering my lungs with the sharpness of a thousand safety pins, as I guide the Jeep down the exit ramp.

Will they follow?

As I pull down the ramp, I watch in my mirror as the truck keeps on going, past the no name town, past the three of us.

"Maybe it was nothing," Luke says quietly, his tense body sinking back into the leather seat.

As I pull up to the red light, my mouth pushes out a small sigh of relief but my muscles refuse to unknot. Because the days of looking over our shoulders, waiting to feel a pistol at our backs, are far from over. And as I lean my forehead against the cold steering wheel, I wonder if this constant fear will ever end.

ELEVEN

"THINK THEY HAVE CHRISTMAS SUGAR COOKIES OR something in there?" Harper asks, her eyes on the convenience store with a neon Bud Light sign flashing in the window.

"It's a gas station in the middle of Iowa," I answer and look out into the darkness, catching a glimpse of a middle-aged man with shaggy gray hair and a deep frown leaning against the counter near the register. "I think the best you can hope for is beef jerky and Hostess Snowballs."

Luke opens the driver's side door and leans his head into the car. The whine of a Muzak version of "The Christmas Song" floats into the car from a tiny speaker hanging close to our gas pump. "I need thirty-two bucks for the gas," he says, and I reach into my backpack to check on our stash of cash.

"Make it thirty-five," Harper says, sliding across the backseat and popping open the door. "If I can't have my mom's cookies on Christmas Eve, I'm at least going to get some type of sugary treat."

"Planning on Santa finding us at our motel?" I ask, pulling out two twenty-dollar bills from our dwindling supply and handing it over to Luke.

"Maybe he will," Harper says, attempting a small smile that looks highly inauthentic on her fatigued face.

"Reagan, got your gun?" Luke asks me quietly, waiting for me to check under the seat before leaving me alone in the car.

"Got it," I answer after I feel the grip of the handle. "All good."

"We'll be back in a minute," Luke says, slamming the car door.

"More like three, I've really got to pee," Harper adds, closing her door, and I can hear Luke arguing with her just to hold it until we get to the restaurant. It's an argument he won't win because as soon as Harper feels that need to pee, she obsesses over it until she goes. She used to get up just as we were about to drift off to sleep during sleepovers to ensure her bladder was completely empty. Even if she had peed ten minutes before. Some people have to go to bed with a clear mind. Harper can't sleep without a clear bladder.

I watch the two of them walk away as the most depressing version of "The Christmas Song" penetrates the car's glass and fills the quiet space. I glance up at the speaker. It's rusty and has a few wires sticking out of it, making the hollow notes sound even emptier.

"And so I'm offering this simple phrase, to kids from one to ninety-two," I sing softly along to drown out the version playing just beyond my pane of glass.

The shrill ring of the satellite phone fills the car, making my entire body jump. I close my eyes and lay my hand over my racing heart for a moment before reaching into the backpack and pulling it out.

"Hello?" I say into the receiver.

"Hey, sweetie," a warm voice replies. Sam. "Just wanted to check in and see how you guys were doing."

"Oh, we're doing okay," I answer, peering back into the convenience store where Luke is paying for gas and several of Harper's treats while she grabs the key to the bathroom. "Just on our way to a lovely Christmas Eve dinner in Waterloo, Iowa."

"Are there places open?" she asks.

"The guy who checked us in at our motel said there's a diner in town that stays open three hundred sixty-five days a year," I answer, cradling the phone in between my ear and shoulder so I can zip up my coat. Without the heat on, the car is getting cold.

"You're still staying away from name brand places, right?" Sam asks. "They'll have cameras at a Motel 6 or Red Roof Inn."

"Of course," I answer. "The shittier the place, the better."

"Where are you staying tonight?" she asks.

"The lovely Waterloo Woods Lodge. The name is pretty misleading. You'd think if you were going to call yourself a lodge, there'd be a little more charm. But the lobby is the worst one yet. Giant stains on the carpet. Depressing eighties flower wallpaper peeling off the wall. Like at least pretend to give a shit."

Sam lets out a laugh and the sudden pain of missing her feels like an ax to the center of my sternum. "Well, just keep doing what you're doing, okay? We're doing everything we can to track these guys. You just keep running and stay safe, okay?"

"Okay," I answer with a sigh.

"Merry Christmas," Sam says. "I really wish we were together tonight."

Tears prick at my eyes and I have to heave out a cough to push them back down.

"Me too, Sam," I answer, my voice raspy. "Merry Christmas."

***

Red. Green. Red. Green. Red. Green.

I stare out the diner window and watch as the Christmas lights flicker.

After driving for two days, living off of gas station pizza, drive-thru burgers, and bad coffee, I can't wait for a dish that's not fast food or Fritos.

They're trying to make it cheerful in here with shiny tinsel stapled along the side of the long Formica countertop bar and over-sized glittery red bulbs and silver stars hanging precariously from the tiled ceiling with pushpins. Our waitress is even wearing a little Santa hat, attempting to be as merry as she can for someone who has to serve just a handful of tables on Christmas Eve. She'll probably make fifteen bucks in tips tonight if she's lucky.

The thought of her counting her measly tips in that Santa hat at the end of the night blackens my already dark mood. As my eyes fixate on the blinking lights, I long for the warmth and excitement that used to bubble at my core on Christmas Eve. It was so strong as a child, like swallowing a million butterflies. They'd flap and tickle every part of me, nearly lifting me off the ground from the inside. That pure happiness subsided as I grew up, but it was still there. Tonight as I sit in a bright-red leather booth, that feeling is nowhere to be found. The only thing bubbling inside me is restrained alarm.

"Two Christmas specials," the waitress says, pushing plates of turkey, stuffing, and mashed potatoes with gravy toward Luke and me, seated together on one side of the booth. "And a pot roast dinner for you."

She slides the last plate toward Harper, who looks up at her with a small smile. "Thanks so much," she says as she picks up a fork, digging in before the waitress has even left the table. Harper's parents supply her with a healthy monthly allowance that allows her to eat at some of the best restaurants in the world, a few blocks in either direction from her dorm. Gas station cuisine has left her crabby during every meal.

"Enjoy," the waitress says with a nod, the furry white ball of her Santa hat flopping in front of her eyes. She pushes it aside as she makes her way to the only other occupied table, a corner booth where a young couple feed each other onion rings.

"Well, I wish we were doing this little Christmas Eve feast at the Dead End Diner in Ohio instead of this place in Who-the-Fuck-Knows-Where, Iowa," Harper says with a mouthful of pot roast.

"Me too," answers Luke as he dunks a piece of turkey into the pool of gravy over mashed potatoes. I take a bite of my own turkey.

"This turkey isn't half bad," I say, trying to brighten the mood as much as one can when it's Christmas Eve and you're not with your family. Oh . . . and on the run from people who are trying to *kill* you.

"Yeah, it's actually pretty darn good," Luke answers, taking another bite. "But we never had turkey on Christmas Eve. Always beef tenderloin or prime rib or something."

"Yeah, us neither," I answer. "My dad's mother is Italian. Like off the boat from Sicily. So even though I grew up only a quarter Italian, we always had the traditional Italian Christmas Eve dinner with the seven fishes and spaghetti and broccoli."

"Spaghetti and broccoli," Harper says, scrunching up her nose. "That sounds disgusting."

"It's actually really good," I answer and take a bite of mashed potatoes. "Really simple. One of my favorite dishes, and we'd only eat it on Christmas Eve. My grandma taught my mom how to make it so even when we didn't spend Christmases with them, my mom would always cook it for me and my dad. With Mom gone, Sam actually surprised me by making it last year in the safe house. I think this is the first Christmas Eve where I haven't had it."

My mind pulls up a memory of the last time my mom made our Christmas Eve meal. We were in the house in New Albany. Mom had spent the day running around, making clams and shrimp and mussels. Sam came over for dinner and we helped her steam the broccoli for the pasta and season the shrimp. And when we finally sat down, Dad had smiled and said, "Well, there aren't seven fishes here, but these three look pretty good to me." He fell asleep on the couch while Mom, Sam, and I watched Bing Crosby and Rosemary Clooney sing and dance in *White Christmas*. And at the end of the movie, as the entire cast sang Irving Berlin's "White Christmas," I looked over at my mother, her eyes glistening with predictable tears. She had caught me looking and smiled.

"This movie gets me every time," she said, swatting tears off her cheek with the back of her hands before taking my cold fingers into her warm palm. "I hope we're always together like this on Christmas."

"Me too," I said, not knowing that would be our very last Christmas together. I guess you never really know when something will be your last. I wish I did. Because maybe I would have lingered longer on the couch with her that night. Asked about her favorite Christmas memories. Tucked away each precious moment in my mental memory box.

"So, Reagan, what was your favorite Christmas present you ever got?" Harper asks, pulling my attention back to our sad little Christmas Eve meal.

"Hmmm ... I don't know," I reply and stare up at the glittering stars, flipping through the imaginary scrapbook in my brain. "We didn't really do a ton of presents. A few toys from Santa and then some practical gifts like clothes or shoes or whatever from my parents. But one year, I remember I wanted an Easy-Bake Oven so badly and Santa actually brought me one. So that was probably my favorite gift."

"Oh my gosh," Harper says, her hand covering her mouth full of potatoes. "I totally wanted one of those but I never got one."

"Making brownies and cakes using the heat from a light bulb," I reply and take another bite of turkey. "What else do you need in life?"

"What about you, Harper?" Luke asks, pointing his fork, glistening with turkey gravy, at her. "What was your favorite Christmas present?"

"Ummm . . . probably my Barbie dream house," Harper answers. "Oh. And my car. That was a pretty nice Christmas gift."

"You think?" I say with a laugh. "What other sixteen-year-old wakes up to a fully loaded Range Rover with a big red bow in the driveway?"

"Being an only child has its perks," Harper answers, raising her eyebrows and pulling at the ill-fitting flannel shirt I let her borrow. She looks back down at her plate, pushing the red-skinned potatoes around like hockey pucks. "They're going to be lonely without me this Christmas."

"Yeah. They will," I answer, guilt flaring beneath my skin.

"Are you sure we can't go home?" she asks, looking up from her plate of food, her eyes suddenly hopeful. "I mean if there's a watcher on my house already, maybe I'd be safe there."

"I'm sorry, Harper," I say and shake my head. "Black Angels' orders are to keep going. To not stay in one spot longer than a day. There's no way there's not at least one of Fernando's guys in New Albany right now. And as much as I want you to be with your family for Christmas, I'd also like to keep you alive."

"I know," Harper says, noisily dropping her fork against her ceramic plate before placing her forehead in both hands. She takes in a heavy breath. "I just really miss them. I haven't seen them since they dropped me off at school. They kept asking to visit but I told them I was too busy. Kind of wish I would have let them come now."

"You'll see them again soon," Luke answers, reaching across the table and touching Harper's forearm.

"Will I?" Harper asks, eyeing us both, suspicious.

"I hope so," I say, not wanting to depress her any further. "We will get this sorted out. I promise."

"It just feels like this won't end until there's a body count," Harper says, rubbing her face into her palms until her cheeks blaze crimson. And she's right. Death feels like the only way out of this.

The all-consuming fear I've pushed down into the deepest parts of my body begins to rise, spreading like poison, crippling my veins. I pull in a breath, trying to control it, and return my body to a state of numbness so Harper can't see the panic swelling behind my eyes.

"I just hope the bodies aren't ours," Harper says, practically stealing the words right out of my mouth. Words I'd never dare say out loud.

Me too, Harper. Me too.

TWELVE

"OH HOLY NIGHT, THE STARS ARE BRIGHTLY SHINING ...
It is the night of our dear Savior's birth ..."

Luke has been scanning the radio on the drive to our nearby
motel, but the only stations we can find are playing Christmas music.
He finally just gives up, and we drive through the city in silence,
listening to the sounds of the season.

We pull up to a stoplight in downtown Waterloo and Luke
puts on his signal to turn left. Across the street is a beautiful stone
church on a small hill. I've always loved church architecture, and
this one is particularly magnificent with its enormous circular
stained-glass window, arched doorways, and titanic towers that flank
each side. A manger scene is lit up in front, complete with the Three
Wise Men and angels and a baby Jesus, swaddled in the Virgin
Mother's arms.

"This is going to sound like an odd request," Harper says, leaning forward and poking her head in between the two front seats.
"But do you mind if we go inside the church for a few minutes?"

"Sure," Luke answers, turning around in his seat to look at Harper. "I didn't know you were religious."

"I was baptized Catholic but my family and I are total Chreasters," Harper answers.

"What's that mean?" I ask as the light turns green. Luke turns left and pulls the Jeep into an empty spot in front of the church.

"Christmas and Easter Catholics," she says, taking off her seat belt. "The bad Catholics who take up room on holidays. We used to go to Midnight Mass every Christmas Eve. I never wanted to go. But it's weird . . . I think I'm going to miss it. I'm sort of yearning all of a sudden for the smell of the pews and old hymnals. I just want to go inside for a few minutes. Light a candle. Say a prayer."

"Of course," I answer, unclicking my seat belt. "We'll go with you."

"Yeah, a little God couldn't hurt us right now," Luke says, putting the car in park and turning off the ignition.

"Hang on a second," I say, placing a hand on Luke's, stopping him from opening the driver's side door. "Let's just make sure no one is tailing us."

The car feels like a vacuum as we each hold our collected breaths. I turn around, studying the road, the parking spaces, the church itself. Downtown Waterloo is deserted. Everyone is at home, setting out cookies for Santa or reading *'Twas the Night Before Christmas*.

"Looks like we're clear," I say but drop my Glock 22 into my purse. Just in case. I button the top of my peacoat and pull my knit cap down until the fraying fabric is covering my ears. I pop open the Jeep's door and my face is immediately struck by a gust of freezing wind that makes my teeth chatter.

"Jesus," Luke says as we race up the church steps. "Did it get colder since we left the diner?"

I hug my arms to my chest as we climb the final steps and Luke pulls open one of the heavy wood doors. When we enter the church's foyer, a priest, dressed in a colorful Christmas robe, is heading in from the main part of the church, his eyes widening at the sight of the three of us.

"Can I help you?" the priest asks, stopping in his tracks.

"I'm sorry, is it okay if we come in?" Harper asks as we step farther inside, already comforted by the foyer's blast of heat.

"Of course," the priest says. His eyes are kind and his voice is monotone (which I bet makes for some very sleepy homilies). "All are welcome here. Especially on Christmas Eve. Will you be joining us later for Midnight Mass?"

"Probably not," Harper answers sheepishly. "We just wanted to light a candle and say a prayer."

"Well, please come in," the priest replies. "As long as you don't mind the choir practicing while you pray, stay as long as you'd like."

"Thank you, Father," Harper says, removing her hat and shaking out her hair. "Merry Christmas."

"And Merry Christmas to you," the priest answers, clutching the tattered Bible to his chest. "May God bless you all."

"Thank you," I answer, my hands immediately drawn together in a clumsy state of prayer. I have to resist the sudden and weird urge to bow, which I know is *completely* wrong. My body flinches awkwardly anyway as the priest gives me a small smile before disappearing down the dark hallway.

"Reagan, what's wrong with you?" Harper whispers but her voice still carries, echoing off the foyer's vaulted ceilings. "What is this, like your first time in a church?"

"I didn't grow up religious," I answer as we make our way into the church's main space. *(Chapel? Sanctuary? Whatever it's called.)* "I've only been to church for a couple weddings and a funeral. What do you want from me?"

"You're supposed to know how to blend in, right?" Harper answers, rolling her eyes. "Isn't that what your parents trained you to do?"

"They skipped the exercise about coming into churches I don't belong to in random cities on Christmas Eve," I whisper back.

"Guys," Luke says quietly and points toward the cross on the altar. "Jesus can hear you."

"Oh, stop it," Harper says, slapping his arm. "Okay, I'm going to go light some candles. I'll come find you guys in a bit."

Harper's boots echo on the stone floors as she walks toward a row of candles, a statue of the Blessed Mother perched benevolently behind the tower of flickering light.

"Shall we," Luke says, placing his hand on the small of my back and motioning up the main aisle toward row after row of uniformed wood pews. It's only the second time he's touched me voluntarily since before the warehouse in Indonesia.

"Sure," I answer and we slowly make our way up the aisle, taking a seat at a pew in the middle.

The pew's wood is dark and smooth and cold. An organ begins

to play somewhere behind us and I immediately recognize the melody: "Angels We Have Heard on High." I stare straight ahead, studying the altar. A large stone cross hangs in the center, flanked by two evergreen trees, simply decorated in twinkling white lights and gold ribbons, while red poinsettias line the altar's steps.

"What's that smell?" I ask, taking in a breath and trying to put my finger on the perfume that seems to be everywhere in this church.

"It's incense," Luke answers.

"But I don't see it burning anywhere," I say, my eyes scanning the altar, the aisle, and the back of the church.

"Catholic churches always smell like this," he answers. "Decades of incense just soak into every part of this place. The pews, the hymnals, the drapery on the altar. It never leaves. Just gets deeper every time they use it."

"How do you know that?" I ask, looking over at Luke.

"I was raised Catholic," he replies, leaning forward in the pew, staring straight ahead at the altar as he rests his forearms on his muscular thighs.

"But . . . I lived next door to you for over a year," I answer, narrowing my eyes, confused. "We used to go on runs on Sunday morning. You used to say that was 'our religion.' I don't ever remember you mentioning going to church."

"Well, we had stopped going by then," he answers, looking down at the ground. He clears his throat as his brain sorts through what he wants to say. "My dad. He was raised Catholic. My mom wasn't, but she'd still go to church with us and stuff. We used to go a lot actually. Not every Sunday, but a couple times a month at least. But after he lost over half of his unit on one of his last tours . . . he just . . . he came home a very different person. Said he didn't want to go to church anymore. So we stopped."

"Not even on holidays?" I ask.

Luke shakes his head. "No. I never really asked why." He looks down, lacing his fingers together then pulling them apart. Together. Apart. Together. Apart. "I think maybe he was angry with God. Being a colonel, you're prepared to watch people die. He knew it could happen. He'd been really lucky in his career up to that point. Hadn't lost a lot of people. He was really close to that unit. So after he lost almost everyone to that roadside bomb, he just . . . was never really the same."

"Is that when he left active duty?" I ask quietly.

"Yeah," he answers, nodding his head, still avoiding my eyes. "It messed him up pretty good. I think he has a lot of survivor's guilt. He still consults and spends a lot of time in DC. He just . . . never wants to be over there again. I can't really blame him. Just like I should probably find a way to stop blaming you for everything that has happened."

Luke finally turns his head, his eyes locking with mine, his face peaceful and still. He's looked at me since Indonesia. But I don't think he's really seen me. I was just a body, a figure in his line of sight. But right now, he's looking at me like he used to. Like I'm still Reagan. And I look back like he's still Luke.

"You can blame me," I answer, the words thick on my tongue, struggling to get out of my mouth. I clear my throat and look away. I pick up a hymnal and flip through it, not really looking at a single gospel or song. The pages might as well be blank.

"But I shouldn't," Luke responds softly.

"I deserve to be blamed," I whisper and Luke leans his body into mine, my voice barely audible over the sounds of the organ. "I didn't listen to you. I was selfish. I didn't care what you thought or what could happen. All I could think about was killing him. And I shouldn't have. I regret it. I regret it so much and I'm so sorry for what it's done to you. To Harper. To all of us. You didn't ask for any of this."

Tears sting my eyes and the tiny printed gospels and songs begin to blur together until all I see is a swirl of white and gray. As the first tear falls, Luke touches my forearm and moves his body toward mine.

"You didn't ask to be a Black Angel. You were born into it," he says, his lips near my ear so I can hear him over the music. His warm breath on my skin sends my body buzzing. "And you certainly didn't ask for your mother to get murdered."

"Yeah, but I chose to go to Colombia," I reply, the tears falling as I mindlessly flip through the book. "I chose to track down Santino for a year. To go rogue and kill him. You didn't."

"I know. And I can't lie and say I wish you had chosen differently, Reagan," he answers, reaching out and stopping my hands from flipping through the hymnal. He slowly closes the book on my lap and slides his hand into mine. "But I chose this because I chose you."

"O come all ye faithful / joyful and triumphant / O come ye o come ye to Bethlehem."

The sound of a little girl singing fills the church. Luke and I turn around to see a small children's choir standing in the church's balcony, dressed in their Christmas Eve best; fluffy dresses and tiny suits and colorful hair ribbons and bright bow ties. The choir director raises her hands and the rest of their tiny mouths begin to sing.

As we turn in our pew and watch the children sing, Luke squeezes my hand and I squeeze back. For a few moments, I forget about Fernando and his team of assassins and the sad motel room where I'll lay my head for a handful of hours tonight. For just a few seconds, I feel those butterflies flapping against my stomach. And I can't tell if it's the warmth that comes on Christmas Eve or the feeling of Luke's hand in mine. Maybe it's both.

I close my eyes, holding on to it. Because I know it won't last. Because I know there are still men searching for us, anxious for our blood on their hands.

THIRTEEN

THE TV LIGHT FLICKERS, CAUSING A STRANGE GLARE against the dark window, hindering my view. I glance at the clock on the nightstand. The red digital numbers read 2:47. I'm supposed to wake Luke up in thirteen minutes to stand watch. But his face looks so peaceful as he sleeps. It's the most serene I've seen him in weeks. I hate to wake him.

I study the curve of his closed eyelids and wonder what he's dreaming about, just as he turns and rolls his body toward the wall. The bed frame lets out a squeaky sigh beneath the changing weight.

The room smells like mold and cigarettes despite our asking for a nonsmoking room. I guess the no-smoking sign—printed with ink that was nearing the end of its life and clumsily taped up over the safety instructions on the door—is a mere suggestion. I stand up from my chair near the window and walk in between the two double beds, turning off the late-night infomercial for some mira-cle nonstick pan. Harper and Luke fell asleep watching the end of *It's a Wonderful Life*.

"It's not Christmas Eve without George Bailey," Harper said, flipping on NBC as soon as we got back to our motel room, two miles away from the church. Harper and Luke zonked out before Clarence could earn his wings. I stared outside at the falling snow, listening to the city of Bedford Falls come together and save the Bailey family from ruin before spontaneously erupting into the chorus of "Auld Lang Syne."

I had my back turned toward the TV, but I've watched the movie so many times, I could see the entire black-and-white scene play out in my mind. I knew the looks of joy and love sketched on every character's face. I always cry at the end of that movie. That last scene used to remind me that there were wonderful people in the world. That good does triumph over evil. But tonight, I cried alone in the dark, knowing that former sentiment, that wide-eyed belief in the goodness of people, was far from true.

There are only a few cars in the parking lot of this roadside motel. A blue minivan. A black Honda civic. A champagne-colored (and falling apart) Lexus. And a granite Volkswagen Golf. Each car has at least two inches of newly fallen snow on its hood and windshield. My eyes scan the dark rooms on the other side of the motel, stopping at one window, aglow behind the closed beige curtains. I wonder what those guests are doing in there at three a.m. on Christmas Eve. What they're all doing here really. On the road, trying to reach loved ones for Christmas Day? Or running away from a stressful Christmas Eve family blowup?

"Reagan," I hear Luke whisper, sending my eyes away from the window. He rubs his face with the palm of his hand before turning the digital clock toward him. "Is it my turn yet?"

"No, I'm okay," I whisper, trying not to stir Harper sleeping just a few feet away, her body spread out on the bed like a starfish. "Go back to sleep."

"You've slept like five hours total in the last few days," Luke answers with a long yawn. He throws on his sweatshirt and socks before climbing out of the bed and making his way toward my side of the room. He picks the Glock 22 pistol out of my lap. "You need to go to sleep."

"Honestly, I don't mind staying up a little longer," I say, although my body is desperate for rest.

"No, go to sleep," Luke says, rubbing me on the shoulder with his free hand.

"Okay," I say, still staring out the window, slow to get up and put on my pajamas. The snow continues to fall in thick, fat flakes, their weight making the descent down to earth somehow seem slower.

"Hmm," Luke's mouth makes a sound behind me.

"What is it?" I ask as I watch what looks like tiny white parachutes.

"It looks like a snow globe out there," he answers, taking a seat in the chair next to me. "I feel like we never got lucky with snow on Christmas Eve like this in Ohio. You'd think we would. It's cold enough there. But I can't remember the last time we got snow on Christmas. I think our last Christmas there it was like fifty-eight degrees or something."

"I remember," I answer with a small laugh. "Your dad drove around with the top down on his convertible."

"That's right," he replies and smiles, and the memory of his father wearing a Santa hat and waving while driving down the street comes back to me. After a few seconds, Luke's smile is replaced with a sigh.

"What?" I ask.

"Nothing," he says, shaking his head. "It's just . . . I can deal with being away from them most of the time. Like the other three hundred sixty-three days of the year, I guess I've accepted that I can't really see my family or have a ton of contact with them. I just wish I could hit the fast-forward button over Christmas Eve and Christmas Day. Magically wake up on December 26."

"Yeah," I answer, nodding and resting my chin in my hand. "These days suck. Makes me feel like an asshole for ever complaining about being too old to build a gingerbread house or wishing I could hide under the table while my uncle fights with my dad over who gets to carve the turkey."

"I'd totally kill for a dysfunctional family moment," he answers, his hands running along his jawline.

"Me too."

"I'll be your pain-in-the-ass family if you'll be mine," Luke says, smiling.

"I thought I already was."

His lips spread now into a full smile, perhaps the first genuine grin I've seen from Luke in weeks. I can feel a smile parting my own lips, relief trapped in a happy sigh in my throat.

The sound of tires hitting gravel turns my head back toward the window. A black SUV pulls into the parking lot and the rush of warmth that filled my body immediately turns cold.

It's nothing. I'm sure it's nothing.

My mind tries to calm the fear that has already vacated air from my chest. And if the sight of a blacked-out car at three o'clock in the morning wasn't worrisome enough, there's one more fact that's causing the alarms to go off in every part of me: their headlights are off. In a snowstorm. They don't want to be seen.

"Reagan," Luke says quietly, his body rising out of his chair.

"I see them," I answer, my voice fighting the terror that's building inside. "Could it be?"

The SUV pulls slowly through the parking lot, bypassing the lobby. Either they already have room keys or the people in that car aren't here to sleep.

They're here to kill us.

As the SUV moves closer and closer to our room, my legs stand, wobbly and straining. And as I search for faces behind the dark windows, tiny patches of black enter my sight and I have to force myself to breathe before I pass out.

The SUV pulls carefully and silently into a parking spot, five doors down from our room. And as the driver turns off the engine, I see it. The barrel of a semiautomatic weapon.

Holy. Shit.

"Harper, wake up," I say, flying across the room and throwing the covers off of her. Harper's eyelids lazily rise, like she's just taking a nap on the beach, and I have to resist the urge to slap her awake. Instead, I pull at her arm. "Harper. Get up. Now!"

"What is it?" she finally asks, the gravity in my voice quickly pulling her out of her state of unconsciousness.

"They found us," I say and that's enough for her to jump out of the bed.

"Oh my God, oh my God, oh my God," she shrieks, her voice building with each word until I put my hand over her mouth.

"Stop," I hiss in her ear, my hand still over her trembling lips. "They'll hear you."

Luke reaches for the half-closed curtains, ready to pull them together completely.

"Luke. No," I whisper loudly a half a second before he can force the shabby fabric shut. "They'll see the movement and know we're in this room."

Luke nods and reaches under the table, pulling another pistol out of our weapons bag. He tosses it on the bedspread and it slides toward me. I let go of Harper and grab the gun, tucking it into the back of my pants.

"How do we get out?" Harper whispers, her eyes feral with panic, her hands involuntarily shaking at her sides.

My head swivels, quickly scanning the room, stopping on the open bathroom door.

The window. I remember seeing it when I brushed my teeth. It's small, but it's our only way out.

I can hear heavy boots outside, attempting to be quiet. They're searching each window, trying to figure out which room is ours.

I put my finger to my lips and point toward the bathroom door. Luke takes three large steps across our small room, reaching it first while I put my hands on Harper's frozen body and push her toward our only chance of escape. Luke pulls back the shower curtain, revealing a small window six feet off the ground. I close and lock the bathroom door behind us (even though they'll be able to kick in this rickety, hollow door in two seconds or less).

"Damn it, it's all rusted," Luke laments as he struggles with the window's lock. "I don't think this thing's been opened in twenty years."

"This is my fault," Harper whispers, her arms wrapped around her chest, her body rocking back and forth, as Luke continues to push and push on the sealed window.

"What are you talking about?" I whisper, turning Harper's trembling body toward me. My own nerves have shut down. I'm robotic. Numb.

"My parents," she whispers, tears now falling silently down her face. "I called my parents from the church."

"Harper, how could you?" I want to scream but control the volume of my voice, knowing any sound will give us away.

"I called from the phone in the church office," she says, her lips quivering so hard, she's barely able to form the words. "No one was in there. I saw the desk. I saw the phone. It was only for sixty seconds. I just . . . I wanted to hear their voices. I wanted to wish them Merry Christmas."

"Harper, their phones are tapped," I say. "Torres's people have been waiting for you to call. What were you thinking?"

"I didn't think they could find us here," she says, now sobbing and shaking her head, her wavy hair matting to the wet patches on her face. "I didn't think . . . I'm so sorry. I'm so sorry."

"Shhh," I say and grab her quivering hands.

Harper finally looks up at me, the rims of her eyes wet and

blazing red. She clasps my hands around both of hers, brings them up to her face, and whispers, "Are we going to die?"

"I don't know," I say, swallowing at the lump that's hardening against the back of my throat.

Maybe.

But I can't say it out loud. All I know is if we don't get out of this room in the next thirty seconds, *maybe* will become *definitely.*

Luke finally forces the window out of its seemingly immovable layers of paint and decades of rust, pushing it open. I glance up just as a gust of wind spits snow through its opening. The gap is just wide enough to fit us through, but we'll each need a boost up.

"Come on, Harper," Luke says, cupping his hands together to lift her up and out the window. I look Harper up and down in my borrowed pajama pants and thin, gray T-shirt as she steadies her hands on our shoulders, her bare right foot pushing down into Luke's hands. I want to run into the other room and grab her shoes. She'll get frostbite in the snow.

They're coming. They're coming. They're coming.

I shake my head, clearing my brain's taunting chant. There's no time. Besides, amputated toes are better than slit throats.

"Harper. Listen to me," I say, my voice urgent as I push her body up the shower wall. "Once you get outside . . . run. Don't stop. Just run."

"Run where?" she asks as she pulls herself up to the window. "It's all woods behind the motel."

"Just run into the woods and keep running until we call for you," I answer as I help push her body through our only chance of survival. "We will find you, okay?"

"Okay," she answers, her voice already sounding so far away. I watch her slip out the window and my chest tightens as I wonder if these are the last words we'll ever exchange, the last time I'll see her alive.

Pound. Pound. Pound.

"Shit," I whisper, pushing Luke toward the window. "Come on. Go. They're breaking down the door."

"No, you first," he says, holding out his hands to boost me up. I hesitate for half a second, but I know arguing with him is pointless. We just need to get out of here. I accept his boost and with shaking limbs, pull myself up the tiled wall, through the window, and climb down on to the snow-covered ground.

A few seconds later, Luke's head pokes out the window. A second more and he's down on the ground. And that's when we hear it.

Crack.

The door frame has broken. They're in our room.

"Go, go, go," Luke commands, grabbing my hand and pulling me toward the dark woods, just ten yards behind the motel.

Thick snowflakes fly up my nose, in my mouth, along my cheek, down my shirt as we sprint into the darkness. I'm lucky to still be wearing my boots, but the snow is cold and deep, up to the middle of my calf, slowing my legs as I run. The tree line gets thicker the farther we run into the woods and after thirty seconds of running, my breath leaves my chest as I realize Harper's footprints are gone.

"Shit," I say and turn around, searching for the deep gaps in white I saw less than ten seconds ago. "Where did Harper turn? I don't see her footprints anywhere."

"Ve, ve, ve!" I hear a voice yelling behind us. *"Encuentralos!"*

Go, go, go! I translate in my head. *Find them.*

"Reagan, we can't," Luke says, pulling me along, fighting my body's urge to turn around and find our friend. "Come on. We have to keep moving."

He's right. If they find us first, Harper is as good as dead.

I scan the ground once more, looking for her trail, then spin my body around, running after Luke in the equivalent of icy quicksand, my breath heaving from my body in puffy, frozen clouds.

Move, Reagan. Move, my mind commands, pushing my legs faster and faster, each muscle threatening to tear in the below-freezing temperatures. I follow Luke and his giant strides, sidestepping trees, ducking under branches, and hurdling over fallen logs. Evergreen needles poke at my face and rotting leaves stick to the legs of my jeans as we run farther into the dark, Iowa forest. My heart twinges with each anguished pound against my breastbone and despite my attempts at Black Angel numbness, my chest feels like it's filling with fluid, hovering on the edge of a panic attack.

"No! No!" I hear Harper's voice scream and every muscle in me seizes up as I jump over a fallen branch. "Reagan! Reagan!"

My feet trip and my body crashes to the ground. Despite the pain of snow down my back and tree limbs against my ribs, I push myself up and turn back toward the motel. Back toward my screaming friend and the men who are trying to kill her.

"Reagan, stop," Luke yells twenty-five yards behind me as I sprint toward Harper's screams. "Wait, Reagan. Wait!"

"No! Please! Reagan! Luke! Help me!" Harper's piercing cries pull me toward her and further away from Luke's pleas to stop.

I know what I'm running into. I know the danger. But without me, Harper will die. And I cannot listen to the sound of my friend being killed. I cannot live with more blood on my hands.

"Reagan!" I hear her cry out one last time, her desperation echoing into the dark void of the endless forest. Then come muffled screams. Someone's hand is over her mouth, but she's still fighting to stay alive.

My body pulls me toward the right, toward the echo of her horrified shrieks for help. I slow my pace, trying to move silently through thick snow. I pull the gun from the back of my pants, positioning my body up against a thick and leafless tree. My shoulders rub against the fraying bark as I peer my head around, waiting to hear Harper once more.

And that's when I feel it.

It corners me, soundlessly, digging into the back of my neck. My body tenses as it presses deeper into my flesh. I recognize it instantly because I've been bracing for it for years: the unmistakable, circular barrel of a loaded gun.

FOURTEEN

"DROP THE GUN," A GRUFF VOICE SAYS FROM BEHIND me. I hesitate, looking at the gun outstretched in front of me, an extension of my own arms, my only certain line of defense. With one breath, I consider my options. Spin around and face the assassin, try to blow his head off before he can blow off mine. Or drop the gun and trust that my fighting skills will give me a chance to escape.

"Drop. It," he says, each word forceful and deliberate.

Click.

Every hair on the back of my neck rises in unison. He's turned off the safety. He's not bluffing. Not that I'd expect anything less from someone trained by a merciless killer like Santino Torres. My fingers reluctantly release their grip on the gun. My eyes stay locked on my pistol as it free-falls in what feels like slow motion, turning on its side, before disappearing into a pile of snow.

"Hands up," he commands, his gun still burrowing into the top of my spine. One pull of the trigger and I'll be dead. My face buzzes, my entire body paralyzed. I stare straight ahead, looking for Harper, praying silently for Luke to appear. But there is no one. Just darkness, leafless trees, and snow.

"I said hands up," the man repeats, his voice transitioning from impatience to anger. I do as he says. My arms slowly lift, my fingers spread apart. Freezing air enters my lungs in small, panicked gasps as I wait for the moment that I can make a move. Any move.

"*La tengo,*" the man yells out. *I've got her.*

"*Donde estás?*" someone calls back. *Where are you?* The voice sounds far away. Hundreds of yards away even. The gun's pressure on my neck begins to ease up enough for me to feel a tiny gap of cold air where the gun's barrel used to be. He thinks he's won.

He's wrong.

With a final, desperate breath, I spin around, stepping into the shooter and away from the line of the gun. I wrap my arm around his and shove my free elbow hard into his chest, knocking his body off balance. I grab his shoulder with my hand as I push my knee into his groin, throwing his body forward, cries of pain springing from his tongue. My hand slides away from his shoulder, up his arm and toward the gun, as I attempt to wrestle it out of his hands.

"*Puta,*" the assailant calls out. *Bitch.* It's not the first time one of Torres's men has called me that.

Despite the pain and pressure on his hand, he grips the gun. Hard. He's not letting go. I slam my elbow into his face again, feeling his nose crack into the point of my bone. Before I even see the blood, I know it's broken.

"*Puta!*" he shrieks. I push my hand up against the gun again, trying to pry it from his hand while the white snow is dotted in crimson polka dots, blood dripping down his face.

I push down again on the gun, knowing if I can get this weapon out of his hands, maybe I will live. Maybe I'll have a chance to get Harper back.

The assailant screams as I twist his arms, and finally the gun goes flying, swallowed by white, lost in the deep snow.

Where is it? Where is it?

My eyes scan the piles of snow, splattered with blood and gaping footprints. It could be anywhere.

Shit. Shit. Shit. Where is it?!

My body dives toward the frozen patch where I suspect the gun may be but before I can begin to dig, the man tackles me to the ground. My face, my torso, my arms and legs are surrounded by snow, his 250-pound body pushing me deeper and deeper into the collection of frozen white flakes. I try to take in a breath, but snow gets sucked into my mouth and finds its way up my nose. My body begins to shake, the cold deteriorating my muscles and weakening my resolve, as his hands find my neck.

No, no, no!

His fingers dig into my flesh, pushing out what I fear could be my last breath.

I pull my trembling hands up to my throat, trying to loosen his grip. But my hands are slick and freezing. I open my eyes, expecting to see white, but this deep down, the ice crystals are black.

No. I will not die like this. Suffocating in snow.

The grip on my neck tightens and I can hear his angry, determined groans even through my snow-packed eardrums. I thrash from side to side but can barely move. I try to breathe, desperate for even half gasp, but no air comes.

Do something. Do something.

The combination of no air and freezing cold means death in a matter of seconds. I push my hands down through several inches of snow until I find solid ground.

Go, Reagan. Go!

My fingers dig deep into the dirt and with every ounce of strength I have left in me, I push up, surprising the assailant, his lethal grip loosening on my neck. With one more push, I scream and roll his body off of mine. Another elbow to his face and I feel the crack of another bone.

"Mierda," he screams as his hands let me free, instinctively grabbing at his eye, his orbital bone now broken as well.

Don't screw with me, I think as I lunge for the gun once again. I dig through the snow. And then, I see it, a black handle in a sea of white.

Boom.

Before I can get my hands on the pistol, my head is knocked backward, a foot thrust into my face at jaw-breaking speed. As I lie on my back, staring up into darkness, the iron taste of blood fills my mouth and then, there's a body on top of mine. Broken-nose and orbital-bone free, a second assailant has found us.

"Luke!" I scream at the top of my lungs, my own blood spitting out across the man's face. He slaps my aching cheek with the back of his hand, my lip splitting and jaw cracking again under the force of his hand.

Help me, Luke. Help me.

I struggle under the weight of the man now straddling my torso. I try to push my body up, attempting to catch him off guard with a head butt. But before my forehead can meet his, my body is being forced back down, my arms pinned on either side. The first assailant has me by both wrists. I try to wiggle free, but as my body lies in the snow, growing frailer with every passing second, I feel my chance to escape slipping away.

"It's over," the first assailant says, his voice thin and out of breath. Blood drips out of his eye and nose and onto my face, mixing with my own. "It's over."

Tears burn the corners of my eyes, a feeling of hopelessness burrowing in my chest. My mind can always play through scenarios of how to escape, but as I lie in two feet of snow, with two trained killers holding me down, for the first time in my life, I don't see a way out. So I stop struggling. I stop fighting. I let them win.

After a few moments of staring at me, making sure I've given up, the two assailants grip me by both arms and pull me to my feet. My sweatshirt and jeans cling to me, every inch of my skin is soaked, every part of me shaking, just minutes away from full-out hypothermia.

"Give me your hands," the first assailant says, pulling my wrists roughly together behind my back. He slips on a zip tie, pulling at the plastic, securing my almost certain doom.

"Don't even think about running," the second assailant insists, a gun now pointed at my skull. So I don't. I know any movement will mean a bullet to my brain. So I put my head down. I stand still. I try to stay alive.

Pop. Pop. Pop.

I can hear the sound of bullets whizzing by me on either side, nearly hitting my two captors. I look to my left. And fifty yards away I see him. Luke.

Boom. Boom. Boom.

The second assailant begins shooting back at Luke as the first assailant pushes our bodies to the ground. My neck struggles against his grasp as I force my head up. Luke ducks behind a tree, the air silent and momentarily still. I try to wiggle myself free but the assailant has my body pinned. I'm trapped back in my frozen prison, surrounded by snow.

Please God. Please God. Don't hurt him. Please God.

I push my chest up off the ground once more, my eyes barely able to see above the line of snow. Luke spins around the tree and opens fire.

Pop. Pop. Pop.

The second assailant shoots back. Luke throws his body back around the thick tree, the bullets barely missing him and exploding against the bark.

I try to crawl, armless through the snow but I still can't move.

"Luke, run!" I scream with the little air I have. I want him to get away from here. To save himself. It's far too late for me.

But he doesn't listen. Luke's body reappears from around the tree again, but before he can fire the first shot, the second assailant has already pulled his trigger.

Boom.

The bullet flies through the air, striking Luke and throwing his body backward. I squeeze my eyes closed for a moment.

Not real, not real, not real, I repeat to myself, like I do when I'm having one of my daymares. When I open my eyes, I expect to be back in the motel room, this whole scene just an anxiety-filled trick on my brain. But as my eyelids rise, I see Luke stumbling backward. I see the blood. I see that this is very, very real.

"Noooooo!" I scream at the top of my lungs as I watch Luke fall to the ground in what feels like slow motion.

Luke, get up! Please get up!

I force my body up once more, fighting to get out of the assailant's hold but he forces his knee into my back, my spine screaming in agony. Still, I struggle.

I have to get to Luke. I have to get to Luke.

Sirens pierce the momentary silence of the woods. Police sirens.

"*Mierda. Policía, policía,*" the second assailant says, his voice panicked. He hurries back toward us on the ground where I'm still battling against the excruciating pain and weight of my captor. "*Vamos ahora. Vamos ahora.*"

"Luke!" I scream out, but before I can take one more breath, my world is black; a cloth bag has been thrown over my head and tied around my neck. I cannot see a thing.

"*Vámonos, vámonos, vámonos,*" the first assailant hisses, the two men yanking my body up by both arms, as the police sirens come closer. Someone at the motel must have heard us screaming and called the cops.

I try to kick my legs but someone knees me in the stomach, knocking the wind out of my gut. My body goes limp as they pull me, blind and hog-tied, through the snow.

Luke, Luke, Luke, Luke, my mind screams out what my mouth cannot. *Please God. Please God. Please God.*

I finally gather enough air and give his name one final shout.

"Luke," I scream with the tiny breath I can muster. I wait to hear a response. A groan, a cry, anything. But I hear nothing. Just police sirens in the distance and the sound of my boots, dragging against the snow.

FIFTEEN

"STOP IT . . . NOW!" ONE OF THE ASSAILANTS SAYS as I twist and turn, my body rebellious against their strong clutches. I don't know why I'm even trying. If I somehow get away, they'll be able to tackle me in a matter of seconds. My hands are forced together in zip ties behind my back, I'm blinded by this hood on my head, and there are trees and branches everywhere that would knock my visually impaired ass to the ground. Still, I struggle. Still, I fight. It's just part of my DNA.

We've been walking through thick snow for what feels like an hour even though it's been barely five minutes. The sirens have stopped and I wonder if the police are now parked at the motel. Clearly the assailants are taking me somewhere else. I tried to scream as they pulled me away but they dug the pistol into my temple, promising to pull the trigger if I screamed one more time.

"Ay! Por qué no la matamos?" one of them murmurs softly to the other. But I can still make out their words. *Why don't we just kill her?*

"*Las ordenes eran mantenerlos vivos,*" the other answers just as quietly. *Orders were to keep them all alive.*

"*Parece que los hemos jodido,*" one says. *Looks like we screwed that one up.*

And then they laugh.

They laugh big. Hearty. Joyful. Like two frat-boys-in-training recalling stories of last weekend's debauchery over plates of fries in the cafeteria. They laugh about killing Luke.

Oh God. Luke.

My lungs burn. The bile at the bottom of my stomach churns over again and again like foamy waves in a storm. It rises, getting caught in my throat. If I throw up, I'll be puking in this bag. It will have no escape.

Not now. Don't puke now.

My mouth forces out a cough, choking down the rancid taste just as it reaches the back of my tongue. Still the nausea lingers in the hollow of my chest, just one foul thought away from full-out puke.

My shoulders spiral against their grip and I let out a shriek as they drag me farther away from my friend, bleeding and freezing in the snow.

"Stop now!" the assailant yells, striking me hard in the back of my head with what I can only guess is the handle of his pistol. The pain radiates from the center of my brain, expanding in circles, like a drop of rainwater on a crystal-clear lake. It gets wider and wider until the agony crashes against my skull. If my world wasn't completely black right now, I'm sure I'd see spots.

"Why are you struggling?" one asks me, the snow around my legs getting shallower and less dense. "Give up."

"Why did you kill him?" I ask, my voice shaking, praying the words aren't true.

"What does it matter?" one responds with a laugh. "You'll all be dead soon. He just beat you to it."

"Why don't you just kill me now?" I spit as the cloth bag gets caught between my lips. "Get it over with?"

"You will see," one answers, a throaty chuckle punctuating the disturbing statement.

"Fernando can't wait to get his hands on you," the other replies, tightening his grip and deepening the bruise on my arm.

What does that mean? Will they torture us? Try to force me to give up intel? Or just use us as bait to lure down more Black Angels? My mind swirls as I try to figure out what Fernando wants from me, why on earth he's insistent on keeping me alive instead of executing me on the spot.

"Let's go," one of the assailants says gruffly, and I hear the sound of a car door opening. He pushes me inside, forcing my body to scoot up against something. Or someone. And then I hear her crying.

"Harper?" I say, wishing I could reach out for her with my hands.

"Oh my God. Reagan?" she answers between sobs. She grabs for my legs. She has the small luxury of having her hands tied together in front of her body instead of behind, and I'm jealous.

"Are you okay?" I ask even though it's a very stupid question. Of course she's not okay. She's tied up in the back of an SUV with a gun most likely pointed at her head.

"Yes, I'm okay," she answers quietly, still pawing at my soaking wet pant leg, trying to find some comfort in touch, even if it's freezing and damp. "What is going on? Where are they taking us?"

"I don't know," I say, wildly shaking my head, trying to see if I can move this hood around and get any type of visual. But the material is too thick. I see nothing. My eyes blink against the black.

"Where's Luke?" she asks and my breath catches, raw and jagged, against my stinging throat.

"They shot him," I whisper. She answers with an audible gasp.

"Is he . . . is he dead?" she asks, her hands tightening their grip on my leg.

"I don't know," I whisper, my voice barely discernable. I think he's dead. I saw the shot. I saw the blood. But I don't want these guys to go back and guarantee it. Put another bullet through his body just to be sure. If it wasn't for the police sirens, I know they would have checked and finished the job.

"Oh my God. Oh my God. Not Luke," Harper says, her cries picking back up again, her fingers digging into my flesh, hurting me even though she doesn't mean to. I bet she doesn't even realize what she's doing. "I'm so sorry, Reagan. This is my fault."

"It's not," I whisper, wishing I could take her trembling body into my own. "If it wasn't for me, you wouldn't even be here."

"What's going to happen to us?" she asks, her voice shaky as it leaves her mouth.

"Stop talking. Stop crying," a voice commands as a car door opens and they climb into the backseat next to me, a gun now jammed into my side. My muscles seize up as the barrel presses against my wet clothing, digging into the organs around my stomach. I pray if they shoot me, they don't shoot me there. It will take minutes, maybe even hours for me to die from a wound to the gut.

And it's painful as hell. If they're going to kill me, I pray it's with one clean bullet to the brain.

I hear Harper suck in a series of shaking gasps, trying to calm herself down. I imagine her closing her eyes, trying to find her center or whatever bullshit she learned in yoga.

My eyes stare straight forward, into the endless darkness. All my senses are heightened. I listen and mentally record every sound. The SUV being put into gear. The sound of its tires on smooth pavement. I wait to hear the gravel from the motel parking lot. There is none.

Where did they take us?

I feel the motion of the car. We're moving forward. We never backed up. They clearly moved the SUV to a different spot or put us in a completely different car altogether. There's got to be more than one car, more than one team. After losing us in Manhattan, Fernando must have been pissed. He probably sent a small army of people to track us down. We've made complete fools of the Torres family time and time again. Killing their guards, executing their family, eluding their captors. But the last laugh may be his.

"Don't even think about trying to fight me off again," one of my assailant's voices says gruffly near my ear. "Or I'll put a bullet in your skull and you can join your boyfriend in the snow."

With one hand, he digs the gun into my side. With the other, he grabs at my thigh. The bile in my throat rises at his threat, at his touch. And I puke.

SIXTEEN

"NO PUEDO SOPORTAR EL OLOR," ONE OF THE MEN IN the car says with a cough. *I can't take the smell.*

My vomit has filled the SUV with its rancid perfume. But it probably smells far better out there than it does in this hood. I've been breathing through my mouth, just to avoid the stench. One whiff and I'm afraid I'll puke again. Vomit clings to my mouth, my chin, my cheeks. It sits in a tiny pool at the bottom of the bag. During our twenty minutes on the road, I've felt it drip, drip, drip onto my legs as it leaks through the tiny, breathable holes in the cloth.

"¡Quitate de ella! No puedo soportarlo," a man in the front seat commands while gagging. *Take it off of her. I can't stand it.*

A small smile spreads across my puke-crusted lips. The threat from the assassin and his hand on my leg made me throw up, yes. But I also knew the smell would be too much for them. They'd be forced to get rid of this hood, give me a chance to see what's going on, where we're heading. I've been trying to pay attention to every little movement of the car. Our speed. The miles we may have covered. How many times we've turned (three times left, two times right). But there's only so much I can do blind. I need to see.

"Okay, okay," the assailant next to me exclaims, unwrapping the rope that's bound around my neck, securing the hood and my temporary blindness. As he begins to remove the cloth, my little pool of vomit cascades onto his hands and my freezing, wet jeans.

I ignore the putrid waterfall because now, I can see. I take immediate stock of my surroundings. Four assailants. Two in front. Two in back. The second assailant from the attack in the woods is to my right with a gun still digging into my side. My first assailant, the man with the broken nose and orbital bone, is nowhere to be seen. Definitely two cars.

"Jesucristo," the second assailant mutters, wiping the vomit off of his body and then my own. He roughly wipes my legs and hands and face, trying to rid the car of the rotting smell. He then rolls down the window, throwing my puke-soaked hood outside and into the snow.

I keep my eyes staring straight ahead, trying to resist the urge to look around, make them think twice about leaving me out in the open, hoodless and hopeful.

Through the windshield, I see we're traveling down a narrow two-lane road, passing by open fields and the occasional farmhouse. We've driven out of the city of Waterloo and past its outskirts. The pockets of subdivisions, grocery stores, and office plazas are long gone. The landscape that's replaced tiny-town suburban life is square mile after square mile of cornfields.

I could live here is the strange thought that pops into my brain. Despite the gun at my side. Despite the fact that Luke is most likely dead and I'm probably being driven to a private airport to be flown out of the country and never heard from again, I think about the life I could have here. Rising with the sun. Tending to my acres of crops until the endless sky is painted in a sherbet selection of oranges, purples, and pale pinks. I'd spend evenings canning vegetables. My winters sleeping under a thick quilt. I'd eat hearty stews and drink lots of coffee and read books while looking out over the acres of dead land. Yes, I could live here.

My eyes glance over at the assailant to my right and I study his face. Dark hair. Pale skin. Doe eyes. Thick lashes. Strong jaw. Maybe twenty-two. He looks like someone I'd see studying brands of granola at the grocery store or pumping gas next to me in Ohio. I want to ask him why he's doing this. Why he's not in college. Why he's become part of the Torres army instead of working at a bank or a hotel or a real estate office. Money, I'm sure, is the answer. He doesn't look evil (which I know is a very dangerous thought). But then I remember his hand, his continuous threat of death shouted or whispered into my ear, and the bile in my throat climbs once again.

My mouth coughs down the urgent need to vomit, sending the assailant's eyes toward me.

"Don't you puke again," he says sternly, eyeing my mouth, my throat, my stomach.

"I won't," I answer, coughing and swallowing down whatever is fighting its way back up.

"No puking on the plane either," he says, waving the gun at my face like he's wagging a disapproving finger rather than a pistol near my brain. "Brand-new jet. Fernando will kill you if you stain the upholstery."

Hmmm. So we *are* going to the airport. And clearly the drug business is still going strong without his brother if he was able to buy a new jet.

Keep him talking. Keep him talking. I hear Mom's voice in my head.

"Where are we going?" I ask, trying to sound casual. Like we're having a conversation in a coffee shop instead of in the back of a car with my hands tied behind my back.

"No, no, *chica*," he says, still waving the gun, like it's an extension of his hand. "What do you think I am? *¿Estupido?*"

He points the barrel of the gun toward his own brain. God, I wish he'd accidentally pull the trigger right now.

"No," I answer calmly. "I don't think you're stupid."

"You may have been trained by the best, but so have I," he says, returning the gun back to my side. "You killed my trainer."

"Santino?" I ask quietly and immediately regret it. Just his name forces the assailant's eyes to narrow, his mouth to scowl. *Shit.* I've said too much. What was I thinking?

"Yes, Santino Torres," he says, spitting out his name with force, as if I mispronounced it. His face darkens even more as he digs the barrel of his pistol hard against my ribs, and I have to remind my paralyzed body to keep breathing.

"I'm sorry," I whisper.

I never dreamed I'd ever end up apologizing for killing the man who murdered my mother. But it seems I've done it more than once. And not just to a member of his army. I've apologized to my father. To Luke. To Harper. The mess I've created. The ripple effect it's had on everyone I love. Luke stood in our Vermont kitchen and told me he knows I wouldn't take it back, even if I could. But as I sit in the back of a car with my best friend tied up next to me and the closest thing I'll probably ever have to love bleeding out in the snow, I know I would. I'd take it all back right this second. But there is no rewind button in life. There are no do-overs.

Tears begin to sting the corners of my eyes as I picture Luke, blood dripping from his nose and mouth, his eyes blank, staring up into darkness, nothingness. Death.

I shake my brain, erasing the image like an Etch A Sketch in my mind. I bite my tongue, redirecting the pain, forcing the urge to cry for Luke and all I've lost back down into their little box. I can't show weakness. I have to be strong. I have to get us out of this. I have to keep Harper alive.

The SUV comes up over a hill, and in the distance, I see a series of lights. The airport. Every vertebra in my back pulls together, the tendons between each bone straining as we draw closer to what will most likely be our last moments inside the United States. Once we leave the country, our already slim chance of getting out of this alive might as well be cut in half. Harper can feel my body tense. Her fingers dig into my kneecap as if to ask, "What's going on?"

Telepathy would really come in handy right now. But I can't speak to her. I can't do anything to jeopardize our last chance to escape.

Maybe someone will see us. Maybe if I make a scene, someone will call the police. Try to stop us from boarding their jet.

I glance at the digital clock in the dashboard: 3:53. Not exactly a high-traffic time at the airport. But there's got to be *somebody* there who will hear me scream. Right?

The SUV begins to slow its speed as the rural airport comes fully into view. Two hangars, one runway, and a tiny air traffic control tower. Still, it's surrounded by high fences, lined with barbed wire. And a gatehouse. Which means a guard. My heart clenches beneath my breastbone.

My chance.

The SUV turns left and slowly pulls up toward the gatehouse.

"Don't you say a god damned word," my assailant warns harshly, the gun now pushed up against my chin. "Do you understand me?"

Breathe, breathe, breathe, my mind begs my incapacitated lungs. My eyes stare straight ahead, my mouth, my neck, unmoved.

"I said, do you understand me?" he repeats through gritted teeth, roughly grabbing the back of my neck and squeezing my skin in his calloused palm.

"Yes." I force out a whisper, the barrel cold on my even colder flesh.

The SUV comes to a stop at the gatehouse and a guard stands up from his seat inside. He barely opens the door when the car approaches his post. No way he can see Harper and me tied up in the backseat.

Awkwardly tall with a thinning hairline, the guard holds a clipboard and gives a quick wave to the driver. "What can I do you for?" he asks with a surprisingly friendly smile. I would expect whoever was working the overnight Christmas shift to be a little bit grumpy.

"Hello, yes. I got a call from our pilot," the driver says, thinning out his accent. "Our jet should be gassed up and ready for takeoff."

"Oh, are you flying out on the Gulfstream?" the guard asks, pointing over his shoulder toward the runway.

Please come outside. Please come closer. Please notice us.

"Yes, that's ours," the driver says with an overeager nod. It's something I'd notice, the forced pleasantness masking anxiety. But it's not something this guard (who looks far more interested in getting back to his tiny TV and Cup Noodles on his desk) is going to take into account.

"She's a beaut," the guard replies, looking down at his clipboard. "Don't get a lot of those into this airport. Mostly crop dusters. Single engines, stuff like that."

Step outside. Please, come closer. Please! My brain is screaming as the gun digs into my chin so deeply, I feel my bone begin to bruise. My eyes burn a hole in the guard's face, begging him to take a step into the snow. But he stays put.

"I just need you to confirm the tail number for me," the guard says, riffling through the papers on his clipboard.

"Of course," the driver says, clearing his throat. Another nervous tic the guard fails to see as a red flag. "N324LE."

"That's the one," the guard says and pushes a button inside the gatehouse. The gate rattles as it pulls back, granting our kidnappers entry. "Have a safe flight."

Before the driver can say thank you, the guard has shut the door, is back in his chair, and engrossed in whatever show is playing in the tiny TV in the corner. I squint my eyes, trying to get a better look. Looks like an old *Law & Order*.

The muscles in my arms constrict with disdain for this man. I hate him for no other reason than he didn't want to step outside into the cold and snow. That he was lazy at four a.m. on Christmas Day. I know it's not part of his job. And of course he would have no idea we were tied up in the backseat, guns pointed at our bodies. It's irrational, but I hate him for not taking that extra step toward our car. That extra step could have been the difference between life and death.

The SUV pulls through the gates and follows a snowy path toward our waiting jet. I see it, majestic and elegant against the dark snow falling peacefully around it. It'd make a beautiful ad for Gulfstream if it wasn't for the fact that it may be the delivery system to our coffins. Who am I kidding. We won't get coffins. We'll be burned in a fire pit or dumped in the ocean. Hopefully, just our bodies. But I wouldn't put it past Fernando to send us to our graves like that, our hearts still beating.

The SUV pulls up right next to the jet and as if on cue, the door opens and steps descend down to greet us.

Oh, what service. I hope they have champagne.

"What's happening?" I hear Harper whisper as car doors begin opening, her voice audible only to me. Her fingers clasp around my thigh, causing a series of finger-sized bruises that I can already feel rising on my skin.

I wish there was something I could do to comfort her. Something I could say.

"Just do what they tell you," I whisper back and her fingers release their tight grip.

"Let's go," the assailant next to Harper says, opening the door and dragging her out by her arm.

My eyes scan the airport, anxious to see any signs of life. Most of the hangar doors are closed but one . . . one is open. A light is on inside. A two-seater propeller plane sits in the dim glow. Is someone there? My eyes stay locked on the hangar door, the plane. But I see no one.

"Move," my assailant barks, pointing his gun toward the waiting jet. I look back at the hangar, searching for a shadow, a figure, anything. And then I see him. A man moves into the light, and into my view. This is it. He's our last hope.

I push my body across the backseat, hopping onto the asphalt, which is covered in a thin layer of snow. A cold gasp of air fills my lungs. My assailant reaches to grab my arm, but I immediately twist and turn and try to run.

"Fire! Fire! Fire!" I scream over and over again at the top of my lungs. "Help" does nothing. "Help" causes people to turn away, run, and save themselves. My stumbling legs race toward the figure in the hangar, toward our only chance of escape. But before I can get even ten yards, my body is tackled to the ground. My face slams hard on the asphalt, burning and freezing my skin all at once.

"Fire!" I scream at the silhouette once more before a hand is shoved violently down my throat, filling my open mouth with fingers that taste of dirt and gasoline.

"Stupid girl. Try something like that again and your friend dies," the assailant on top of me says, gripping me at my chin with his free hand and forcing my face toward Harper. First, all I see are her feet, still bare and probably near frostbite. Then I see her ice cream cone pajama bottoms, her shaking, tied-up arms, the hood pulled over her face, and finally, the gun pointed directly at her skull.

Click. The safety is off.

"We're not kidding," he says, pulling my face back and slamming my forehead into the impossibly hard ground. The blood comes fast and warm as it drips down my face. "We don't need her. Try that again and she dies."

I don't say anything (not that I could with this guy's fingers in my mouth). I don't move. I don't nod. I just stare at the ground. The white snow smeared with my blood.

The two men pick me up by each arm. And then I see him. The silhouette is walking toward us. Now he's running.

Oh my God. Oh my God. He sees us. He's trying to help!

The men force me toward the jet steps, but despite their warnings, I turn around. I search for the man who's come to save us. But as he gets closer, I feel my heart drop several centimeters in my chest. He looks up at me, reads my grave face, and waves a gun. He's one of them. I risked Harper's life for nothing.

You fool. You careless fool.

"Move it," one of the assailants yells at me, forcing my body up the stairs and through the jet's doorway. The men move me roughly through the cabin, pushing my body down onto a buttery leather seat next to Harper. Her hood is now off. She looks at me with swollen, red eyes and a bloody lip. Her mouth drops when she sees my beaten face. I can feel the bruises forming, my cheeks and right eye pulsing. The cut on my forehead drips and warm blood trickles down my face.

The man I thought might be our savior comes up the jet stairs and through the cabin door. When he sees me, he smiles, walks to my seat, and slaps me hard across the face. I close my eyes, my left cheek stinging and my ear ringing from the strike. The shocking force sparks sobs in my chest. But I trap them in my throat before the cry can escape.

"Thought I was here to save you, little girl?" the man says, leaning so close to my face I can smell the stale coffee on his breath. "No one can save you now."

With those words, I hear the cabin door close. The jet's engine roars to attention, the plane taxiing down the runway. I open my eyes as each of these monsters settle into their seats, preparing for a quick takeoff. My head turns slowly toward Harper, and as the jet speeds down the runway, the tears she's been struggling to contain in her hazel eyes slip free, running down her pink face. I know what she's thinking. Because I share the same thought.

The nose points toward the sky, lifting the multi-million-dollar jet into the air. And as I watch the patches of Iowa farmland get smaller and smaller, that thought repeats louder and louder, like a battle cry.

We're as good as dead. We're as good as dead. God help us, we're as good as dead.

SEVENTEEN

THEY'VE THREATENED TO SPLIT US UP TWICE NOW. Once for talking (Harper was crying so hard, she was on the verge of a panic attack. I was just trying to calm her down). The second time was because Harper dared to grab my arm.

"No touching," the second assailant who attacked me scolded, pointing at her chapped hands, clasped around my forearm. Harper immediately pulled away and looked down at the floor.

"Can't you just untie us?" I asked, squirming uncomfortably in my seat, my hands forced awkwardly behind my back. "We're thirty thousand feet in the air. Where are we going to go?"

"What do you think we are? Idiots?" one of the men answered.

Okay, fair enough. With my arms free, I could disarm one of the guards, get his gun, and do some damage. Doubtful I'd be able to kill them all. But even if I could, the whole landing a plane thing would be kind of difficult. Never got to take that class at CORE (yes, there really is a class at the training academy where operatives learn to land jets and helicopters).

After that very hard no, I tried to convince them to at least tie my hands in front of my body.

"Please," I asked calmly, trying not to beg. "My arms and shoulders are killing me like this."

"Like we give a shit," the same man replied.

They refused. Which, if I'm being honest, is probably a smart move on their part. If my hands were in front of me, I could probably still kill someone (like I've never practiced choke holds with zip ties on?). And I could most likely get out of the zip ties altogether. With my hands tied behind my back and a seat belt forced across my lap, it's nearly impossible.

Over the last two hours, one by one, each of the six men has fallen asleep. All but one. My first assailant sits kitty-corner across the aisle with his bloody nose and black-and-blue eye, staring us down. I heard the other men talking. He's *supposed* to stand guard. But his eyelids are heavy and when I sneak a glance at him, they flutter closer to unconsciousness. He's gotten the shit beaten out of him. This guy can only fight sleep so long.

Go to sleep. Go to sleep. Go to sleep, you asshole.

I close my own eyes, trying to look small and sleepy, nuzzling my head against the luxurious headrest (PS: Nicest plane I've ever been on. Hand-stitched leather seating, TVs everywhere, freaking gold cup holders. It's ridiculous). I change my breath, pulling in slower, deeper gulps. After a few minutes of fake sleep, Harper nudges me in my side. When I open my eyes, I see that he's out. They're all asleep.

"Finally." Harper whispers so softly, I can barely hear her above the roar of the jet's twin engines.

"Thank God," I whisper back, my tense shoulders dropping a fraction of an inch. I turn toward her, the concerned words on my tongue for hours are finally free to tumble out. "What the hell happened to you out there? Are you okay?"

"I don't know. I'm so sorry," she answers, shaking her head slowly, strands of hair still matted to her blotchy, tear-streaked face. She's no longer crying but I can see where the tears fell, like tiny, fading rivers on her raw skin. "I ran and ran and ran and I found this hollowed-out tree and I thought maybe I'd be safe in there. So I hid and then next thing I know, there's a gun pointed at my face and an arm pulling me away. And that's when I started screaming for you. Maybe I shouldn't have."

"No, you did the right thing," I say. "Did they hurt you? Are you injured?"

"My feet really hurt from being out in the snow without shoes," Harper answers, looking her body up and down. "But they feel better with the socks."

One of the men felt bad for Harper and gave her a pair of fuzzy blue socks. Like the kind they give you on overnight flights to Europe with the little white gripping pads at the bottom. It was such a random, weirdly timed gesture of kindness. Like giving a Kobe beef cow a massage or letting it drink a gallon of beer before cutting off its head.

"Reagan . . ." Harper whispers before biting down on her lip, tears filling her eyes again. "Do you really think Luke is dead?"

My body stiffens and for a moment, I can't breathe. I hear the shot. I see the blood. His face. The fall. It comes back to me, in pieces and out of order. I've been trying desperately not to replay it in my mind. To not deliberate whether he's dead or alive. I've pushed that moment into the darkest corner of my mind because if I really think about it, if I contemplate Luke being gone, I'll lose myself completely. And I can't. I cannot afford to lose my mind, my will to live and to save Harper. Not now. So I swallow the emotional tumor trapped in my throat and try to find a suitable answer.

"I don't know," I finally say, my voice thin and far away. Like the words aren't even coming out of my own mouth.

Harper reads the restrained sorrow on my face and softens her own. She gingerly reaches for my arm, glancing quickly at the men to make sure they're all really asleep.

"Maybe he's okay," she whispers, her hands grasping at my still-damp sweatshirt.

"Maybe," I answer, but the hopeful word leaves my mouth with very little weight. My body shivers and I try to push the image of Luke, falling onto his back, out of my mind before the anxiety that's blossoming inside of me pushes its way up.

My head shakes with tiny microbursts, trying to erase every emotion and lull me back into the feeling of half dead. I look past Harper, out the window and into the night. The sky is still mostly black, but out on the horizon, I can see the first promise of daylight. A deep blue outlines the night sky's edges, creeping up and up and up, promising to scorch this blanket of darkness with the morning sun and paint the sky a fiery orange. That hopeful blue color feels alive, almost human. It whispers: *It's coming, it's coming, it's coming.*

"It's Christmas," Harper says, her eyes focused on the sky's changing colors.

"It is. I forgot. Merry Christmas, Harper."

"Merry Christmas, Reagan," she says, squeezing my arm and turning her eyes back toward mine. She smiles, but her crooked lips make her face look even sadder than before.

Harper stares out the window again, her chest rising with a deep gulp of air. Several seconds of silence pass before she turns back toward me and I know what she's going to ask before she even opens her mouth.

"What's going to happen to us?" she asks, her eyes desperately searching mine. "Are they going to kill us? Is this how it ends?"

"I won't let that happen," I answer even though I know I may have zero say on whether Harper lives to see the New Year. "Look, if they wanted us dead, they'd have killed us already. They wouldn't have put us on a plane bound for who knows where."

"Why are they keeping us alive?" Harper asks.

I shake my head. "I have no idea." And I really don't.

"So, what do we do now? I mean, should we try to get away at the airport? Should we run, scream, do something?"

"No, we should just keep our heads down and get in the car."

"What?" Harper says, her whisper swelling too high, causing one of the assassins to stir. I quietly shush her and turn toward the guard, making sure the man drifts back to sleep. He does.

"We do nothing," I whisper as I turn to meet her face, still frozen with surprise.

"Are you crazy? Have you never seen an episode of *Dateline*? This may be our last chance to be in public. If we don't do something or try to get away, our chances of survival are like cut in half or some really scary statistic."

"Look, whatever private airport they're taking us to is staffed by people who are on this cartel's payroll," I whisper, awkwardly twisting my shoulders and trying to turn my tied-up body toward Harper. "If we want to stay alive, we can't try to run now. We have to wait."

"But what if we . . ."

"No," I whisper and shake my head. "I should never have tried to draw attention to us at the last airport. If I do it again, they will kill you. Okay? I mean it. They. Will. Kill. You."

The blood drains from Harper's face, turning it a sickly shade of pale gray in a matter of seconds.

"I'm sorry, I don't mean to scare you," I whisper. "But I'm begging you. Don't do anything. I will get us out of this."

"How?" Harper asks, her jaw shaking, her eyes blinking back tears.

"I'll think of something," I answer.

"I hope you do," Harper says, her voice breathy and body starting to shiver. "Because I'm terrified, Reagan. I'm so fucking terrified."

I close my eyes, take in a deep breath of recycled air, and push it out of my mouth.

Me too, Harper. Me too.

EIGHTEEN

"OPEN UP, PRINCESS," MY FIRST ASSAILANT SAYS, dangling a pack of cellophane-wrapped peanut butter crackers in front of my face. I glance at his hands. They're speckled with blood (probably mine and his) and dirt. I'd rather go hungry than have him feed me.

"Can't you just untie me?" I ask, trying to make my voice as small and timid as possible. Make them think I'm not as strong as they've been warned.

"I untie you, I know what happens," he says, tilting his head to one side, his dark hair falling across his black and bulging eye.

I push my body back into my seat, my stomach grumbling, desperate for just one cracker. I eye the tasty squares, the crackers dyed a shade of bright orange not found in nature, but what I really want is the peanut butter. At least the tablespoon sandwiched between the squares has some protein. Who knows when they'll feed us again.

"Can't you just give them to her?" I ask, nodding toward Harper, who can feed herself with her arms in front of her body.

"You want them?" he asks, his voice rising, bordering on offended. He stands up from his seat, opens the package, and shakes them over my head, dumping the six crackers and their crumbs onto my lap. "You eat like a pig."

Asshole. You effing asshole.

He throws the cellophane wrapper in my face, like an exclamation point on his disgust at my rejection. He settles back down in his seat as the men around him laugh. One gives him a high five. I stare down at the crackers and can feel the heat rising up my neck, no doubt painting my skin a fiery red. And suddenly, I feel naked, exposed. They're just crackers on my lap, but I feel like I've been stripped down and put on display. Humiliated and vulnerable, all at once.

I look over at Harper, who is quietly eating her own crackers. Her big eyes stare back at me, silently trying to calm me.

It's okay. It's okay, I can almost feel her mind pulsing, sending waves of comfort toward mine.

"Here," she whispers, slowly raising her hand and offering me one of her crackers. I open my mouth but the assailant immediately stands up, smacking it away from her hand and forcing it to fall onto the ground.

"Don't you feed her," he yells at Harper. "You eat like a pig or you don't eat at all."

Fuck you. Fuck you. Fuck you. Fuck you.

He stares back down at me, the right corner of his blood-crusted mouth turned up, smug with power. I wish I was untied so I could throw my elbow into his other eye socket, remind him just how powerless he is when we're on an even playing field.

His eyes hold on to mine as he slowly backs up and flops his giant body into his seat, his limbs outstretched and casual, like a king on a throne who's lost interest in his crown. I finally break our shared stare, turning my eyes downward to the broken crackers, spread out into pieces across my lap.

I will kill them. I will kill them. I will kill them.

I bite down at the inside of my cheek as I think about getting away. We can't escape at the airport. It's too dangerous. And Harper would be dead in seconds. But I will not let us die at the hands of these cowards. After Santino, I never wanted to kill again. But that fire has reignited in my core. And it's starting to climb.

I look toward the window and see we're getting closer to the dark blue ocean. I've felt us descending for the last ten minutes and I'm anxious for us to get over land so I can see the terrain, try and figure out just where they're taking us.

"Abrochense los cinturones," a voice says over the built-in speakers of the plane. The pilot. He hasn't said two words the entire flight. The men follow his command and settle back down in their seats, fastening their seat belts tight across their laps.

My eyes are fixed on the ocean, its color growing lighter the closer we get to land. With each mile and changing shade, that dark cloud of dread pulls taut on my lungs, not knowing just what awaits us on the other end of this flight.

And then . . . there it is. Land. We fly over a busy port and adjacent shipyard. Large ships are stacked high with rectangular shipping containers, all painted different shades of red, blue, black, and green. From several thousand feet up, they look more like Legos than cargo. Beyond the industrious port, a sprawling city with the occasional high rise that I'm sure charges a premium for ocean views. As we get continue to descend, I see rickety shelters along a river and mud-covered roads. Slums. I try to piece together where we could be but I just can't tell. Colombia would be my best guess. A coastal town where drug trafficking is still a major problem. Buenaventura, perhaps? I'm hoping there will be some sign at the airport or along our route that will give our town away. Not that I'll be able to tell anyone. It's not like I can radio back to CORE our location. And with Luke potentially gone, it might be a couple days before my father and the other senior leaders even realize we've disappeared. By then, it could be too late. There may be nothing left to save.

I shudder, trying to push away the oncoming daymare, but it seeps into my brain anyway. Usually in my daymares, I'm alive. But this time, I'm dead. I'm in dark blue water; my hair floats around me like a mermaid. My hands and feet are tied together, anchored to a cinder block. My skin is gray and peeling. Dozens of tiny fish feast on my flesh. And suddenly, my eyelids lift. My eyes are gone.

My limbs begin to shake and I swallow the shriek buoying in my throat.

Not real. Not real. Not real.

I shake my head, clearing my brain, and stare back out the window as the plane gets lower to the ground. Distinguishable buildings and cars and people are finally coming into view. And then, black. A tarmac. The wheels touch down and I feel my body thrown forward as the plane hits the brakes, but I dig my feet into the jet's plush carpet, trying to stay in my awkward state of upright.

"Toto, I don't think we're in Kansas anymore," Harper says

quietly as she glances out at the palm trees, blue skies, and men directing our plane, dressed in shorts and T-shirts. We're much closer to the equator than to the cold and snowy tarmac in Iowa.

"Silencio!" my second assailant scolds, an angry grimace carved into his face.

Harper presses her lips into a thin line and turns back toward the window, her chest rising in a crescendo of tiny bursts.

I stare at the men with their orange vests and tiny green sticks, directing us into an assigned spot at the private airport. Harper sees them too. Her eyes grow wide and I know what she's thinking: maybe they can help us. My heart enlarges hideously in my chest with each painful, rapid beat, knowing they could truly be our last hope. But if we try to signal for help and it doesn't go our way, they will kill Harper. Maybe not on the runway, but within the hour. They'll drive us out of town to a secluded spot, force her to her knees, and put a bullet in her brain. If we run or scream or try to escape, Harper won't live to see another sunset.

The jet begins to slow its taxi, pulling up next to two waiting SUVs. The windows are dark, tinted, and probably bulletproof. In fact, the entire black body is most likely bulletproof. A cartel, though powerful and feared, is always a target. For police, for rival cartels. They live in a precarious state of luxury, control, and danger.

As the pilot brings the jet to a complete stop, the men begin unbuckling their seat belts, stretching their arms and wearily standing up from their seats as if they each just ran a marathon. It's hard work kidnapping two girls in the middle of the night.

"Don't move," the first assailant spits in my face, his gun back in his hands. He holds it out in front of him and then slowly raises the barrel up, pushing it to the center of my forehead, its steel cold on my warm skin.

"I'm a little stuck here," I say, glancing down at the belt tied around my waist, my arms aching and still secured behind my back. "We're not going anywhere."

"You wait here," he says, like I have another choice in the matter. He pushes the gun against my skin one more time, his finger moving near the trigger, and my heart claps like a summer thunderstorm inside my body so loud, I'm surprised he can't hear it. He returns the gun to his side and backs down the aisle, his eyes still on me. I watch him as he ducks out the jet door and bounces down the plane steps, joining the other men in the sunlight. He brings a pair of sunglasses to his face and tilts his head toward the blue sky.

The passenger door of the first SUV opens and a man with large aviator sunglasses and a black baseball cap climbs out of the car. He greets each man with a handshake before placing his fingers along the hips of his dark jeans. His face, though hidden, looks strikingly familiar. I know I've seen that jawline, that five o'clock shadow before. My mind filters through the catalogue of guards and assailants I've encountered over the last year dealing with Torres. Perhaps he was one of the guards at the ranch where my mother was killed? I squint my eyes, trying to take in his face, trying to place him, but I can't.

"Reagan," Harper whispers, even though there's no one on the plane to hear us. "The traffic control guys..."

She doesn't finish her sentence. She doesn't need to. My eyes glance at the lone traffic control worker still near our jet. He fiddles with his orange vest, glancing occasionally toward the meeting of Fernando's soldiers just outside the jet's door, careful not to keep his eyes on them for too long. Just the way he looks at them, with a mix of curiosity and fear, tells me he knows who they are. What they do. What they're capable of.

"We can't," I simply say and shake my head. But even as the words leave my lips, my head is swiveling around the cabin, searching for another exit, another way out. But there is none.

When I turn back around, the man in the black ball cap and glasses is hurrying up the jet stairs, leaving the others still talking on the ground. He enters the plane and quickly makes his way up the aisle toward us. As he takes off his mirrored frames, Harper gasps, her fingers digging into my forearm. And before she says his name, I know exactly who he is.

"Mateo?" she says, her voice thin and shaky, her eyes slick with sudden tears.

He gives her a small smile and nods his head, his eyes warmed by her emotional greeting. He comes closer to us, leaning over her to help her unbuckle her seat belt.

"You bastard," she says, her voice swelling, her fists lunging toward him, connecting hard against his shoulder. He catches her wrists before she can strike him again, shaking her and shushing her rising emotions.

"Stop, stop. Stop, *mi amor*," he says, still holding on to her wrists as she tries to wrestle her arms free to swing at his face.

"*Mi amor*? Fuck you," Harper says, her voice still rising. Mateo puts a hand over her mouth and looks out the window onto the tarmac. The men are finishing up their conversation, one of the assailant's legs bounces up and down on the first step, just moments away from climbing the stairs back onto the plane.

"Stop, stop," he whispers, shaking her again, his hand gingerly placed over her trembling lips. "Don't do anything foolish. Okay? Either of you."

He glances over at me and I nod my head. Mateo (if that's even his real name) turns back to Harper, carefully removing his fingertips from her lips. A tear breaks free, falling down her weary face, her eyebrows stitched together, angry. They stare at each other for a moment, an intensity passing between them. Betrayal and heat and love and hate, all in one breath.

"*Vámonos,*" a voice commands at the jet's door. Mateo snaps to attention, picking Harper up by her arm, still holding her gaze. As he turns around, he confidently puts a hand on her back, guiding her out of the jet and down the steps. My first assailant walks toward me, bruised and broken and still bloody. He tears off my seat belt and yanks me to my feet.

"You see my face?" he asks as he pushes me closer to him. "I'll do far worse to you later, little girl."

"Yeah, but only because I'll be chained up." My lips speak before my brain can stop me. He grabs at my arms, twisting them even tighter behind my back as he pushes me down the aisle.

"Keep talking," he says, pushing me toward the jet's stairs. "Keep talking."

My head ducks out of the oval jet door and I step into the tropical sunshine. I take in a breath, knowing it could be one of my last moments in fresh air. I wish for sweetness or salt from the ocean. But the smell of toxic fuel fills my nose instead.

I shudder, another daymare sweeping into my brain. I'm lying in the dark, hog-tied, a thick white cloth tied around my mouth. Liquid is being poured onto my body. I smell it. Gasoline. I struggle and try to scream but no sound comes out of my gagged mouth. A match is lit, illuminating a man's face, before that tiny flame is dropped at my feet.

NINETEEN

DESPITE THE SUNNY WEATHER WHEN WE ARRIVED, clouds have begun to form the farther we travel away from the city center. Harper stares blankly out the window next to me as we pass through a slum on a small river. We're outside of Buenaventura, Colombia (a sign near the airport confirmed that location), on our way to what I can only guess will be a guarded mansion in the countryside. Fernando lives like a king while thousands live in shacks made of plastic tarps and rotting two-by-fours.

Harper and I sit together in the center of the SUV's backseat, Mateo to her left, my first assailant to my right, loaded guns in their laps, their fingers near the triggers, ready to be pointed in our faces at any moment. I was surprised they didn't bring hoods for us to wear on the drive. But someone up front made the comment that we'd be dead soon. So why did it even matter?

His declaration sparked a shudder in Harper, but I certainly wasn't going to turn down the opportunity to drive to Fernando's compound with full sight. At least I'll know where we are, where we could run to. That is . . . if we can make it out of this drug cartel's grip.

Mateo keeps looking over at Harper, and I wish I could read what's written in his eyes. It's like he's trying to get her to look at him, but she flat-out refuses to give him even a passing glance. I document and try to decode Harper's body language. Her straight, almost rigid upright posture and deep frown tells me the first emotion lingering beneath her skin is no longer fear. It's anger. She is freaking pissed. She's behaving more like a scorned girlfriend who found out her boyfriend has a side piece, not like someone on her way to face one of the most dreaded cartel leaders in the world. But that's okay. I guess after hours of raw anxiety and terror tearing apart her stomach, betrayal is a welcome distraction.

We drive in silence for forty-five minutes, past lush green mountains and scarcely populated villages. We've passed exactly eight people. Four in cars passing in the other direction, two on bikes, and two walking between villages, a bucket in one man's hand, a fishing pole in the other's. But for the past five minutes, I've seen no one. No cars, no people. No signs of life. The car weaves around a mountain and then I see it. A fifteen-foot-high wall, lined with barbed wire that seems to go on forever. The compound.

Shit. There's no getting over that thing.

If we can somehow get out of the house or wherever we'll be kept, I have to figure out how the hell we can get off of these grounds. My head swivels slowly. I pretend to be looking at my hands, still tied behind my back, but I'm really double-checking what's behind us. Nothing. Just mountains and tropical vegetation and a poorly paved two-lane road. If we escape, we'll have nowhere to run to.

I face forward just as the car pulls up to a guarded gatehouse. The guard stands at attention, dressed in a dark green uniform, a machine gun in his hand. He looks very official, like a member of the military rather than a trained assassin, his paycheck coming in the form of dirty drug money.

The driver rolls down his window as our car slowly approaches the guard post and the enormous wood-and-iron gate. The wood is stained a deep chocolate brown with clusters of dark pink bougainvillea flowers growing like ivy up either sides. It looks more like the entrance to an exclusive Florida golf course or five-star resort rather than a drug compound. But then again, these guys are billionaires. They can afford the lavish touches of flower-covered gates and chrome-wheeled SUVs with all the money they make from keeping the world addicted to drugs.

"Tenemos a las chicas," the driver says when the guard approaches the front window. *We've got the girls.* The guard looks at Harper and me, tied up in the backseat, and gives the driver a small smile.

"Fernando estará contento," the guard responds, pointing his square chin in our direction. *Fernando will be pleased.*

I inhale through my mouth, air entering my body with the same density of lead, and I feel my lips start to tingle. The guard looks at me one more time, his smirk growing in size, then clutches his semi-automatic weapon to his chest and walks back toward the gatehouse. I watch as he enters the tiny building and hits a button at the top of his desk. The wood-and-iron gate shakes and then pulls back, disappearing into the high wall. The guard waves us through and the driver lifts his foot off the brake, slowly rolling the wheels of our car closer to the compound, Fernando, and our waiting dungeon.

He wants something from us. I'm not quite sure what it is yet. Information on the Black Angels? To draw more agents into the mouth of his heavily armed, illegal army? That lead-laced breath cuts into my chest as I think about the torture that awaits me. I'll be wishing for the interrogation tactics of the CIA. Sleep deprivation and wall standing sound like a picnic compared to what Fernando will probably do to me. Nothing is off-limits. The tingling in my lips begins to spread, numbing me in preparation for sadistic cruelty and unrelenting pain.

The SUV pulls through the gate, gravel crunching beneath its tires. But as I look out the window, I can clearly see this is rich-people gravel. Tiny polished pebbles make up an opulent driveway, with enormous trees lining our route to a colossal white stone house. We pass by a tennis court, two helipads on the left, and an enormous stone building on the right. I make mental notes of every spot, every guard, every wall. There are two guards stationed outside the building. But there are no guards at the helipads or tennis court. And while there are high stone walls around most of the property, as we get closer to the mansion, I can see that in the back the high walls disappear and are replaced with a tall chain-link fence with imposing barbed wire on top. That's the spot. If we get out of the house, that is the spot I'm going to run like hell toward. It's our best chance of escape.

The SUV turns into the circular driveway, winding its way past a beautiful fountain surrounded by well-trimmed hedges, and finally the driver puts the car in park at the front door. I look up at the house with its peaked roof, dormers, and black shutters and feel like I've pulled up to a house in the south of France instead of Colombia. The formal, symmetrical architecture seems supremely out of place in this tropical climate.

"Welcome home, ladies," says the assailant next to me as he looks up at the mansion. He turns back in my direction, a devious smile crawling up his swollen, bruised face. "Fernando will be happy his Christmas presents have arrived."

"Let's go," Mateo says before my tongue can strike back with a harsh comment or scream out of fear. Right now, I want to do both.

Harper's eyes widen and stay anchored to mine as Mateo grabs her by the arm and guides her out of the car.

Help me, her face calls out to me. I nod at her, trying to keep my own expression calm despite the storm at my core, threatening to unravel me at any moment.

"Move," the assailant snaps. I hadn't realized he'd opened the car door. He points at me with his gun, motioning for me to get my ass in gear and slide out of the SUV already. I awkwardly scoot my butt along the leather seat and slide onto the pebble driveway.

"Nice, yes?" the assailant says, looking up at the mansion beside me. The delight on his face is borderline prideful. Like he built this place. Like he's responsible for the billions in dirty income it took to create this compound and the dozen others spread around South America. But he's just a small piece of this illegal machine, a pawn in Fernando and Santino's fruitful enterprise. They're smart for making a man like this feel proud. For making him feel like he's part of something bigger when in reality, he's replaceable. He means nothing to them. Without him, the product will still get processed. Drug mules will get them out of the country and into the hands of dealers. And other men with a good shot and a desire to play God will kill for the Torres family. Or at least, what's left of them.

I look up at the stone estate, pretending to admire it but, really, I'm counting and recording every door (just one at the front) and every window (eight downstairs, ten on the second floor) I can see. Two guards anchor either side of the stately dark wood and iron door, but there are no others I can see at the sides of the house. Perhaps there are more guards out at night. But for now, there are only two lone guards . . . carrying guns that can fire six shots in a single second.

"Shall we?" the assailant asks me, his arms waving toward the house, as if he's inquiring whether I'm ready to take my seat at a dinner party.

Like I have a choice in the matter, you dick. But I swallow the sour rhetoric on my tongue and resist the urge to roll my eyes.

The guards open the front door and stand at attention as Harper and I are forced through, our personal and assigned assailants holding on tight to our restrained arms. I step into the two-story foyer and my eyes are immediately drawn up to a titanic crystal chandelier. A long second-story bridge leads to a curved staircase, its steps sweeping elegantly down to the first floor.

My eyes glance to my right and catch my reflection in a large oval mirror. I shudder at my image, somehow surprised by the red welt on my cheek, my blood-crusted lip, and the deep bruises on my face. I guess my fear and anxiety have been overriding the blistering pain. I try to remember how many times I've been struck in the past twelve hours but begin to lose count after eight. I stare back at a blond girl I barely recognize. My short tresses are covered in dirt, my sweatshirt torn and speckled with blood and mud and leaves. I look like I've been to hell and back.

But I know the worst is yet to come.

TWENTY

DRIP. DRIP. DRIP.

The pipe next to me has been dripping with a rhythmic beat for the past twenty minutes. The sound has gone from mildly annoying to edging me toward lunacy. Harper and I sit side by side on the cement basement floor, our hands still tied, the cinder-block wall digging into our shoulder blades and spines. There's a single light bulb, hanging precariously from the low ceiling, illuminating our wretched little space. It's hard to see much in here, but from what I can tell, there's a furnace and water heater in the back corner and rows of shelves to our right, each one lined with brown cardboard boxes. I can see pieces of yellow fabric sticking out of one. Colorful plastic flowers in the other. A ratty teddy bear and doll missing an eye in a third. It's a storage room. For both unwanted people and possessions.

"I'm having some serious déjà vu," I say to Harper, who has been surprisingly quiet during our time in this damp, ominous space.

"Why?" she asks, slowly turning her head toward mine.

"I just . . . am," I say, my voice tight in my throat. What I really want to say is, *It reminds me of the room where I watched my mother die.* But I don't. I need to keep Harper calm. I don't want to spark her hysteria. As soon as they left us alone, I was expecting Harper to break down into tears and beg me to get us out of this. But she's been so calm for the last half hour, she's bordering on comatose.

Harper's head swivels sluggishly away from me. Her face cringes as she gingerly pulls her legs toward her chest and cradles her knees in her tied-up arms. I want to ask her what she's thinking. Why she's so quiet. If she's okay. But all of these questions seem like they have horrifying answers. So instead, I simply say, "Love you, Harper."

"Love you, Reagan," she answers after a beat. I never told a friend I loved her until Harper. But we said it to each other all the time. When we'd split off in the hallway, on our way to different classes. When we'd get off the phone at night. When we'd end long text conversations. It almost always came from her first. "I love you" flowed off her tongue with such ease. But she didn't say it to so many people that it lost its meaning. Just me and Malika. It became almost habitual. I told her I loved her more often than I told my parents. But I meant it every single time.

"Do you remember that time we made a list of all the people we'd take a bullet for?" Harper asks, her eyes empty, staring straight ahead but looking at nothing.

"What?" I ask, trying to wipe the dust off my mental scrapbook and pull up the memory.

"In study hall," Harper responds, her voice monotone. "We were talking about true love and Malika said her idea of true love was

167

taking a bullet for someone, no questions asked. Do you remember that? And then we made a list of all the people we'd die for?"

"Yeah," I say.

"Your list was long," Harper says, nodding her head. "It was much longer than ours. I think I even faked my list. But you. You meant yours. Didn't you?"

"I don't know. I guess so," I answer, trying to remember who was on my list. I close my eyes, dragging up the memory buried in my brain. I see the names, scrawled in the corner of my notebook. My parents. My Nana. Sam. Harper. Malika. Luke.

"I'm too scared to die," Harper says and I can hear her swallow. "I don't think there's anyone I'd truly die for. Not like you."

"I've been trained my entire life to maybe die one day for someone else," I answer. "You can't really compare yourself to me."

"Yeah," Harper says, still nodding so slowly, I wonder if she even feels her chin bouncing up and down. "But I think you still would. Even without your training."

"I don't know," I say and shake my head, staring down at a crack in the basement's cement foundation. "I don't know how much of it is nature and how much is nurture."

Harper bounces her knees up and down, still staring straight ahead and then suddenly stops. She shakes her head, her wavy hair falling into her face. She sniffs and says, "I shouldn't have called out for you. I should have just let them take me."

"Harper, if they took you, I'd have figured out a way to come after you," I reply, wishing my hands were free so I could touch her, comfort her in some small way.

"I know," she says, listlessly rotating her face toward mine. She raises her eyebrows over her sleepy hazel eyes and adds, "See. Nature prevails."

The deadbolt on the door to the storage room clacks loudly back into its holder, announcing the arrival of a guard like a thunderbolt. Every nerve in my spine ignites and I feel like the skin along my back is on fire. The door swings open, slamming against the unfinished wall and my second assailant is standing there, an M4 carbine in his hand.

"Stand up," he commands gruffly, and we both struggle to our feet. "Fernando wants to see you."

Every curse word in every language I've been taught echoes in my brain as the second assailant grabs my arm and Mateo grabs on to Harper. Together they march us through the finished basement, complete with a twenty-seat theater and a fifties-style diner (no, seriously. Think red booths, chrome everything, a neon jukebox, and a sparkly Formica countertop. Someone wishes they were a teenager in America . . . or just really likes reruns of *Happy Days*). Then they take us up the basement steps and through a long hallway. The floors are a dark wood. The black-and-white photographs that hang on cool gray walls look extremely familiar. It takes me a moment to realize they're almost exact replicas of the photos that hung in Santino's ranch in Tumaco. Or were at least taken by the same photographer with a similar aesthetic. Delicate open flowers and a white chapel against a cloudless sky. Fields of tall wildflowers at sunset and green-covered mountains surrounded by low, foggy clouds. Each photo captures the same gentle subjects and emotes the same surprising softness.

I hear Victoria Browning's voice in my head. *Pay attention to the details*, she used to tell us during our class on surveillance and targets. *Sometimes it's the little things that pull it all together.* My pace has slowed as I look up at the photographs and study the angles and lighting and landscapes. The guard is finally forced to pull me along.

"Walk," he grunts, tightening his grip on my arm as he yanks me down the illuminated hallway, lights strategically positioned to highlight each piece of amateur artwork.

I turn my head away from the walls and concentrate on putting one foot in front of the other. My hands begin to tingle and I cannot tell if it's my nerves absorbing the panic I'm attempting to stifle or the fact that my arms have been permanently tied behind my back for over twelve hours. The buzz radiates up my forearms, lighting up my biceps with unwanted electricity. I gently shake my arms, trying to prevent the million pinpricks from reaching my shoulders, my neck, and my already throbbing skull.

The guards turn us down another hallway, past an enormous library with shelves and shelves of antique books and a sunken living room with matching light-gray linen couches, a dark-blue marble coffee table, and an elaborately decorated Christmas tree in the corner. There are boxes and wrapping paper and bows littered around the tree. Toy bulldozers and miniature cars and a tiny tea set are still under the evergreen. It's difficult to wrap my head around the fact that it's Christmas. And even more difficult to comprehend that there are children somewhere in this mansion. That's why we're here and not at some warehouse or underground bunker. Fernando wanted to be with his children on Christmas Day, hostages be damned.

My feet have slowed again and my guard sighs loudly, tightening his grip on my arm and dragging me down the hall, away from the remnants of a beautiful holiday morning. As we pass the dining room, with its enormous driftwood table and twelve matching chairs, I hear chatter. Then a round of laughter. Pot lids clanging shut and the sound of a food processor slicing or dicing or mincing. The guard turns me down one more hallway and pushes my body through a white wood-paneled arch. And there I stand in Fernando's kitchen.

Five men (including some of the men from our trip ... I mean kidnapping) are seated at a massive white and gray marble island watching a man slice tomatoes. He's dressed in dark jeans and a black polo shirt, a red-and-green Christmas-themed apron tied around his body. His salt-and-pepper hair sweeps across his deeply wrinkled forehead while he concentrates on slicing. A well-maintained mustache hugs a wide smile, a crooked upper tooth catching his lip.

Is it ... could that be him?

The man looks up, his gray eyes meeting mine, and despite his smile, my warm blood chills. I know those eyes. His brothers had those same cold, wicked eyes. He needs no introduction. I know he's a Torres.

Fernando Torres.

"So glad you ladies could join us," Fernando says, pointing his knife down into the cutting board and waving his free hand around the room, inviting us to step closer (which we only do because we have guns pointed at our sides). I can hear Harper's shaky breath next to me as we're pushed farther and farther into the massive kitchen.

Fernando carries his cutting board, full of finely chopped

171

tomatoes, toward a pot on the stove behind him, scraping the butcher knife across the grooved wood and dumping the pieces into the steaming liquid. He picks up a wooden spoon from its resting place on a small blue plate next to the six-burner stove, and stirs the tomatoes into his sauce. He opens the drawer beside him, pulling out a tasting spoon, and dips it into the pot. He scrapes it along the side and pulls out a tablespoon of dark red sauce.

"Now, who wants a taste?" Fernando asks, turning toward Harper and me. He carefully cradles his hand beneath the spoon as he carries it to our side of the island. Harper and I must have twin looks of shock on our faces as he brings the spoon closer to us, because he laughs and says, "What? Think Colombians don't know how to make spaghetti and meatballs? It's delicious."

I imagined my first interaction with Fernando quite differently on the plane. I pictured him in an office, sitting behind an enormous mahogany desk, his feet up, gray smoke circling his face. The curtains would be drawn and dark woodwork would cover every square inch of the walls. In my head, he'd be counting stacks and stacks of money, puffing on a cigar, and stroking his mustache. A true stereotype, I know, influenced by movies and pop culture imagery. I never dared to imagine I'd meet one of the most dangerous men in the world wearing a Christmas apron and trying to feed me with the same enthusiasm as my Sicilian grandmother.

Fernando blows gently on the still-steaming tomato sauce (so nice of him to be concerned about burning my tongue before he kills me, right?) before shoving the spoon near my mouth.

"Go on, now," he says, bringing the spoon centimeters away from my lips. "Taste."

"No, thank you," I reply, staring down at the dark red color. I press my lips together and hold them between my teeth, hoping he'll take the spoon away.

"What? Do you think I'm trying to poison you?" Fernando says with a throaty laugh. He pulls the spoon away from my mouth and opens his own. The spoon disappears around his full lips and he smiles as he pulls it out. "Think it needs a little bit more salt."

He shakes the spoon near his head with a smile, congratulating himself on his fine cooking, and turns back toward the stove. He pinches salt from a small dish between his fingers, sprinkling it into the sauce and throwing what remains over his left shoulder. For good luck, I guess.

Fernando turns back to the kitchen island, picking up his butcher knife and chopping up pale pink, raw chicken breasts.

"Some people hate cutting up raw chicken," Fernando says, slicing his knife cleanly through the slimy meat carcass. "I've never minded it though."

"I imagine you've dug your knife through much worse," I speak before my brain can stop my sharp tongue. Fernando stops, staring down at the raw meat, a small, nauseating smile on his face as he begins slicing again.

"You could say that," Fernando replies, slicing each breast into eight uniform pieces. "Some are easier than others." He looks up at me, waving the butcher knife in the air, its glint catching my eye and making me sick. "You would be difficult. Muscle is harder to slice through than fat."

A scream swells in my throat. I trap it, trying to swallow it down, but it only grows and grows and grows, like a jagged stone, piercing deeper into the fragile flesh with each purposeful blink from Fernando's provoking eyes.

I stare at Fernando as he jabs at me with silence and a growing smile. Out of my peripheral vision, I can see every face turn toward mine to watch my reaction.

I pull a quivering breath through my lips and roll my shoulders back, trying to suppress the tremble in my hands. "Is that what you're planning to do to us?" My voice is stronger than I expected it to be.

Fernando's gray eyes look my body up and down, his fingertips grip the handle of the butcher knife as he spins it, its tip puncturing the cutting board.

"I haven't decided," he replies informally before turning back to his chopping.

"Well, why don't you just do it now?" I ask and turn toward the assailant behind me. I nod toward the gun at my side. "Seriously, have him put a bullet in my skull. What are you waiting for?"

"Well, what would the fun be in that?" Fernando replies, the right corner of his mouth turned up as he changes knives and begins dicing an onion. "Besides, I'm a big-picture person. Santino was impulsive. He thought something should be done, he did it. He thought someone should be killed, he killed them. But I'm the more thoughtful brother. And honestly, I may not even kill you at all."

"Oh really? And why is that?" I say, not believing him for a second. "What are you going to do to me? Torture me for Black Angel secrets?"

"There's nothing you can tell me that I don't know already," Fernando answers, glancing up at me and then back down at his finely sliced onion. "I probably know more about the Black Angels than you do. How do you think we found you? Luck?"

Holy shit.

My muscles seize up and the little breath I was holding on to is immediately dragged from my fatigued body. It wasn't Harper's call to her parents that tipped Fernando off to our location. It was the mole. It was the fucking mole.

Who? Who?

My mind pulses with that question, the single word cracking against my skull over and over again. Who is feeding them information? Who is selling out the agency? Who wants me dead? I can feel the blood drain from my face as I struggle to contain my shock and focus on getting us back downstairs to our little dungeon. I'm desperate for silence. For time to think about just who the traitor might be and how I can keep the two of us alive.

I push down all my mole-related questions and focus on the pressing one in front of me. "Then what the hell *do* you want from me?" I ask, my mouth spitting out the words.

A wave of fury contorts Fernando's face and I immediately regret the agitation in my tone. He slams down his knife and takes several large, commanding steps around the island before standing directly in front of me. He crosses his thick, muscular arms in front of his chest and stares directly into my eyes, that chill returning to my spine.

"You have taken everything from me," he says, each word deliberate, his voice shockingly calm. But his face gives him away. Crimson streaks across his cheeks and crawls up his pale neck. "Your parents killed my nephew. You killed not one, but two of my brothers. You've sent my cousins to prison. You've weakened my business. So now . . . you will help me get some of the pieces of my life back. You will do what I tell you to do."

Spit lands on my cheeks, forcing my face to cringe and turn away. But Fernando grabs my cheeks with his brutal fingers, crushing my jaw and pulling me toward him, so close I can smell the acidic tomatoes and potent rosemary on his breath. His gray eyes pierce into mine. "Do you understand me?" he says through gritted teeth. I don't speak. I don't blink. I just stare. After a few seconds of silence, he tightens his grip, shakes my face, and booms, "Do you?"

"Yes," I somehow manage to whisper.

"I know where everyone is," he hisses. "Cameron Conley. Your father. Anusha Venkataraman. I will go after them one by one if you don't give me what I want."

His eyes narrow into slits before he pushes my face away in disgust. He turns his back toward me, returning to his side of the island, where he picks up his knife and starts chopping again.

"What do we do with the girl?" one of the men at the island asks, his eyes on Harper. "Should we just kill her now?"

Harper sucks in a sharp breath, her gasp echoing in her throat. I turn to look at her and wish I hadn't. Her body trembles, her eyes are filled with fresh tears, her mouth opens, and I pray a scream or sob doesn't escape.

Fernando looks up from his chopping and slowly walks over to Harper, the heel of his polished black shoes echoing against the cathedral ceilings, the knife gripped in his hand with the blade pointed out, one quick and easy thrust away from ending someone's life. He holds out his free hand, silently halting the assassin rising from his seat.

Fernando makes his way around the island until he's directly in front of Harper. He looks her up and down, slowly raising the tip of his knife up to her face, pushing back the wavy hair that hangs over her face. Her face shudders as the shiny blade passes just centimeters away from her eyes. Fernando scans her body, dressed in a gray T-shirt, my pajama pants, and borrowed fuzzy socks from the plane. He lowers the knife to Harper's chest, the harsh blade a half an inch away from the center of her sternum, and I feel my own body begin to tremble.

Dear God, no. Please. Don't kill her. Don't kill her.

"No, please no," Harper whispers, trying to keep her pulsating body still and away from the knife. Tears claw their way up my throat and I am paralyzed, helpless. I want to jump in front of her, knock the knife from Fernando's hand with my forehead. Scream at him to leave her alone. But if I move, they'll still kill her. One act of defiance from me won't save her. It will only guarantee that knife will be plunged into Harper's heart.

After a moment, the blade finally leaves her body and is returned to Fernando's side. He shrugs with indifference before saying, "Keep her alive for now. Reagan, I will send for you later. And you will help me." He then points again at Harper with the tip of his knife and threatens, "Or you'll watch me slit her throat."

As Fernando lowers his blade once again and walks back toward the island, tears break free from Harper's eyes and she sucks in her bottom lip, trapping the cry that's surely lingering in her throat.

My tight shoulders fall. We're still alive. But as I stare at a trembling Harper, I realize an hourglass with the remaining moments of our lives has been flipped upside down. Those precious grains of sand pull through, counting down the seconds until we meet our end.

I close my eyes. And in that gray space, I see my mother, her arms reaching for me, and I cannot tell if this is a memory or my imagination.

Help me, Mom. Please. Help me.

TWENTY-ONE

THEY PULLED IN TWO SINGLE MATTRESSES FOR US TO sleep on. They're thick with quilting and an extra pillow top that's kind of luxurious compared to what we've been sleeping on during our time in hiding. But they smell like dogs. One of the guards told me this is what Fernando's pets normally sleep on. Lucky pups. The mattresses are in reasonably good shape except for one corner of my mattress that's been chewed up. I can't look with my hands behind my back, but I pray for a metal spring or something I could use lying just beneath the fabric. Something to get us the hell out of here.

Harper lies on her mattress next to me, staring up at the ceiling, her hands resting on her quivering stomach. Without a sweatshirt, her skin must be freezing in our windowless room. I'd give her my own sweatshirt if I could get it off of my body.

"Are you cold?" I ask as I lie on my side, watching her body shake.

"Yes," she says, her quaking voice barely above a whisper. "I can't stop shaking."

"It's not just the temperature. It's your nerves," I answer, clumsily scooting my body onto her mattress. My hands are still tied behind my back so while I can't hug her, at least I could provide some much-needed body heat.

Harper rocks herself back and forth to make room for me and I rest my body next to her trembling frame. "Shhh, shhh, shhh, shhh," I whisper methodically near her ear, trying to comfort her the same way you'd comfort a crying baby. "It's okay. It's okay."

Harper's shaking escalates and a tear runs down her cheek. She pulls her tied-up hands to her face, swatting the tears away, angry that they've made their escape. "It's not okay, Reagan," Harper says, her voice trembling as the tears fall faster. "We're going to die in this place."

"I know you're scared. I'm scared too," I say, trying to keep my voice composed and even, the way my mother spoke to me when I was freaking out. "But we both have to be strong right now. We both have to try to remain calm, because if we don't, we might as well just give up."

"Well, I feel like giving up," Harper says, burying her face in her hands. "I don't know if I can take another second of this."

"I will get us out of this," I say quietly as Harper takes deep breaths into her palms.

"How the hell are you going to do that?" she says, her voice echoing into the small cave of her hands. "You can't even wipe your own ass right now. So how the hell are you going to get us out of here?"

"I need to figure out what they want from me first. If it's something I can give them to save us, I will."

"And if it's not?"

"Then...then I'll just have to manipulate the shit out of them. But I will get us out of here, Harper. I will," I say, the words light as they leave my tongue, their promise hollow. But it's enough to get Harper to uncover her face and look at me. "First, I need to figure out who is feeding them intel."

"The mole?" Harper asks, widening her bloodshot eyes.

"Yes," I answer and nod my head. "I thought it was the call to your parents that tipped them off to where we were but now I don't think so. Did you catch what Fernando said?"

"No," Harper says, shaking her head. "I was too busy worrying about being stabbed to death."

"Fair enough," I answer, wiggling on the mattress, attempting to find a more comfortable spot for my aching back and shoulders. "He said 'How do you think we found you? Luck?' He was basically saying the mole tipped them off to our motel."

"Well, who knew where we were?" Harper asks, her voice getting stronger.

"Just my dad and Cam. And neither of them could be the mole," I reply, shaking my head. "No one else knew where we were..."

My lips stop moving, my mouth paralyzed and open as her name enters my brain like a hurricane. Words are replaced by a gasp and air enters my lungs like a thousand freezing knives.

No. Please, no.

"What is it?" Harper asks, her eyes widening.

"Oh my God," I whisper and stare past Harper, my muscles compressing, my limbs immovable.

Every memory of her is turned upside down, shredded into pieces.

"What, Reagan?" Harper asks, her voice rising with panic. But I don't move, I don't speak. Harper shakes my shoulders as I stare at a single spot on the cinder-block wall behind her, my mouth still open and tears forming in my eyes, fogging my vision. She shakes me harder and asks, "Reagan, what is it?"

"It's Sam," I whisper, my eyes now blurring to the point that I can't make out the details of Harper's face.

How could you? The words rattle around my chest as I see Sam's face, smiling down at me, her blond hair in a ponytail and blue eyes wide and kind. I try to place the memory, but can't.

"No way," Harper says, furiously shaking her head. "It can't be Sam. She's like an aunt to you."

"She was more than that," I say, my voice raw with emotion. I swallow hard, struggling to form the words that are clattering around my brain. "She was like a second mom. She was my only mom now."

"I know," Harper argues. "She would *never* do that to you. She's been with you for every part of your life."

"Exactly," I answer, my deep love for her draining from my blood until I'm freezing, the tips of my fingers tingling, numb. "She's the only one who has been there for every phase. And for every bad thing that's ever happened."

"What are you talking about?"

"When I was sixteen, a Torres assassin came to my house in Philadelphia to try to kidnap or kill us. We locked ourselves in the panic room and were safe but . . . Sam knew exactly where we lived. I remember my dad screaming then that there had to be a mole. There had to be someone who gave us away. And when my parents were taken in Ohio and I was nearly kidnapped at school . . .

again . . . she was right there. She knew where we were. She tipped them off. And then she did everything she could to keep me from going on that mission to rescue them. She wanted them dead. And last year when a group of Black Angels was attacked by Torres's people on a mission, she was the only one who survived. And she survived without a scratch on her. How is that possible?"

"Maybe it's all just a coincidence," Harper says, her hands still heavy on my shoulder, trying to reason with me. "Just because you're near an explosion doesn't mean you built the bomb."

"Then how can you explain last night?" I answer, turning my eyes toward Harper. "She called me on the satellite phone at the gas station. She *specifically* asked where we were staying. Not just the town, the motel. I told her the name. She was the only one who knew the name. And when Fernando made his threats tonight about who he'd go after if I didn't cooperate, he mentioned Anusha, my father, and Cam. He didn't mention Sam. Because Sam is the mole. She's the one who's been conspiring with them this whole time."

"Oh my God," Harper whispers, turning her body away from me and staring up at the ceiling. "Maybe it really is Sam."

Et tu, Brute?

My mind races with a thousand furious thoughts, a hundred agonizing questions. But for some reason, this quote from Shakespeare's *Julius Caesar* rises to the top. *Even you, Brutus?* It was the last piece of literature I read in Honors English at New Albany, and I remember thinking then how I'd never felt betrayal like that. But there she is. My Brutus. My constant confidante and protector.

Sam has to be the Black Angel mole.

My body feels empty and pained all at once. Like someone

183

reached inside and stole all my vital organs, leaving my body hollow and gutted.

Memories of Sam start to flash before me. Her kissing my knee when I fell off of my bike when I was little. Her teaching me how to use a tampon. Her lying in bed and gossiping with me about the boys I liked in school. It was all an act. It was all to keep us close. Close enough to know everything. To know every strength and every weakness. All to feed it back to these monsters.

How could you? How could you? How could you?

My eyes can't contain their tears anymore. They fall fast and hot, leaving long trails down my skin like boiling, angry rivers. I trusted Sam with my secrets and fears and hopes. I trusted her with my life. My lips tremble as I try to take in new air that won't come quickly enough. That hollow spot in my gut that never seems to close shrieks with familiar agony. And I feel like I'm losing my mother all over again.

"I'm so sorry, Reagan," Harper says softly, trying to pull my body toward her and into a disjointed hug. "I don't understand how she could do this to you."

"She's a spy," I answer sharply, wishing I could wipe the tears off of my face. "It's what she was trained to do."

It's what we were all trained to do.

TWENTY-TWO

I HEAR THE CLANG OF GLASSES. REAL PLATES, REAL silverware.

I open my eyes and, at first, all I see is Harper's still-sleeping face. I've fallen asleep on her shoulder, her hands still looped behind my neck. I haven't been asleep for too long. I know this because the ratty gray shirt Harper's wearing is still damp with my tears.

The clang of dishes fills our small space again, forcing my head up. I look past Harper's shoulder and toward the doorway. The door is closed, but Mateo stands just inside, balancing an oversized tray. Water fills two long glasses. Sandwiches, cut into quarters, sit on white plates.

"I'm sorry. I didn't mean to wake you," he says, his voice startling Harper out of her sleep. She gasps as she opens her eyes. When she sees me next to her on our mattress, her face falls. It wasn't a nightmare. We're really down in the hollows of Fernando's giant estate, waiting for three options: to be rescued, to escape, or to die.

Harper hears the metallic ping of silverware as Mateo steps cautiously toward our makeshift beds. She cranes her neck, looking back at him.

"What are you doing in here?" she asks, her voice raspy from a lack of liquid. The girl usually has a water bottle permanently in her hand or at the very least, her bag. She literally wouldn't drive the five minutes from my house to hers without taking a water bottle for the road.

"I thought you girls might be hungry," Mateo answers, his brown eyes incredibly warm for someone who works for a psychopath.

"What was your first clue? That all we've had to eat all day is crackers?" Harper snaps, pulling her arms from around my neck and pushing her body up.

Mateo sets the tray down at the edge of our mattress. The wood tray has a glossy dark stain and legs, like the kind you'd use to serve breakfast in bed. The white plates are outlined with a silver rim. The silverware shines; the glasses look thick, hand-blown even. The elegant tray sits in stark contrast to our drab and gray concrete room. All the tray is missing is a clear vase with a single red rose.

"I'm just loving the five-star service," Harper quips, crossing her arms over her body. "Aren't you, Reagan? Isn't this Christmas dinner of cold sandwiches and tap water just so lovely?"

Mateo's face visibly cringes with each of Harper's sarcastic lashes, confirming the soft heart I suspected, the innocence the other guards lack. These characteristics mean he's primed for my manipulation. As long as Harper doesn't bitch him out and screw it up.

"Thank you, Mateo," I say, trying to be overly gracious to compensate for Harper.

"Is Mateo even your real name?" she asks sharply, leaning her back against the cinder-block walls.

"Yes, it's my name," he answers as he stands back up.

"Wow, something that's actually true about you," Harper snaps, her chest heaving with an annoyed sigh. "So, how exactly do you expect us to eat with our hands tied together?"

"I'll untie you for a few minutes," Mateo answers, pulling out a pocketknife along with a pair of fresh zip ties. He looks up at Harper, nervous. "But I have to tie you back up once you're done."

"Why not leave us untied?" Harper asks, her face twisting with every angry word. "Afraid you guys won't be able to rape and kill us if our hands aren't behind our backs?"

"No, I wouldn't. I'm not that kind of guy," Mateo answers, shaking his head, his eyes cast down at the ground. His sneakers scrape along the concrete floor, as if he's kicking at imaginary pebbles.

"So what kind of guy are you, then?" Harper scoffs, her voice rising as she offers Mateo her hands to cut free. He runs a blade through the zip ties and it snaps, releasing her hands from their plastic chains. "Are you just the kind of guy who spends hours and hours getting to know someone but really you're just setting up a trap for them to get kidnapped? Is that the kind of guy you are?"

"Look, I didn't know it'd end up like this . . ." Mateo says unconvincingly. He walks toward my side of the mattress and runs the blade through my ties. My arms and shoulders fall forward, my strained and aching muscles finally released.

"What did you think would happen?" Harper yells. "What the hell did you think these people were going to do to us? Feed us cupcakes and have a tickle fight?"

"I didn't know what I was getting myself into with Fernando," Mateo answers, his face sincere. His chest rises and falls twice with deep, contemplative breaths before continuing. "Look, he's my mother's cousin. I didn't grow up in this world. I grew up in a little village a hundred miles away. I only met him once or twice in my life. I didn't want to do this. But my mother didn't give me much choice. He's been taking care of her and my brothers and sisters since my father died. I'm working for him as repayment for all that money."

She looks up at Mateo, her eyes releasing from their narrowed slits. She pushes her lips together and shakes her head before tempering her voice. "I really liked you, you know. I looked forward to your phone calls and messages. This wasn't a game for me. And what's worse than the fact that you're just a big liar who didn't really care about me at all, is that I'm now tied up in the basement of a drug lord and I'll probably be dead in a couple days."

"I'm trying to do everything I can to make sure that doesn't happen," Mateo says, rubbing his hands over his face. "I care about you, Harper. I know you probably don't believe me. But I was just doing what I was told. And now that I know you, I don't want to see you die."

Conscience. This boy has a conscience.

"Then let us out," I try quietly. "If you care so much about her, leave us untied. Accidentally leave the door unlocked or something."

"I can't," Mateo says, shaking his head. "They'd kill me. And then they'd kill you too. You won't make it out of this room without getting shot. There's a guard right outside that door."

"Are there cameras in here?" I ask.

"I don't think so," Mateo answers, shaking his head, his eyes scanning the corners of the room. "This is Fernando's private residence. There aren't a ton of cameras. He doesn't normally bring . . . people here."

People. Fernando struggles to find a more acceptable word than what we really are. Prisoners. Captives. Hostages. Dead women walking.

"Where are the other cameras in the house? Do you know?" I ask.

Mateo shakes his head, rubbing his hands nervously along the thighs of his dark jeans. "I don't know for sure," he answers. "I've only been working for Fernando for a few months. They still don't tell me everything."

"Do you think you could find out?" I ask. Mateo's mouth twists as he looks over his shoulder toward the door, anxious that someone may be listening. I lower my voice, bringing his nervous eyes back to mine. "Look, I'm not trying to get you in trouble. I don't want to get you killed either. But if you care about her, give us a chance to stay alive. Please."

Mateo stares at the door for one second, two seconds, three. He then looks back at the two of us, his eyes lingering on Harper.

"I'm sorry. I'm really sorry," he says quietly, fearfully shaking his head, his feet slowly scraping against the ground as he backs out of the room. "I can't. Please. Eat. And please don't do anything stupid. If they walk in on you trying to get out, they'll . . . just . . . behave yourselves. I'll be back in a few minutes."

He finally turns around, opens the door, and quickly closes it behind him. The bolt slides back into place with a loud bang, locking us inside. Harper and I stare at the door and the room falls silent once again.

"God, I'm so stupid," Harper finally says after a few quiet moments. Her wavy hair swings between her shoulder blades as she shakes her head, still staring at the thick wood door.

"Why do you say that?" I ask even though I know what she's thinking.

"I thought . . . I thought I was falling in love with that guy. What a fucking idiot I am."

"You didn't know," I say and reach out to touch her for the first time in hours with my stinging but free hands. "How did you meet him, anyway?"

"He liked a photo of mine on Instagram like a month ago," she says, pressing her lips together. Harper closes her eyes and shakes her head again. "He was really cute. Said he went to Penn. So I followed him back. Then we started direct messaging and before you knew it, we were texting and talking every day. Like, literally we would stay up until three a.m. talking on the phone about just . . . everything. I wonder if anything he said was true."

Harper twists her face back toward mine, her eyes gleaming with a different kind of emotion. Instead of terror, they read pain. Heartbreak.

"Maybe some of it was," I reply, trying to give Harper something to hold on to. "Maybe it wasn't all a lie."

She stares at our untouched sandwiches and rubs her sore wrists with the opposite hands, her face soft and fragile in the faint light. "I just thought we clicked. It was . . . easy. I thought I finally might have with him what you had with Luke."

My lungs stop working mid-breath. Just the mention of his name flips a vital switch, turning off the survival reflex we're all born with. I've been desperate not to think about him, but his presence throbs at the center of my body with every heartbeat.

Luke. My Luke. The image of him being shot tries to rise, but I close my eyes, clench my fists, and push it down. It obeys, descending back into the black. Behind my eyelids, I see his face. Not the short dark hair and colored contacts he has now. But the way he was. The face I used to think about as I fell asleep.

I see him dressed in his JROTC uniform, the military cap covering some of his blond hair. With that uniform on, Luke stood a little bit taller; his pale blue eyes smiled even when his mouth did not. I haven't seen him in that uniform in well over a year. And I miss the pride, the excitement that seemed to beam off of him. Tears sting the corners of my eyes as I realize I'll never see him happy like that again. When I open my eyes, the shelves in the storage room are a messy, scary blur as I realize I may never see Luke again. Period.

"Oh God, Harper," I whisper and every inch of my body instantly radiates with an almost unfathomable pain. My stomach heaves, punched by furious imaginary fists.

"What is it? What is it?" Harper asks, grabbing my arm.

"I think he's dead," I say. "I think Luke's dead."

"You said you didn't know," Harper responds, her voice almost offended. "You said he might still be alive."

"I know, but I think I was just playing tricks on my brain," I answer, biting down on my tongue.

"But maybe he is okay," Harper answers, her voice unconvincing and thin. "Maybe he's just wounded and pretended to be dead."

"No. I saw the shot," I say, my voice straining. "And I just let it happen, I just let him die."

"Stop. You did not," Harper argues, rubbing my throbbing arm.

"But I did," I answer, sniffing back the snot that is now threatening to leak down my face. "I yelled out to him. I screamed for help when I should have just let them take me. I should have known what would happen if he came and tried to rescue me."

I try not to picture him, but the image comes anyway. An aerial shot of Luke lying motionless on the ground. His mouth unhinged. His eyes open, cold, and dead. His body white. The snow red.

"He never knew," I say, my mouth struggling to form the words that have been floating around my brain for hours.

"He never knew what?" Harper asks gently.

I try to speak, but the tears start to roll, stealing my words. I cry for what I've lost. For all I'll never get to do with him. What I'll never get to say. Harper holds on to my shoulder as I sob. She shakes me gently, trying to coax the sorrowful confession off of my tongue.

I take a breath, trying to slow down the tears and pull together the words that sit like an anchor in my gut. "Luke never knew that I loved him," I finally say, my hands pushing the tears off of my cheeks. "I never told him. I was scared to even think it, let alone say it. But I did. I loved him."

"He knew . . ." Harper starts, but I cut her off.

"How could he?" I yell, my voice much louder than I meant it to be, startling Harper and even myself. "I pushed him away and pushed him away. Every time it felt like we were getting close, I found a way to put up a wall or humiliate him or drive him off."

"But he always came back to you," Harper replies, her voice soft.

"Always. He's been in love with you since like the first week you met. You were his person. And he knew you loved him too."

Harper's trying to comfort me, but her words only make every inch of me throb. With Luke in my life, despite how broken I'd become, there was at least that small trace of hope; there was the potential for happiness. Without him, it's like the next sixty years of my life, everything I'd secretly envisioned for us, has been wiped away. And now all I can see is black.

Luke chose me. He ran after me, emotionally and sometimes quite literally. He chose me over and over and over again, without hesitation, without doubt. Even when I wounded him, even when loving me was horribly inconvenient, he still chose me. And I chose him back. Even as I pushed him away. I only hurt him to protect him. Because I loved him. He was mine. He was always mine.

My stomach aches with an unrelenting emptiness, suddenly homesick for a person instead of a place.

"It's okay, Reagan," Harper whispers, wrapping her hands behind my neck and pulling me toward her. "It's okay."

It will never be okay, my mind screams, wanting to push her away. But I give in. I let her pull me into her body. She kisses me on my forehead, as my body heaves once again, fresh tears falling onto her shoulder.

TWENTY-THREE

MY HANDS SLIDE BACK AND FORTH BEHIND MY BACK, testing the tightness of my newly fastened zip ties. Mateo walked in on me crying. He simply said, "Please eat. I'll be back in five minutes." He slipped back out the door, locking it behind him. I forced myself to calm down, and Harper and I quickly ate our sandwiches.

I thought about breaking one of the plates and saving a shard of porcelain to use on one of the guards later. But I was afraid a broken plate might get Mateo killed. Giving two hostages glassware was probably not a smart move on his part.

After we were finished, Mateo silently cleared our plates, tied us up, and left. After he was gone, I found three tissues on my mattress. He must have left them there for me. If someone has to die on this compound for us to get out, the last person I want it to be is Mateo.

I look over at Harper as she sits with her back against the concrete wall, her knees pulled toward her chest. She stares straight ahead, her eyes scanning rows and rows of boxes on gray plastic shelves.

"I wonder what he keeps in there," she says, finally breaking her self-induced silence. Her eyes stay glued on the boxes. "I'd say severed heads, but it smells too nice in here for that."

"Well, I can see some fabric sticking out from some of the boxes," I answer, my chin nodding toward an open box with a pale yellow blanket spilling out. "And it looks like one of the boxes has holiday decorations in it. I see green and red ribbons, so I've got to assume that's a wreath."

"I find it kind of unnerving that this man has anything resembling a normal life down here," Harper says, her eyes still studying the stacks of brown cardboard. "Like, it'd be less disturbing to me if this basement was filled with trophies from murder victims and machetes."

A voice outside our door immediately causes our chests to seize up mid-breath. Our heads swivel slowly toward the door, almost in unison. The bolt slides, cracking into its holder and the door swings open.

"Good evening, ladies," Fernando says, bounding through the door with irritating enthusiasm. He twirls a ring of keys around in his fingers, catching them in his palms with each turn as he walks toward our mattresses in the corner. Two guards, carrying M4 carbine semiautomatic guns, follow him into our makeshift dungeon, slamming the door behind them with a deafening bang that makes Harper jump.

What do you want? I feel like snapping at Fernando but stop myself, knowing this visceral reflex to show disrespect will only get me pistol-whipped. Or much worse.

I stare up at him, studying his body for weapons. He's dressed in a deep maroon V-neck sweater, pressed black pants, and black polished shoes. His mustache is neatly combed and hair slicked back, making his large forehead appear even bigger. He looks like a businessman, which in a way, I guess he is.

"Sorry to keep you waiting," Fernando says as he stands over me. "But I wanted to have Christmas dinner with my family before we talked business."

"How nice for you," I answer, picturing Fernando sitting at the head of that long table in his dining room, surrounded by his children and wife and team of assassins as they enjoyed his spaghetti and homemade tomato sauce.

"It was quite nice actually," he replies, rocking back and forth on his toes, the shine from his shoes catching my eye. "Although I think the cake may have been a little overbaked . . . oh well. I'll just have to try the recipe again. So, shall we have a chat?"

Fernando opens his palm and casually waves toward the door, as if he's inviting me up to his living room for tea and scones.

"Fine," I answer, gracelessly rocking my body forward and struggling to get to my feet. As I get to my knees, Fernando reaches out and gently helps me up off the ground. My muscles involuntarily flinch at his touch. He ignores my cringe, wrapping his fingers around my bicep and pulling me to my feet.

"It's okay. I'm not here to hurt you," Fernando says with an unnerving calmness as he pushes me toward the two guards with loaded guns, their fingers poised near the triggers.

Yeah, right, I feel like barking. As I take a few steps away from the mattress, Fernando tightens his grip on me and my core begins to quiver. I can feel the contents of my stomach turning over. I swallow the lingering nausea that's stirring as he holds on to my tied-up right arm and carefully escorts me to the door. I turn around to look at Harper, curled up in the corner, looking impossibly small. She hugs her knees to her chest. Her eyes are the size of silver dollars.

"Don't worry," Fernando says mildly as he pulls me away from my best friend. "She'll be just fine. We don't want to hurt her either."

"Then what do you want?" I finally say as he pushes me through the storage room door and out into the luxurious home theater with a giant screen, plush leather couches, and enormous recliners. The door behind me slams shut. I turn toward the sound and watch as one of the assassins bolts the door from the outside with a simple lock.

Interesting, I think as I watch him, taking in every detail. It's just a deadbolt. Like the type you'd find on a door leading in from a garage or back patio. I have to find something to jimmy that later. Not that I expect to find a lot of pocketknives lying around the storage room.

"Let's sit down in my office," Fernando says, pulling my eyes away from the door and back toward him. "Then we'll talk, okay?"

My chin bobs up and down with a silent nod as my eyes inconspicuously scan the room. A single guard is stationed outside our room. Right now, he's standing at attention, a Glock 22 at the end of his muscular right arm. But there's a chair to his left. I'm surprised he's even given the option to sit, but let's hope he does. Fernando pulls my feet forward as I quickly search the corners of the rooms for surveillance cameras. Left corner, right corner, front corner, back corner. I don't see any. My eyes survey the metal end tables and dark wood entertainment center. None. At least that I can see.

Fernando shifts his hand farther down my arm and the skin below his grip begins to smolder. I desperately want to yank my arm away, but it won't do any good to piss him off. I keep my heated face as still as possible, careful not to move my neck and alert Fernando or the guards to my quick examination of the property and its security measures. But my eyes are working overtime. I search the ceiling for cameras as we walk toward the stairs. We pass a massive wine cellar, the fifties diner, and an exquisite bar with dozens of martini and wineglasses hanging over a blue marble counter. Nothing. I can feel the two assassins behind us, eager to shoot me if I make the wrong move. Fernando pinches the skin on my arm between his fingers as we climb the stairs to the first floor. Once we reach the top, I check the corners and ceilings again. Still nothing. The cool gray walls hold only the black-and-white photographs, and I can tell from their thin frames, there's no way a surveillance camera could be hiding beneath the glass.

Fernando pushes me to the left, away from the dining room, living room, and kitchen and toward a section of the house I haven't seen yet. On our right, we pass a large playroom, child-free at the moment, but filled with colorful blocks and princess costumes and enormous beanbag chairs and books. A small stage has been built along the back wall, complete with a red curtain and gold ropes tied to either side of the thick fabric. We pass a butler's pantry with cerulean-blue cabinets and a white marble prep station. And directly across the hall to the left is a sliding glass door that leads out to a small patio with an expansive grill; beyond that is the backyard and a high chain-link fence. On the other side, the Colombian wilderness. Freedom. I take another quick glance as we pass by the door. There's razor wire across the top of the fence, but it's still our best chance of escape.

"Right this way," Fernando says as we reach the end of the hallway. He lets go of my arm and opens a set of French doors.

I step through the doors, a guard positioned on either side of me, and into Fernando's private office. A fire roars in a gray stone fireplace to my left, two oversized dark leather wingback chairs flank either side, a small table and chessboard set up in between. A dark wood desk sits on the opposite wall across from the fire. Behind it are shelves and shelves of books. Antique books with muted colors and gold printed titles and brand-new books with colorful jackets and perfect spines. There must be over a thousand of them. I squint my eyes, looking at the titles. Classics and memoirs and biographies and commercial fiction, some in English and some in Spanish, fill the floor-to-ceiling shelves.

"Yes, I'm a big reader," Fernando says, looking at my face and then back at his collection of literature. "I don't care much for television. I prefer to read. How about you?"

I can feel my eyebrows cinch together, the familiarity of his tone rippling at the nausea in my gut. But I will play along, act like we're old friends, just catching up on life over the holiday weekend.

"I like to read," I answer, following Fernando's lead, pretending that I don't have my arms tied behind my back and a gunman ready to kill me on command. "Especially the classics. *The Great Gatsby* is probably my favorite book."

"I prefer the classics too," Fernando says, settling into his seat behind his desk. The dark leather squeaks as his body adjusts to find just the right spot. "My favorites are probably *1984* and *In Cold Blood*."

"Both equally haunting," I answer, still standing at the edge of his desk. I can feel the body heat from the two guards lingering just a few feet behind me and I have to bite down hard on my tongue to suppress the shudder threatening to slide up my spine.

"Indeed," Fernando says, leaning back in his chair, examining me. His eyes start on my tied-up arms and then slowly move up my frame before circling around the features of my face. Finally, he lands on my eyes, his stare penetrating through mine before he says, "I prefer stories that stay with you long after you've finished the last word."

Fernando and I stare at each other, the fire and wood cracking and popping behind me, filling the strange and silent space.

What do you want, old man? My mind whispers as I try to keep my face unmoved and expressionless.

"Please, take a seat," Fernando finally says, gesturing toward a dark leather chair on the other side of his desk. I look at him and then back at the chair, like this is some kind of trick. I wait for razor blades or nails to rise out of the rich upholstery. Like he has a button on the other side of his desk, ready to cut me after one harsh word. I stare at the chair for another beat. Nothing happens. I shake my head, clearing my mind's wicked imagination, and then carefully sit on the chair's edge, unable to lean back with my restraints.

"Okay," I say quietly, looking back up at Fernando. "What is it you want from me?"

"It's not what I want," Fernando begins, resting his elbows on both armrests and bringing his fingertips together, like five little points. "It's who I want."

I stare at the diamond shape Fernando's fingers are creating and shake my head, my eyes returning to his. "I'm sorry, you want a person? Not information?"

"We want Cameron Conley," Fernando answers, his voice gruff, and I can feel my face contort.

"Cam Conley," I say slowly, his name curled around my heavy tongue. "What do you want with Cam?"

"I need him on my team," Fernando answers, settling his hands on his desk blotter. "He's one of the best hackers in the world. My source tells me his skills have guaranteed him a spot in the training academy. I need his expertise."

"For what exactly?" I ask, my eyes narrowed and mind racing with what in the world Cam could do for a drug enterprise.

"With technology, our business is getting more complicated," Fernando answers, leaning forward, his chair whining under the changing weight. "We need someone who can help us hide assets. Transfer money. Pay off our network. Visible money trails are getting businesses like ours in trouble and landing people like me in prison. We need someone who can keep us underground. Help us run this empire. Cameron Conley knows how to do that."

"Why can't you just get someone down here?"

"Tech prodigies in Colombia are attending college in America. MIT. Stanford. Harvard. And they're not coming back. I need someone like Cameron. And you will be the one to get him down here."

"He'll never agree to work for you," I spit out, my mind reeling from the request. "His parents were nearly killed by your people . . ."

"That was Santino," Fernando says, throwing his hands in the air like he's an innocent man. "That wasn't me."

"It won't matter to him," I say, shaking my head. "He'd never agree to work for you."

"This isn't exactly a job opening I'm hoping he'll apply for," Fernando answers, his voice rough and edging toward anger. "You are the one who damaged our business. So you *will* do this for me. You will get Cameron away from CORE. We will take him. And he will be flown down to Colombia."

"Yeah, in zip ties and against his will," I say, my head tilting to one side.

"We will give him a nice life here," Fernando says, his hands waving around the stunning room. "Look at this home. He'll live in luxury. And so will you. We're already preparing the guesthouse for you and your friend. Once Cameron is down here, we'll move you two in there. It's gorgeous. Two bedrooms. Your own bathrooms. A small kitchen and living space. Fireplace. I designed it myself. It has everything you could ever need."

Including bars on the windows and guards stationed outside the door.

"You'll all have access to great cuisine," Fernando continues. "The finest of everything. We'll treat you well if you do this for us. And we'll treat Cameron well. You have my word."

"No, you won't. Because he'll refuse to work for you. You'll torture him until you kill him. And I won't do that to him. Do you think I'd really put him in that position and—"

"You do it or he dies anyway," Fernando explodes and pounds his fists against the desk. Pens and a silver lighter jump on the desk blotter before landing back in place, forty-five degrees from where they started. Fernando takes in a shaky breath, trying to control his growing temper. He rubs his left hand over his eyes and down his cheeks before returning his icy stare back to me.

All three Torres brothers have the exact same eyes. You'd think their dark shade would come across as warm, even deceptively kind. But their shape and short eyelashes make them appear cold and on the dangerous side of crazy. Their clothes and demeanor tell a different story, paint a much more elegant, even sophisticated, picture. But their eyes give away exactly who they are.

"You will get him down here," Fernando says, each word measured and deliberate as his finger jabs in the air, pointing at my face. "Or I'll keep going down my list."

"What's that supposed to mean?" I ask, my arms suddenly roaring with pain behind my back.

Fernando leans back in his chair, staring into my face, studying me again, and in that splintered silence, every nerve within me ignites. He wants to remember this. Whatever he's about to tell me, he wants to remember this moment, the look on my face before I knew so that he can relish in the aftermath.

He watches me as he opens his desk drawer and pulls out a piece of paper, folded into a perfect square. His callous eyes sparkle and a small smile rises up his right cheek, as he unfolds it once, then twice, opening it up. He looks down at the paper in his hand, clearing his throat, as though he's preparing to read a speech in front of a crowd. "'New Albany High School Lacrosse Star Found Dead,'" he reads from the paper, looking back up at me.

The room spins, colors blur, and I feel the desperate need to throw up. I try to steady myself on something. I grab for the arms of my chair, but my hands are immediately pulled back together, still tied behind my back.

The guard at my side turns his eyes to me, but I do my best to just stare and stare and stare.

"Luke Weixel, age eighteen, was found shot to death in the woods behind a Waterloo, Iowa, motel early on Christmas morning," Fernando continues, his voice deepening, as if he's a news anchor reading the words off a teleprompter. "The shooting death is being investigated as a homicide, though family and friends say they don't know why Weixel was in that part of Iowa over the holiday. Weixel led the New Albany High School Lacrosse team to their first State Championship during his sophomore year. He was a member of the local JROTC branch and an honor roll student. Blah, blah, blah . . . accolades, accolades, accolades . . . boring, boring, boring . . . such a nice guy . . . etcetera, etcetera, etcetera. He is survived by his mother, father, and younger sister. Oh . . . how sad for them." He looks down at the paper, his lower lip pouting with a fake frown. Fernando then looks back up at me and smiles. "And how sad for you, Reagan."

I try to breathe, but air won't come. Invisible hands grip my neck, pressing down on my throat. "I don't believe you," I somehow spit out, even though I do. I can feel my muscles beginning to twitch underneath my sweatshirt, but I try to overpower them, control the overwhelming urge to scream or pass out or spin out of control.

"Take a look for yourself," Fernando says, turning around the piece of paper and leaning across his desk to bring it closer. It's an article printed out from the *Columbus Dispatch*. He points at the date in the corner. "Look . . . December 25. Dead on Christmas Day."

"You didn't have to kill him," I say through gritted teeth. "If it's me you want, you didn't have to kill Luke."

"But it's not just you I want," Fernando says, his voice unnervingly composed. He stands up and walks around to my side of the desk. He bends his knees, lowering his body until he's eye to eye with me. "Killing you, that would be easy. I want Cameron Conley down here in twenty-four hours. You will figure out how to get him away from CORE. And you will make sure he gets down here. Or I will start killing the people you love. One by one. Until there's no one left but you. Torture of the heart is far worse than torture of the body."

"You don't know where they are," I say, my eyes filling with tears. I try to swallow them down, but they rise, insistent on making their presence known despite my frantic attempts to make them disappear. "You can't hurt them."

"But I do. And I can," he says and smiles, noticing the gleam in my eye, and I hate myself for being weak. "You know I'll find them. You know I'll kill them all if you don't do what I want. So what's it going to be?"

I snap my eyes shut, struggling to contain my tears, hoping darkness will push them away, but I feel a single tear escape and run down my cheek. When I open my eyes again, Fernando has moved closer, his face beaming, his hand outstretched. And before I can stop him, his thumb sweeps across my face, wiping the tear away and my already scalding face inflames at his touch.

"There, there, Reagan Hillis," he says in a voice that's fatherly. "Don't cry yet. That's just one death. One body. If you refuse to help me apprehend Cameron, there will be more."

"Leave them alone," I say, my voice trembling. "They've done nothing to you. Leave them alone."

"Just like you left my family alone?" he answers, now standing up, his lunatic smile fading and voice rising.

"So then kill me!" I explode, my eyes filling with tears again. "Just kill me. These are innocent people you're talking about."

"You don't get to make the rules, Reagan," Fernando booms, throwing the article in my face. "So if you don't get Cameron Conley down here by sunset tomorrow, I will make sure you suffer the way I've suffered. I will keep you alive to watch every person you love die. I'll start with that blonde in the basement. You don't think I'll slit her throat in front of you? Because I will."

With that, Fernando turns on his heel and heads for the door. "Take her back downstairs," he yells over his shoulder. "And only bring her back up when she's ready to contact Cameron."

The guards yank me off the chair. I hear Fernando's heavy footsteps walking down a different hallway before he slams a door behind him, the sound rattling through the quiet house.

He's going to kill them. He's going to kill them all.

I suck in my quivering lip, trying to control it between the grip of my teeth. I look down on the floor and see the crumpled article and Luke's pale blue eyes staring back at me. I recognize the photo. It was taken on our first day of senior year for the yearbook. He hated that picture and his lopsided smile. But I always loved that photo. I had it tucked away in my nightstand. *Love, Luke.* That's how he signed it. I remember my heart leaping at that one word. *Love.*

My eyes stare down at the headline, fixated on two words.

Found Dead. Found Dead. Found Dead. Found Dead.

I read them over and over again, wishing there was a way to rewrite them. To undo everything. To bring him back.

"Move," one of the guards says, dragging me forward. I cannot feel my legs and struggle to put one foot in front of the other. As they push me from behind, my heart falls through my body. It's like that aching organ could slide out of my toes and through this wood floor, disappearing and never stopping.

Luke, Luke, Luke, Luke, my mind whispers over and over again as they practically carry me down the hallway, down the basement steps, and through the storage room door. They push me inside, slamming the door hard and locking it behind them, the finality of the sound echoing in my brain several seconds after they're gone.

"Reagan," Harper says quietly from the ground, her small body still curled up against the wall, watching me. I lift up my heavy head, my eyes a blurry haze as I stumble toward her, my knees giving out, collapsing next to her onto the mattress. Harper lunges forward, grabbing me by the shoulder. "What is it? What's wrong?"

"He's dead," I whisper, staring down at the white, quilted upholstery. "Luke is really dead."

My face finally turns toward hers. Harper's cheeks are already streaked with tears, like she knew it from the moment I was shoved back into the room. Luke is gone.

We collapse into each other, crying until our ribs ache and eyes burn. Crying until there is not a single tear left.

TWENTY-FOUR

DRIP. DRIP. DRIP.

I stare at the pipe next to me, counting the number of drips.

Fifty-one. Fifty-two. Fifty-three. Fifty-four.

It's been dripping on and off all day. I wonder if it only makes that sound when someone is showering or running the dishwasher or doing laundry.

Fifty-five. Fifty-six. Fifty-seven. Fifty-eight.

I lie on my side, shivering, my hands still tied behind my back. I feel like I've been cut open, my blood slowly dripping from my body and soaking into the mattress. My skin feels like it's barely above freezing and I cannot stop shaking.

Fifty-nine. Sixty. Sixty-one. Sixty-two.

My brain counts to stop me from thinking about Luke. But the dripping and the counting and the made-up distractions are fruitless. All I see is his face. All I hear is his voice. And I swear, somewhere in this room, I smell his cinnamon gum.

When Santino Torres killed my mother, he stripped away pieces of me. The pieces that were good and kind and joyful. But with Luke, they've stolen so much more. All that I had hoped for and wished for and pictured are now black and blank and empty. And layered in between this boundless grief is a searing guilt. Because it's my fault that he's dead.

I rub my face against the mattress and think back to the conversation we had on that snowy, tense drive to New York City. How one moment, one decision can change your whole life. If he'd just gone to that AP bio class, he'd be at West Point right now. He'd miss me, he'd wonder what happened to me, but he'd be safe.

He'd still be alive.

"Reagan, are you sleeping?" Harper whispers softly next to me. I stare at the pipe, my back still turned toward her. I think about not answering, pretending to be lost in the bliss of a REM cycle. But then I remember, she's lost Luke too. And I don't want her to be alone.

"I'm awake," I answer, my voice still hoarse from sobbing. I stare at the pipe, too sore and too tired to turn around and face her. But I feel her stand up and step over my body. Harper sits down on the mattress beside me, her back against the wall. Her hands reach out and stroke my hair. The wet strands that stuck to my tear-stained face have dried into clusters. They scrape across my face with each stroke, the short length forcing them back down toward my chin again.

"What are we going to do?" Harper asks, her voice timid.

"About what?" I ask.

"About staying alive," Harper responds. I finally push my body so I can look up into her face. We stopped crying an hour ago, but the fair skin on her face and neck are still blotchy. She always does that. When Harper cries, it's hard to hide the evidence. It lingers on her for hours. "What are you going to do about Fernando? About Cam?"

"I don't know," I answer, my breath pulling from my body through my mouth, the wound inside of me growing until it feels like it's about to split.

"Are you giving up on me?" Harper asks, her mouth pressed into a straight line.

"No, I'm not giving up on you," I answer even though part of me wants to. I feel dead already. And if I don't get Cam on a plane, even if we somehow manage to escape, who will be left? What will I have to live for?

I squint my eyes, looking away from Harper as an epiphany needles at the center of my chest.

"What is it?" Harper says, her hands touching me gently on my shoulder.

"Nothing, I just…" I begin, rolling my body away from her, my eyes focused on the heavy aluminum HVAC chambers running across the ceiling.

"You just what?"

"I just realized that I've never really lived for myself," I answer, the sudden insight tumbling out of my mouth. "I've only lived for other people."

"Don't we all live for other people?" Harper asks.

"We do, but…" I say, my voice trailing off as I stare up at the overlapping wires and piping and exposed wood. "Like you… you've

211

lived for your parents and friends. But you've also lived for the unknown. The excitement of not knowing what's going to happen to you next. The hope of what could."

"And you haven't?" she asks.

"No," I say and shake my head. "I trained my whole life to be a Black Angel. There was no real question about what I'd do. So I've lived for the people I love. And I guess I'm just terrified of making the wrong move here because if I screw this up, if I somehow lose them . . . even if we escape . . ."

I won't know how to keep living, my mind finishes, my mouth unable to compose the weak and feeble words.

My eyes make their way back to Harper, who is staring down at me, the splotches on her skin burning an even brighter shade of red. She opens her mouth to speak, but closes it again, still thinking. "I don't know," she finally says quietly. "I don't know how you go on living when everything you love is taken from you."

"I know I can't just lie here," I answer pushing my body up with my shoulder. "I have to reach out to Cam. I know that. But I can't let them get to him. I just hope he'll hear my warning. I hope he'll pick up on the fact that we are not okay."

"Don't you guys have like distress signals or codes?" Harpers asks, shrugging her shoulders. "Or is that something that only happens in the movies?"

"No, we do," I answer and nod. "But they are usually mission specific codes. I'm not on a mission right now."

"Is there anything you could say? Anything you could do on the phone?"

"I think so. I just have to make Fernando think I'm playing along.

And I've got to hope Cam doesn't react. He doesn't have a great poker face. But . . . we don't have another option."

The keys jingle at the door behind me and my body freezes. I hear it open but I'm too terrified to turn around. I look up at Harper and watch her tense face fall with relief.

I crane my neck and see Mateo standing just beyond the doorway, the dark wood tray in his hands again. But this time, we don't get expensive glassware and sandwiches cut into fourths. There are plastic bowls and paper cups. Someone must have yelled at him for daring to bring us real silverware and plates.

"Something to eat, ladies?" he asks, kicking the door closed behind him with his feet. I hear the metal bolt click on the other side, the guard locking us all in.

"Thank you, Mateo," I offer dimly, trying to push my body all the way up without the use of my arms, but my stomach and ribs are still sore from crying. Harper grabs at my shoulder, helping me sit up the rest of the way.

"Here, let me cut you out of those ties," he says, setting down the tray and removing the pocketknife from his pants. Harper offers him her hands first and he flips out the sharp blade. My eyes stare down at the knife, desperate for it, my brain suddenly racing with all the ways I could use it to get us out of here.

With Harper free, Mateo turns to me. "Turn a little for me if you could," he says, almost apologetic. I rock my body back and forth on the mattress until Mateo can reach my hands. He slips the knife through the plastic, setting me free. I pull my arms around toward the front of my body, cradling each wrist with the opposite hand, and my forearms and biceps finally go lax.

"Thank you, Mateo," I say, rubbing my fingers along my raw, inflamed skin.

"You're welcome," he answers, handing us each a plastic bowl full of pasta and marinara sauce.

"Is this what Fernando was cooking today?" I ask, recognizing the red sauce he shoved in my face.

"Yes," Mateo says with a nod. "But I promise, it's fine. It's actually really good."

"So the drug lord serial killer is a good cook?" Harper asks as she takes in a greedy spoonful of the pasta.

"He is," Mateo says, settling his body down on the concrete floor in front of us. "He's good at a lot of things actually. Cooking. Photography."

"Did he take all those black-and-white photographs?" I ask.

"Yup, he did," Mateo answers with a nod. "He's even had some showcased in art galleries around Colombia. Under a different name of course. He's very artistic. He even has a room upstairs where he makes pots and jars and plates out of clay. Has a kiln and everything."

I try to imagine Fernando sitting down at a potter's wheel, his hands shaping wet clay into a bowl. It takes such patience and precision. I would know. We did pottery for a semester in art class at New Albany and I sucked at it.

"It's hard to picture him doing such delicate work," I say between mouthfuls of pasta.

"I know," Mateo says, nodding his head. "His brothers were really the ones who ran the business. He's done his share of dirty work of course, but he's always been more interested in other things. He enjoyed the wealth and luxury his brothers and the cartel afforded him."

"So is the cartel suffering without them?" I ask.

"It's definitely damaged," Mateo answers with a deep nod. "His brothers ran this like a true business. Fernando doesn't really know what he's doing. If he doesn't get control of it soon . . . it might fall apart. Split into smaller cartels. Things are pretty tense among some of the other leaders. People aren't exactly confident in his ability to keep it all going."

"No wonder he needs Cam," Harper says, raising her eyebrows at me.

"He does," Mateo answers and turns toward me. "Reagan . . . just . . . do what he wants. If you do, you stand a chance. But if you refuse . . ."

A voice at the door stops Mateo's warning cold. But he doesn't need to finish. I already know what he's going to say and that shiver returns, crawling up my skin like a giant centipede. Mateo's and Harper's heads whip toward the sound. My eyes stay locked on the pocketknife, still on the mattress in front of Mateo. But before I can reach for it, Mateo picks it up and slips it into his pocket. Damn.

The bolt unlocks and Mateo swiftly rises from the ground. The door swings open and Fernando and two guards carrying automatic weapons step into the room, slamming the door behind them.

Shit. Shit. Shit.

The muscles in my arms tighten. They've come for me. I take in a tremulous breath, a strategy of deception bouncing around my mind, creating unsteady beats in my chest.

"What are you doing down here?" Fernando asks irritably, his eyes watching Mateo who is rubbing his hands along the tops of his pants.

Stop, I want to scream. Mateo looks nervous and sweaty.

"Just bringing down some food," he answers, his voice cracking, as he points to our plates. "I was just about to tie them back up."

Mateo takes the zip ties out of his pockets and waves them in the air as evidence.

"Leave us," Fernando spits, his lips pinching together.

"Yes, sir," Mateo says quietly. He lowers his head and makes his way toward the door. He turns around once he's reached it, glancing back and taking us in for a beat too long. A good-bye look. And maybe it is. He knows what could happen to us soon if I refuse to give in to Fernando. His worried eyes tell me he's seen the carnage before.

My biceps and shoulders tighten, my lungs seizing up with sudden dread as Fernando walks closer and Mateo slips quietly out the door.

"Plotting with Mateo?" Fernando asks, his voice unruffled despite the suspicion in his words.

"Of course not," I answer quickly, shaking my head. "I'm not interested in dying today or getting him killed."

"Really?" Fernando says, now walking around our mattress in a slow rainbow, my stomach twisting as I wait for this snake to strike me. "So you've agreed to my demands?"

"Yes," I answer, my nails digging into my palms. "I will reach out to Cam over email and you can expect a call within a few minutes. You just need to get me a secure line and a number that looks like he's calling somewhere in the United States. Preferably, with a Virginia or Maryland or DC area code so he won't be suspicious. We can't make this work if we don't have one of those area codes. He'll never believe me."

Fernando raises his eyebrows, perhaps surprised by my willingness not only to betray my friend, but also to ensure his kidnapping is a success.

"Consider it done," Fernando says, his lips pursed into a contorted but pleased smile. The two guards step forward and pick me up off the ground by both of my arms. Fernando points to Harper. "Tie up the girl as well."

One of the guards spins me around, tying my hands behind my back with zip ties, while the second ties up Harper.

"Let's go," Fernando says, waving us toward the door. The guard whips me around and grips my bicep with one hand and his gun with the other. The second guard follows quickly behind us. I glance over my shoulder to get a look at Harper, making sure she's okay. She looks back at me, her eyes fierce and unafraid for the first time in days. She nods at me as if to say, *You've got this.* And I hope I do.

As I'm dragged out of the storage room, I notice the guard stationed outside our door has changed. This one is younger and thinner than the guard who was there before. I pray he stays our guard throughout the night. He has weapons of course, but I have a better chance of overpowering someone of his size than the tall and muscular guard who was positioned outside our door just hours ago.

I search the room one more time for cameras, just to ensure I didn't miss them the last time I was hauled from this room. But there are none. The guard tightens his hold on my arm, creating long, finger-shaped bruises on my skin, as they rush me through the basement, up the stairs and into the first hallway. But instead of turning left toward Fernando's office, we turn right and make an almost immediate left down a new hallway I haven't seen before. This hallway is dark and lined with four closed doorways. There isn't a photograph or piece of artwork in sight.

And up in the corner of the ceiling, I spy the unmistakable pin-sized red light of a surveillance camera. I make a mental note to avoid turning right down the main hallway. Even if we don't come down this hall, that surveillance camera will pick up our movement.

As we reach a dead end, Fernando removes his keys from his pocket and unlocks the last door in front of him. He flips a switch, illuminating a series of overhead lights, and the sudden brightness makes my tender and tired eyes sting. I cringe, my feet frozen, and the guard has to yank my arm to push me farther into the window-less conference room. A sleek, dark wood table is surrounded by ten matching high-backed leather seats. A laptop is set up in front of one of the middle seats, its screen saver a flurry of colorful beams of light. A large and outdated satellite phone sits to the right of the computer. They were prepared. They expected me to betray my friend. I can't decide whether to be pleased or insulted.

"Are you ready to make contact?" Fernando asks, taking a seat to the right of the chair with the computer.

"Yes," I answer quietly, rubbing my hands together, my wrists aching against the restraints. "Can you untie me? I can't type very well without my fingers."

"Fine," Fernando answers, pointing at the guard standing behind me, signaling for him to cut my hands loose. I turn to watch him pull a pocketknife from his coat and flip it open, exposing the serrated blade I'm so desperate to steal. With one motion, he cuts through the plastic and the blade quickly finds its way back to his pocket.

I pull my hands forward and stare down at my wrists. I've been in zip ties for less than twenty-four hours, but the tight plastic has started to create deep, pink grooves on my olive skin. A couple more days in restraints and that skin will be bloody and raw. That is, if we live that long.

"Take a seat," Fernando says, hitting the back of the leather chair next to him. I force my paralyzed body to take a few cautious steps toward him. As I stand next to him, his scent, a combination of musky cologne and tobacco, overwhelms me, getting trapped in my septum, and I have to concentrate on not throwing up. My weary arms pull the chair out from under the table, the wheels screeching against the hardwood floors. As I take a seat, his eyes linger on my face.

Be calm. Be calm. Be calm.

The growing lump in my throat descends as my skin stirs with a subtle, lukewarm buzz. Numbness. I clear my mind, forcing half-dead Reagan to rise. As I settle in my seat, I wrestle down the last remaining trace of panic pulsing against my sternum, and that persistent alarm finally falls silent.

"Before I do this," I say slowly, my hands in my lap, my face staring at the changing colors of the screen saver. "I have to know. What is going to happen to Harper? To my family? To me? If I get him down here, will you let us go? Will you leave us alone?"

Fernando leans his elbow on the slick tabletop, his cheek

resting in his hand. He tilts his chin up at me, a faint smile tickling his lips, and simply says, "Of course."

Liar. Not that I'd trust anything he said. But his body language and the devious flicker in his eyes tell me all I need to know. Even if I deceive my friend, get him kidnapped and down to Colombia, we'll still be killed. Or at least be kept alive until Cam submits to Fernando's demands. Torturous bait until he becomes a slave to the cartel.

"Okay," I finally answer, the putrid taste of half-digested tomato sauce still rising until it reaches the back of my tongue. I turn toward the screen. "I'll email him. What number should he call?"

Fernando reaches into his pocket and hands me a number with a Chevy Chase, Maryland, area code scrawled on a piece of paper.

"Tell Cameron to call this number," he says, sliding the paper in front of me. "Tell him to meet you in Lincoln Park near the Eleventh Street entrance tonight. We'll pick him up there."

Pick him up. As if he's just giving him a ride to a bar or dinner or something. More like tackle him to the ground, put a bag over his head, and throw him in the back of a van.

"Okay," I answer, my fingers now typing on the keyboard, logging into my email account. When I sign in, there are several messages from my father and Cam. The subject lines start out concerned, *Please Check In* and *Where Are You?* Then grow increasingly more frantic as the hours pass. *Respond NOW, Reagan. Find a phone and CALL US. Where the hell are you? Freaking out.* The last one is from Cam. It screams at me from the screen, *REAGAN! CALL ME. NOW!*

I open up that email and hit reply, my fingers stiff as I carefully type out:

Get to a secure conference room. Tell no one. Call me at 240-555-9349.

I hit send and lean back in the chair, the metal springs whining against my frame. The guards, Fernando, and I all stare at the phone in silence. The room is so quiet, I can actually hear each one of them breathing. Fernando's nose whistles with each pull of air. The guard behind me sniffs back congestion and the guard to my right exhales strangely and loudly through his mouth.

I dig my fingers into my hipbones as I wait for Cam to call, my mind racing through the plan in my head, the signals I'll say to let him know I'm in trouble.

Ninety seconds after the email is sent, the satellite phone begins to ring, its shrill tone piercing through the thick silence in the room.

Fernando nods at me and then presses the speaker button on the phone. I lean in closer and say as calmly as possible, "Hey."

"Jesus Christ," Cam says, his voice hoarse and completely out of breath. "Where the hell are you guys? Are you okay?"

"Yes, Cameron," I answer, deliberately using Cam's full name, something I never ever do, hoping that through his flood of emotions, he'll somehow notice it. "We're *totally* fine."

I change the normal cadence of my voice, elongating my words, praying he picks up on my cues that someone else is listening. That we're not okay.

"Well, where have you been?" he says, his voice still frantic. I need him to take a breath. I need him to calm down and pay attention to my words, notice my signals.

"Cameron, Cameron, Cameron." I repeat his name, hoping he'll listen and realize just what is at stake at the other end of this phone. "Take in a deep breath for me. Okay? Cameron?"

There is silence on the line for one second, two seconds, and I know Cam has noticed and is processing it all. "Okay, Rea Rea," he answers, a signal back. He knows. "Just tell me where you are so we can come and get you."

I feel the strained muscles in my shoulders loosen with a small sense of relief. I gather my thoughts, trying to string together the next sentence. "Cameron, you can't tell anyone at CORE we're okay," I say, both for Fernando but also for myself. The mole. If they find out Cam knows we're in danger, its game over for Harper and me. "I need you to meet us in Lincoln Park on Capitol Hill near the Eleventh Street entrance. You got it?"

"Okay. When?" he answers quickly.

"Can you get away tonight?" I ask, my voice rising up an octave at the end of the question.

Please say no. Please say no.

"I can't," Cam answers. "You know how locked down CORE is here at night. There's no way I can get out of here."

He's lying. He's gotten us out at night before. He knows, wherever I am, he needs to give us time. Time for me to get out and time for him and my father to find us.

"I can be there tomorrow morning. But probably not until seven thirty. Any earlier and the senior leaders will get suspicious," he answers. I glance at the clock on the wall across from me. It's 10:13 p.m. I only have a handful of hours to get us out of here. Because if Fernando's assassins get to the park and Cam doesn't show, Fernando will kill us before breakfast.

I turn toward Fernando and he nods.

"Okay, Cameron," I answer. "Seven thirty tomorrow. Harper and I will be waiting."

"Stay safe, Rea Rea," he responds. "I'll see you soon."

And with that, the line goes dead. Fernando turns to me.

"Thank you for doing the right thing," he says, his voice eerily kind and his head bowed.

"You're welcome," I answer, my voice quiet.

Fernando pushes his meaty palms against the table as he stands, leaving behind sweaty handprints on the sleek veneer. "Hopefully, tomorrow Cameron will be on a plane and all of this will be over," he says.

Or I'll be over, I think as I follow suit and stand up beside him.

"Take her back downstairs," Fernando says, nodding toward his guards and they both grab me harshly by my arms. "Gentle, gentle. She's not a hostile prisoner anymore. Right, Reagan?"

He raises his eyebrows and I find myself nodding in agreement. "Right," I finally answer, my voice as strong and confident as I can make it.

As the two guards pull me toward the doorway, Fernando calls after me, "Be good, Reagan."

And I can't tell if it's a salutation or a warning. Either way, even if he distrusts me, even if there are ten guards stationed outside our room tonight, I have to get us out. The clock has been set and its countdown clicks loudly in my ear, like a bomb just waiting to go off.

Tick-tock. Tick-tock. Tick-tock.

TWENTY-FIVE

MY EYES PRICK WITH EVERY BLINK, WEARY BOTH FROM crying and getting only an hour of sleep since Harper and I were taken. Who am I kidding? I barely slept in the days leading up to our kidnapping. The brain matter behind my eyes aches with exhaustion while the rest of my skull pulses, alternating between rapid beats of fear and flushes of adrenaline.

We have to get out. We have to get out. We have to get out.

Those words roll around my brain. Every time I look at Harper. Every time I think of Cam back at CORE, plotting to find us. Every time I picture Luke's face. Every time I wonder who might die next if I don't set us free.

We have to get out. We have to get out. We have to get out.

Timing is everything. We have to try to break free in the middle of the night. We can't try to escape while people are still awake. Measuring time down here is nearly impossible. I learned how to tell time in my training by using the sun or the placement of the moon or even the North Star. But ten feet below ground, I've got just my internal clock and the sounds of the pipes.

After hours of dripping or rushes of water, the pipes have been silent for the better part of two hours. I pray that means everyone is asleep. I've set my internal clock to three a.m. At that hour, any night owls should be tucked in but early risers will still be asleep.

I keep telling Harper that we have to be patient. We have to be calm. I told her to try to get some sleep but she refuses. Her body won't rest; her legs are in a continuous state of spasm.

"Do you think it's three o'clock yet?" Harper asks for what feels like the millionth time.

I lean my body closer to the pipes, making sure there's no new noise. It's still quiet. "I think we've got to be close," I answer quietly as I scoot back to my spot on the mattress. We've each refused to move but a few inches since I was returned to our miserable little space. It's like these mattresses are our lifeboats, buoying up and down in an endless ocean, the two of us terrified to step out beyond our small rectangle of self-created safety. I've been desperate to start searching the shelves for something to cut us loose and pick that lock. But I've been terrified of a trigger-happy guard walking in and executing us on the spot.

"Time to go?" she asks, her body now rocking back and forth, her eyes growing manic from lack of sleep.

"Almost," I answer, clumsily pushing my body toward the edge of my mattress. "I have to find something to cut us free from these ties."

"Like what?" Harper asks, shifting her body onto her knees. "I doubt they keep like big blades or scissors in here."

"I know," I answer and rock my body off of the mattress, my hands retied tightly behind my back once I left Fernando in the conference room. At midstep, I look toward the door, listening for any sound. There is nothing. My legs carry me toward the shelves of boxes twenty feet away from us. "There has be something in here that will help. Something made of glass. Or even like a string. If we can find a string, with your hands in front, I'll teach you how to cut yourself free."

"Here, let me help you," Harper answers, picking herself up off the mattress. She turns toward the door and whispers, "Do you think we're safe?"

"Of course not," I answer, nodding toward the boxes. "But Harper, we have to try. Once we untie ourselves, there's really no turning back. If a guard comes in and sees our hands are free, they'll know we're trying escape. And this torturous little game Fernando is playing will be over. But we have to risk it. If we don't try to escape right now..."

My voice trails off, not wanting to finish that anguished sentence, terrify her even more. Harper blinks hard, her eyes red and slick with restrained tears. Finally, she answers, "Okay."

Harper and I begin looking through poorly closed boxes. With her tied-up hands in front, she flips open one box and I look inside to find deflated floaties and colorful buckets and half-used sunscreens; items for the beach or pool. The next is filled with colorful Christmas twinkle lights. But I can tell just from looking at them they're plastic. I was hoping for the old-fashioned bulbs that could be broken. But they aren't there.

"Next," I say, and Harper opens the next box. It's filled with race cars and Legos and coloring books. I look on the side of the cardboard box and see his name. *Alejandro* is written in black letters with the thick tip of a permanent marker. *Alejandro*, my mind repeats. The name of Santino's son. The young boy who was killed on my parents' failed mission last year.

As Harper rummages through the box, I think back to the article written about him in one of the Colombian newspapers. His dark, haunting eyes, his sweet smile, all come back to me, gutting me with a one-two punch. His death didn't start this war, but it was certainly the catalyst for what feels like its longest, hardest battle: over a year of bloodshed since Alejandro was killed. First the four-year-old boy, then my mother. Black Angel agents. The attempt on Cam's parents. Our Black Angel trainer Michael. Four of Santino's guards and Santino himself. Luke. And if we don't get out of here now, our bodies will be added to that list.

The weight of all of those deaths, all of those injuries, pulls down on my anxious heart, slowing its rhythm, forcing my body to stop in mid-motion. If only Alejandro had lived. I'll never know if it was the Black Angel's bullets that took that little boy's life, but I can't help but wonder what would have happened had he not been playing hide-and-seek during that hostage rescue.

"Found something," Harper announces, pulling out a colorful plastic telephone with a rotary dial, big blue eyes, and a red handle. And attached to its end is a long red string.

"That's perfect," I answer and walk back toward the mattress. Harper follows, the telephone in one hand and the long string in the other. "See if you can pull it off?"

"Are you serious?" she asks, looking down at the well-fastened cord.

"Yes," I answer with a nod. "Here, let me sit on it and then you pull. Come on, Harper. You're stronger than you think."

I plant my butt on the plastic phone and signal for Harper to start pulling. She stands up, gritting her teeth and pulling hard for about five seconds before the string pops up, throwing her body backward. She stumbles for a moment before catching herself. She holds the string up in the air and for the first time in days, smiles at her accomplishment.

"Great, okay. Let's get you free," I say and motion with my chin toward the spot next to me on the bed. Harper sits down on the mattress, the string lying across her open palms. "Now, what you're going to do is create friction. You need to make a loop and tie one end of the string super tight around the arch of your foot."

Harper follows my instructions, securing one end of the string around her sock-covered foot. She looks up at me, waiting for the next step.

"Slip that string through the zip tie and then tie the end around your foot," I instruct, nodding toward the string. "You're going to create a friction saw with this."

With her hands tied together, Harper's fingers shimmy the string through the zip tie. She grabs the red plastic end with her teeth, pulling it through and letting it hang down. She looks up at me again, waiting on my direction.

"Good," I say. "Now tie it just as tightly to your other foot."

She pulls her knee forward, tying the string around her free foot, double knotting it, just to be sure. "Okay, now what?" she asks once the knot is tied.

"Now lean yourself back and do the bicycle back and forth," I say, leaning my own body back to show her just what I mean. "That friction should act like a blade on that plastic and cause it to pop off."

Harper leans back, bicycling carefully, creating very little friction against the plastic ties.

"You've got to go much harder and faster than that," I say, and Harper begins to move her feet more rapidly, pulling back her own wrists and creating extra tension. Back and forth. Back and forth. Back and forth. Finally, the zip ties pop.

"Holy shit. I actually did it," Harper says, her voice breathless as she slowly holds up her free hands. Wide-eyed and mouth agape, she examines her palms as if she's seeing them for the very first time. It's crazy the basic everyday functions we take for granted until they're stolen from us.

"Okay, now you've got to do the same thing to me," I say and motion toward my hands behind my back. "Hurry, Harper. Now that you're untied, we've really got to move."

With Harper free, the bomb has officially been set, the timer ticking closer and closer to detonation. There's no going back. If they walk in on us now, we're dead.

Harper quickly stands up and runs the string through my zip ties.

"Same thing?" she asks from behind me. "Tied to both of my feet?"

"Yes," I answer and hear her hands working quickly behind me.

"Okay, you ready?" she asks.

"Ready," I answer, my stomach beginning to bubble with anxiety.

I pull hard against the string as I hear it sawing against the plastic. I can feel Harper's legs moving back and forth, back and forth. After several tense seconds, it pops and my arms fall forward.

"Freedom," Harper says as I push my aching body off the ground.

"Not yet," I answer quietly, my warning catching in my raw throat, as I head back toward the shelves. "We still need a couple things. We need something for me to pick the lock and then something for me to use to hit the guard with. You look for something heavy in the boxes, I'm going to check our mattresses for springs or something metal to help pick that lock."

Harper and I make quick and quiet work with four free hands. She opens up boxes and digs through the contents while I rip back the chewed-up fabric at the corner of my mattress (thanks, puppies). The luxurious fabric doesn't want to give at first, but I pull and pull and pull until it finally tears, exposing several metal springs, all linked together. I look for a spring in the corner that has fewer attachments and yank on it hard. It doesn't move. I grab hold of it with both of my tired, aching hands and pull with all the strength I have left inside me. Finally, the spring pops out of place and my body falls backward. I catch myself before I fall onto the mattress, terrified any sound inside this room will alert the guard on the other side of the door.

"This will totally work," I announce, beginning to bend the wire spring into a curved tool, perfect for picking.

"I think I found something too," Harper says with a loud whisper, pulling out a long piece of rounded metal from a box. A pipe. She hands it to me. "It's pretty heavy."

Despite its hollow middle, it is. I cradle the thick pipe in my hands before picking up one end and slamming it into my open palm. This is definitely enough to knock someone out. As long as I get to the guard first. Because in a gun-versus-metal-pipe fight, I'll lose.

"This will do," I say, slamming the makeshift metal weapon into my hand once more for good measure. I look toward the door, eyeing its lock, thankful that there's only one deadbolt holding us captive. If there was a chain or a bar on the other side, we'd be screwed.

"Okay, I'm going to pick the lock," I answer, pointing toward the door. "So I'll need you to hold on to the pipe. But then as soon as the lock is picked, hand it back to me and watch my hands. I'm going to count you down. Then I'm going to need you to pull open the door and I'll hit the guard over the head with the pipe."

"Do . . . do you think he has a gun?" Harper asks, her voice thin with apprehension.

"*Of course* he has a gun, Harper," I answer. "Everyone in this god damned house has like three guns on them right now. And they're asleep!"

"Okay, okay," Harper says, shaking out her thin, freezing arms before biting down on her bottom lip.

"Listen to me," I say, my fingertips touching her exposed skin. "Once we get outside of here, we have to be silent. So here's what we're going to do. Once the guard is knocked out, we're going to go up the stairs and then take a left down the hallway. When I went to Fernando's office, I saw a sliding glass door that leads out to the backyard. That's our best bet to get out. There are no cameras in that hallway but there could be an alarm on the door. We just have to pray the alarm isn't on."

"What if it is?" Harper asks, her eyes expanding. "What if the alarm goes off?"

"Doesn't matter," I answer, shaking my head. "We have to get out that door, through the yard and over that fence."

"There's barbed wire on the fence," Harper says, her voice edgy.

"I know," I answer, placing the pipe on the floor and peeling off my outer layer to give Harper a fighting chance against the barbed wire. "Here, put my sweatshirt on to protect your arms and hands. Whatever you do, don't touch the razor wire. Just follow me. We'll have to climb up at one of the corners. There should be a bar and a gap between the razor wire, connecting the fences together. At least, I hope there will be."

If there's not, our skin will be shredded. But we just have to do it. We just have to scale that fence. No matter what.

"What about you?" Harper asks, looking down at my now bare skin. "What about your arms and hands?"

"I've scaled fences in training camps," I answer her, thinking back to my training at an Israeli camp a few summers ago where I was trained in the skillful art of climbing both barbed wire and electrically charged fences. "I'll be okay."

The truth is, I cut or shocked myself several times before getting it right. I'm hoping my muscle memory remembers how to do it and I can make it over the top of the fence without cutting a major artery and bleeding out.

"Then what?" Harper asks, shaking her head. "It all sounds impossible, but say we take down the guard and get out of the house and over the razor wire fence. Then what the hell do we do?"

"We run," I say, not having a better answer than that.

My mind keeps circling back to our car ride to the compound. Five minutes down the road, I remember a small village. Maybe we can find a phone there. Even then, I'm not quite sure who to call. It's not like CORE has a switchboard or something. But maybe we can find someone who can hide us. Who can help us. We'll just have to pray we make it to the village before Fernando realizes we're gone. With the desolation of the countryside, it's the first place they'll look. But we don't really have a choice.

"You ready?" I ask.

"I think so," Harper says, forcing a brave nod. And as I search her face, I realize these could be our last moments together. Our last moments alive. Because once I pick that lock, we'll come face-to-face with either our first steps toward freedom or our final steps toward death.

My heart tightens as I look at Harper. She could be dead in the next two minutes.

I take a breath, stopping the guilt that keeps attacking my lungs, attempting to fill them and drown me. I will not let it paralyze me anymore. I push that searing guilt to the bottom of my gut and feel it catch in the reignited flame at my core. This guilt must fuel me. It must get us out of this mess.

I pull Harper's shoulder toward me, wrap my arms around her neck, and pray to a God I'm not even sure I believe in.

Keep her alive. Keep her alive. Dear God, take me. But keep her alive.

"I love you," I whisper in her ear, putting my hand on the back of her head as she tightens her grasp around my midsection.

"I love you too," she whispers, her voice muffled by my shoulder.

"We're going to be okay," I say and squeeze her harder, hoping that extra grip on her body will force her to believe me even though I don't quite believe myself. "You ready?"

"I'm ready," she answers, nodding her head and pulling her body out of my arms, her hands still holding on to my rib cage.

Harper's eyes meet mine, terror and grit sparking among the hazel. I steady her shoulders in my hands. "We can do this," I whisper, and she nods. Like she already knows.

I pick up the pipe and silently hand it to Harper. We turn away from the shelves and tiptoe toward the door. Once we reach it, I examine the brass lock. It looks like a pin tumbler lock, which means it will have a series of pins inside. If I can push each one of those pins aside, I can unlock the door.

My body is at once flushed with relief and then flooded by terror, that dark cloud of dread slipping through my open mouth, coiling around my lungs and freezing my muscles. Every part of me stops moving.

Concentrate. Concentrate. Concentrate, I tell myself, rolling back my shoulders and stopping my body from falling any deeper into its coma of fear. I stare at the lock and shake out my hands. I don't have time to be afraid.

I steady my hand and slowly stick the metal spring into the lower part of the keyhole. I silently jiggle it against the pins until I feel one. I push with as little weight as possible, careful not to make a sound and alert the guard on the other side. I hear the first pin pop. Four more to go. I push again. *Pop.* Again. *Pop.* I turn the screw again. *Pop.* Last one. *Pop.*

Okay. Now the deadbolt.

I slowly turn the spring, easing the deadbolt into its holder, the delicate tissue in my lungs burning with my held breath. Finally, I feel the bolt slide into the holder.

Click.

I hear Harper gasp at the sound. That tiny click could give us away. My own eyes expand with panic.

One Mississippi. Two Mississippi. Three Mississippi. Four Mississippi.

I count the seconds, waiting to hear the sound of the guard standing up on the other side, waiting for the door to fly open and a gun to be pointed at our foreheads.

Five Mississippi. Six Mississippi. Seven Mississippi.

Nothing. I let out a held breath, my lungs scorching, greedily sucking in new air. I slowly slide the piece of metal out of the lock and stick it into my pocket. I hold out my hands to Harper and she places the metal pipe in my palms.

This is it. This is it.

My entire body begins to tingle, fear and adrenaline ripping through my veins, my blood filled with a dangerous heat, like I've just downed a gallon of gasoline. I turn to face Harper, taking in her pieces, one last time. Her wavy hair, the beauty mark beneath her left eye, her tiny ears and big eyes. I memorize her face, knowing it may be the last thing I ever see. She holds my gaze, perhaps doing the same. Our chests rise together with matching breaths. I hold up my fingers to count her down.

Five. Four. Three. Two. One.

Harper sucks in another breath as I grip the metal pipe in my hands. After a fretful beat, she pulls open the door, hiding her body behind the wood, and there, sitting to the left of the door is the young and skinny guard, a gun on his lap. As I step forward, his sleepy eyes widen, shock registering on his face, just before I slam the pipe into his face, breaking his nose and knocking him off of his chair and onto the floor.

His gun falls next to him and I quickly kick it away. The pistol spins and slides across the acid-stained concrete. The guard tries to lift his head, groaning, his pale face splattered with blood that just keeps coming. He's not out yet. I hit him one more time with the pipe on the side of his temple, knocking him out. His head collapses to the floor, but as I stand over him, I can tell that he's still breathing. He's still alive. I could hit him once more, kill him. Make it impossible for him to warn the other guards that we've escaped. But as I lift the pipe back in the air for the deathblow, I see his chest rise and fall. And I can't. I can't take another life. Not if I don't have to.

I fly across the room, stashing the blood-covered pipe, then search the guard's body for extra weapons. I find just a radio and tuck it into the back of my jeans.

"Harper, come on," I whisper and she sticks her head out from around the door. Her eyes immediately expand at the sight of the guard, bloodied and beaten, on the floor.

"Is he dead?" she whispers as she takes a cautious step out of the storage room. I walk quickly across the room to pick up the pistol. I double-check it. It's loaded. Good.

"No, but if we don't get out of here now, I may have to kill him, so let's go," I whisper, walking back toward her and grabbing her by the wrist with my free hand, pulling her through the dimly lit basement. Once we get to the foot of the stairs, I put my hand up, stopping us both. I stand at the base of the staircase, the Glock 22 pointed in the air, my finger poised by the trigger. And I listen. For footsteps, for voices, for anything. But the house is still. I grab on to Harper's wrist and carefully climb up the stairs, stepping lightly, trying desperately not to make the floorboards creak.

One. Two. Three. Four. Five.

I count the steps as we climb. I reach the sixth and final step, I place my weight on it lightly, and then ...

Creeaaak.

Shit. I hold my breath, waiting to hear movement in the dark house, my finger still hovering near the gun's curved trigger. But still, I hear nothing. I reach the top with Harper trailing behind me and skipping the creaky step.

Clever girl.

Harper comes up to the hardwood floors behind me. I hold my hand up again, stopping her from moving any farther, as I listen for sounds in the house. Down the hallway in front of us, I can see the glow from a light somewhere. Perhaps a light is on in the kitchen? Perhaps someone is in there making a snack? Or was it left on by mistake? Still, I listen for even the almost silent shuffle of tired, slippered feet. But there is nothing.

The hallway to my left is pitch-black. But I know the sliding glass door is that way. I turn to look at Harper, her eyes broad but her face still, the panic momentarily buried somewhere in her body. I point my head down the dark hallway and slip my free hand through hers. She squeezes me tightly, all her fear contained in that grip, as I guide her slowly across the floor.

One. Two. Three. Four. Five. Six.

I take each step slowly, careful to touch down with my toe and not the clunk of my heel.

Toe. Ball. Heel. Toe. Ball. Heel.

Like dancers, we move soundlessly through the hallway, me counting the number of wary steps and the seconds I've been holding my breath.

Seven. Eight. Nine. Ten.

After seventeen steps and even more seconds without air, we reach the sliding glass door I saw earlier with Fernando and his guards. I squeeze Harper's hand before letting it go. I turn my head, searching the shadowy hallway, listening again for the sound of someone rising in the house, alerted that a guard is down and the captives are trying to flee. Stillness.

I look out the glass door. Beyond the dark patio, the backyard is dimly lit with just a few floodlights, but even so, I can see the fence and the barbed wire. I search for the corner, hoping that where the side and back fences meet, we'll get a break from the sharp razors, but I can't see that far. We'll be running blind.

The muscles in my tense forearms ache as I scan the backyard once more, waiting for guards on their rounds to walk in front of me. But after what feels like an eternity, no one walks past. The back-yard may not be manned by a guard at all. But I know nothing can really be that easy. There could be guard dogs, waiting to run us down. Shooters on the roof. Traps in the grass. Not to mention, a god damn alarm to shriek as soon as I open this door. But if we don't get out of here now, death is not a question. It's a certainty.

I look over at Harper. She's staring down at the door handle, biting her lip, her arms twitching in my sweatshirt, just waiting to run. Her eyes look back up at me, her chest rising and falling quickly with uneasy breaths, and nods. As if to say, *I'm ready. Let's go.*

With one hand, I grip the gun, and with the other, my fingers wrap around the door handle.

Please be unarmed. Please be unarmed.

And as I put my fingers on the door handle, I look into the glass. And in my distorted reflection, I see my mother's face.

Help me, Mom. Help me.

I hold my breath and pull. It slides with ease. For one second, there is silence. And then . . . sirens.

"Shit. Run," I yell to Harper over the grating cry of the alarm and we sprint through the patio and into the backyard. I immediately begin running to the left, toward what I hope will be a corner in the fences, with Harper on my heels.

Lights begin to turn on in the backyard, and I can hear voices yelling from somewhere inside the mansion.

Go, go, go, my mind is screaming, my legs pushing me faster and faster across the solid earth, my heels inflamed. And then I see it. A corner in the fence. A break in the barbed wire.

Forty yards. Thirty yards. Twenty yards. Ten yards. Five yards.

The fifteen-foot chain-link fence feels even higher when you're standing underneath it, armed gunmen just seconds away from filling the backyard.

"Come on, we've got to climb," I yell to Harper as I begin to scale the corner of the fence. My hands and feet crawl up the metal chains with ease and reach the top. I grab on to the metal post between the barbed wire that links the two fences together and throw my feet on the other side.

When I start climbing down, I see Harper is frozen, halfway up the fence, unsure of how to get over the barbed wire.

"Don't think, just do it, Harper," I scream, and suddenly, I hear the pop of a gun.

Boom. Boom.

It comes again, scurrying her up the fence. In the chaos, Harper forgets my warning, grabbing on to the barbed wire with her sweatshirt-covered hands, and screams as it tears into her flesh.

"Get yourself over, get yourself over!" I'm screaming and Harper throws her legs over to the other side, pulling her hands from the wire, half climbing, half falling to the ground.

"Para! Para!" I hear a voice command over a booming loudspeaker. *Stop! Stop!*

Boom. Boom. Boom.

Bullets are now whizzing near my frame, but I don't have time to look into the backyard for the guards. I lean down to Harper, crumpled on the ground. Her hands are torn and bleeding. Still, I pull her up harshly by her wrists.

"Run, Harper," I scream, yanking her body into the thick vegetation just beyond the fence. "Run!"

And so we run. Away from the screaming guards and the gunfire. Away from Fernando and our meeting with death. But if we don't run fast enough, if we get caught, that meeting is still on today's calendar. In red. And underlined.

TWENTY-SIX

RUN. RUN. RUN.

My mind repeats only one word, screaming it like a siren. The vegetation is thick. Harper and I keep tripping over tree branches and getting stuck in bushes. But still, we run north. We're far enough away from the roadway so we don't get spotted. But close enough that we know we're heading in the right direction and won't get lost in the thick of the Colombian wild. Because getting lost out here is almost as dangerous as facing Fernando and his hired gunmen.

Almost.

I hear the sound of a slow-moving car on the roadway again, twenty yards away.

"Car," I whisper and grab Harper's wrist, my hands tacky with her blood. I pull her deeper into the overgrowth and we both slide onto the ground, our bodies parallel with the earth.

I try to slow my heavy breathing so I can hear the car again. This is vehicle number four since we started running. And at this late hour, with so little around, I know it's Fernando and his army of assassins looking for us.

Harper moves next to me, cracking a branch, and immediately her body freezes.

I can see the headlights going north. The driver creeps the vehicle slowly along the two-lane roadway, the car almost coming to a full stop just yards away from us. They're close enough now that I can hear the sputter of their engine.

Please keep going. Please keep going, I plead with the driver, who has probably been instructed to kill us on sight.

Harper's trembling fingers grab at my hand, her wounds still bleeding. The running doesn't help. Her heart is working harder, pumping blood faster throughout her body. As soon as we got far enough away from the house, I quickly looked her over to make sure she didn't hit one of the radial arteries in her wrist. Thank God she didn't. Because between that laceration and her heart pumping extra hard as we run, she'd be dead by now.

The car slows down even more and above our heads, more light. Shit. They've got a flashlight.

Harper gasps next to me and I slap my free hand over her mouth, keeping her silent. The beam moves forward with the slow speed of the car, the light still dancing among the overgrowth, looking for us. Finally, that penetrating light disappears and the car begins to speed away. They're going in the same direction as us. But with the unknown to the south and absolutely nothing to the east and west besides mountains and tropical forests, we don't really have a choice. We have to make it to that village. And quickly.

"Come on," I whisper to Harper, pushing my body off the ground. "They're gone."

"How much farther to the village?" Harper asks as I gingerly pull her up by her wrists, careful not to push into the deep cuts on her hands.

"I don't know," I answer. We've been running for at least thirty minutes but with so many obstacles and stops and starts, progress has felt slow. "Maybe another mile."

"God, I'm so tired," Harper says, her body hunched over. In the moonlight, I can see her bloody hands on her knees, my pajama bottoms smeared red and tattered from the barbed wire.

"I know. But we have to keep going," I answer, my own breathing labored, my body throbbing with pain. But at least I have the luxury of shoes. Harper is still in the thick socks the guards gave her on the private jet. Her feet must be killing her. I'd give her my boots, but I know they're two sizes too small for her feet.

"Okay," Harper says, standing up straight once again and tossing her wavy hair behind her shoulders. She puts her hands on her narrow hips, sucks a deep breath through her pursed lips, and nods. "Let's go."

My legs carry me once again through the darkness, and suddenly, I can hear Michael's voice calling out to me, as if I'm running intervals back at CORE.

"Come on, Reagan. Let's go! You can run faster than that."

I've tried to push our beloved trainer, killed at the hands of Santino in Indonesia, out of my mind. It's almost too painful to think about him because all I see is his dead eyes and the deep, red tissue around his slashed throat.

So much bloodshed, so much death. So many people I love are gone. I have to keep running. So I can reach that village, reach a phone. Alert my father that they're all in danger. That Sam is the mole. I have to save the few I have left.

One hundred yards in the distance, I see light. But it's not the light from a car. It's the very dim glow of a scarcely populated town.

"We're almost there," I whisper to Harper, holding out my arm to slow her exhausted stride. "We need to be quiet. One of the guards could be stationed at the village just waiting for us."

"Should we keep running?" Harper asks, her voice thin with lack of oxygen. "Go to the next village or something?"

"The next village is at least another five or six miles by car," I reply, my mind carefully going back over our route to the compound. "I'm afraid we won't make it there before sunrise."

"But if Fernando's people are hiding here..." Harper begins.

"They are probably hiding everywhere," I whisper over the sound of animals starting to wake from their slumber. The sky is still dark, but it's like animals can feel the promise of morning. "If I think it's unsafe, we'll keep running or hide out or I'll think of something. Okay?"

"Okay," Harper relents and reaches out for my wrist. "I trust you."

You shouldn't, I feel like saying. What have I done for her? Except get her kidnapped and nearly killed. We may be out of that storage room and miles away from the compound, but we have yet to truly escape. The center of my chest feels like it's collapsing in on itself at the thought of making it this far and still being forced to watch my best friend die.

I feel for the gun in the back of my jeans. Amazingly, it's still there. I pull it out and unclick the magazine, running my finger along the ammunition, feeling for the smooth and rounded end of each bullet. Fifteen. Fully loaded. I slam the magazine back into the pistol and it clicks into place.

"Think we'll need that?" Harper asks, eyeing the Glock in my hands.

"We might," I whisper, but I'm not sure if she hears me over the sound of the cracking branches and songs from nocturnal insects.

The light pierces through the thinning vegetation, bringing the village into view. Tin roofs cover several homes on reedy stilts and as my eyes look from house to house, I realize some don't even have the luxury of a sturdy roof over their heads, protecting them from Mother Nature's wrath. Some homes are covered by straw or reeds.

"Hang on," I whisper, putting a protective arm across Harper's rib cage as we near the edge of the overgrowth. "Let me check first. Stay here."

Harper freezes, and in the very dim light, I can finally make out all the features on her face. Blood is smeared across her right cheekbone, most likely from her hand but possibly a cut from a branch striking her. Her hazel eyes are weary and exhausted but her jaw is tight, her face surprisingly fierce, readied for fight or flight. As I turn away from her, I pray we won't have to do either.

"Be careful," she whispers and I nod without glancing back. My feet step cautiously through the last of the foliage until I'm standing within the last few feet of cover. One more step and I'll be fully visible to anyone on the other side.

With my gun pointed in the air, my finger poised near the trigger, I push away the final bits of branches and leaves, peering out onto the empty roadway. My head swivels north and then south. I listen for the sputter of an engine in the distance, for the sound of rocks scraping against the dirt and crunching beneath tires. I hear nothing. In front of me are two dozen small houses, all built with a varying array of manufactured and earth-made tools and products. Thatched roofs and aluminum and two-by-fours and plywood make up these dwellings, and I have to wonder if this little village will even have a phone. They barely have electricity. I step farther out onto the road, pointing my gun out in front of me, readying myself for the pop of gunfire. But nothing comes. The village lightly hums with the hush of sleep.

"Harper," I whisper. I hear movement in the brush before her face warily peers out from behind a bush. "We're clear. Come on, we've got to move."

With my gun outstretched in front of me and my eyes searching every home and every tree for a shooter, we sprint across the open roadway and immediately duck our bodies back into the cover of darkness between two small homes.

"Stay close to the house," I whisper to Harper, and push my hand against the center of her chest until her body is parallel with the unsound house, hidden from the sporadic light of the roadway. "Let's keep going."

Harper pushes every inch of her frame up against the wall, moving her feet carefully from side to side, as if she's standing on the ledge of a building, just one strong gust of wind away from free-falling to the ground. We move along the wall, my gun still pointed in the air, my finger suspended near the trigger. We need to explore this village and see if we even have a hope and a prayer of finding a phone or Internet access or some way of reaching Cam and my father. I'd take messenger pigeons at this point if they could fly all the way up to DC.

Crack.

A startled breath sucks through my open lips and the two of us freeze midstep. Someone is here.

Is it a villager? Fernando? An assassin? An animal?

Harper grabs at my arm, digging her nails into my flesh, the same questions most likely swirling through her frantic mind.

Crack.

It comes again. And it's close.

Harper's nails dig deeper into me, her fear forming a death grip on my much-needed limb. I turn toward her, mouthing the words "Let go." I need to get myself to the edge of this house and see just who may be on the other side. Her fingers finally relent, dropping from my skin and falling to her side.

"Stay here," I mouth to her before turning back around, my feet immediately carrying me closer and closer to the sound.

Crack.

It comes again. And I know it's not an animal. It's a footstep. It's a human trying to be as silent as me.

I press my body closer to the wall, trying to hide any hint of shadow on the ground that could give me away. My hands reposition themselves around the gun and my sternum feels like it's tearing apart. My lungs blister, but I'm too terrified to breathe.

Twenty feet. Fifteen feet. Ten feet. Five feet.

I reach the edge of the rickety structure, my shoulders rubbing against the weather-battered wood.

Crack.

Another step, just yards away from me now. My heart pumps, my palms, even my fingers are moist with sweat. I grip the pistol with both hands, readying my finger to pull the trigger.

I look at the ground, searching for a shadow in the moonlight, but they must be pressed up against the corner of the building as well.

Shoot or get shot. I ready myself, taking a final breath and counting down.

Five. Four. Three. Two. One.

My body pulls around the edge of the building, my gun pointed at the forehead of a face I recognize, her pistol just inches from my chin.

"Holy shit," I reply, sucking in a breath.

"Jesus Christ, Reagan," Victoria Browning says with a small smile, pulling down her pistol while lowering and grabbing the still-pointed gun from my hand.

"Harper, it's okay," I say, poking my head around the structure and inviting Harper to join us on the other side. "Harper, this is Victoria Browning. She's a director within the Black Angels, Director Browning, my best friend Harper."

Harper sticks out her hand, the impulse to always be polite deeply rooted in this Midwest girl, even while running for her life.

"We don't have time for pleasantries," Browning says firmly, putting her hands on both of our shoulders and pushing us deeper into the village. "Come on, I've got a car waiting. Let's get you somewhere safe."

Harper and I follow Victoria as she runs toward the other side of the village where an SUV is hidden behind one of the last battered homes.

"Get in, get in," she orders, opening the back door. Harper and I both slide in and only when Browning climbs into the front seat and turns on the ignition do I take in my first truly relieved breath.

"Oh my God, Browning," I say, putting my elbows on my knees, my body sinking forward, my head hanging between my two hands. "Thank you so much for finding us. Is my dad okay? Cam?"

"Everyone is fine," Browning answers, looking back at us in the rearview mirror. "Let me just tell everyone I've got you."

Browning puts her finger up to her ear and pushes the talk button on her two-way radio.

"Team two, I've got the girls," she says, taking a right and heading back north, away from the compound. "Copy. We'll see you at the meeting point."

"How did you find us?" I ask, my legs now completely drained of their adrenaline, my calf and thigh muscles stinging like I'd just run one hundred miles.

"We had surveillance outside the compound," Browning answers, glancing at us again in the mirror. "We were trying to get in to rescue you two, but with about fifteen minutes from our planned attempt, we heard the alarms and knew you guys must have escaped. So one team went south, I went north, and here we are. We figured you'd try to make it to one of the villages to look for help."

"Well, thank God you got us before they did," I reply, sinking back into the leather seat. "I thought we were going to die."

"Me too," Harper says, taking my hand into hers. "But I also thought you'd find a way to get us out."

"Oh my God. I'm so tired," I say with a small laugh, rubbing my face with my free hand. "I want to take a shower and eat something and go to bed for like two days."

"You can rest on the jet back to DC," Browning says, turning off the two-lane road and onto an even smaller dirt one. "We've just got to meet up and regroup with the team."

Trees and shrubs, thick with leaves, hide whatever we're driving toward. I squint my eyes searching for a home or warehouse or structure. Finally, a two-story building comes into view. We are the first car to arrive.

"Team two, we are at the meeting point. What's your location?" Browning says into her earpiece. She releases the talk button, listening for instructions. She pulls past the building, parking in the back, out of sight from Fernando's team who might drive past. She puts the car into park and nods her head, and I wonder who is speaking on the other side. She then turns around to us. "They're still a few miles out. Your dad says to go ahead and wait inside."

"My dad came down?" I ask, my voice brightening as I unbuckle my seat belt. "He hasn't been on the ground for a mission since Mom died."

"You're his daughter," Browning says, pushing open the driver-side door. "Of course he wanted to be a part of the team to rescue you."

We slam the car doors and walk toward the structure. Browning takes a single key from her coat pocket, unlocking the deadbolt on the back door. She puts a hand on my back and shepherds us inside the lightless space.

She flicks on a light near the doorway and a few fluorescent bulbs two stories above my head buzz to life. In the dim glow, I can see shelves and shelves of aluminum and small tables set up in the middle of the building.

"What is this place?" I ask, turning around and taking it all in.

"They supply tin to local villages," Browning answers, running her hands along the slick metal, stacked in dozens of thin sheets on one of the shelves. "We've used this building for missions before."

"Missions with the Torres cartel?" I ask.

"Of course," she answers. "Believe me, they are not hard to find. Here, sit down. You must be exhausted."

Browning pulls two metal chairs away from the tables. They scrape along the concrete floors, and for some reason, the irritating sound causes the bile to surge in my stomach. I take in a breath, trying to quell the nausea that has taken over any sense of relief, and sit down next to Harper.

After a few seconds of silence, I hear the rumble of an engine and tires knocking against rocks on the dirt road.

"Who's here?" I ask, my eyes widening and nerves beginning to fire. I look around the building, searching for a low window that looks out onto the driveway. But there is none.

Browning puts her finger to her ear, nodding at the conversation on the other side. "Copy," she replies and shakes her head at me. "Don't worry, it's just the second team."

Tears begin to gather in my throat at the thought of seeing my father in just a few seconds. But that nagging nausea won't subside. Perhaps it's just the unknown. The fear of getting to the airport without Fernando finding us. Luke's face flashes in my mind and that sorrow comes roaring back. Maybe that's it: guilt and sadness curling around my gut now that the adrenaline is gone, now that we're safe.

I hear the car engine cut off and the sound of car doors slamming.

I breathe in again, a smile tickling the corners of my mouth as I think of the look on my father's face when he walks through that door. Will we run to each other? Hug? Cry?

I hear the crunch of gravel, the sound of several footsteps. The door opens with a heavy whine. And my heart, my mouth, my stomach, all drop to the center of the earth.

"Hola, cariña," Browning says, a wide and wicked smile spreading across her face. *Hello, darling.*

"Holy shit," I whisper.

"You naughty, naughty girls," he says as he walks toward us, his pace slow, his voice both teasing and menacing.

His boots clunk louder and louder against the concrete floors as he steps closer to us. After a few large steps, he's standing over us, and my body begins to shake.

"What the hell is going on?" Harper asks, exasperated.

I look up into Fernando's face and then back again at Victoria Browning, her arms outstretched, the gun she so cleverly took out of my hands pointed at my face.

"She's one of them," I whisper to Harper.

That traitor. She's one of them.

TWENTY-SEVEN

"OH MY GOD," I WHISPER TO NO ONE, MY HEART constricting with mournful beats in my chest. Harper hangs her head next to me, tears silently falling down her face, the relief from our supposed rescue exchanged in a single second for unrelenting sorrow.

My hand reaches out for hers. She threads her fingers through mine, squeezing it hard, as I look around the building. Three guards stand near the back entrance, M4 carbines in each of their hands, just waiting for the command to kill us. One of the guards is the assassin I beat the shit out of. I'm sure he can't wait to pull the trigger.

I take in a breath, quickly running through any possible martial arts move that could get us out of this. But it's five against one. Five heavily armed and trained killers against one. And as I look up into Fernando's chilling eyes, I know our fate is sealed. This is it. *This* is how we die.

Every curse word I know enters my mind in bursts. How could

I be so wrong? How could I focus in on Sam so fast? She was never the mole. It was always Browning. And I never even considered her. How could I be so stupid?

My stomach twists but doesn't knot. It twists and twists into one long and painful rope. My eyes look beyond Fernando and hold Victoria Browning's gaze. I look for something in her gray eyes. A twinge of remorse. A hint of misgiving. But there is nothing but an icy, piercing stare.

"Why?" My mouth finally forms the simple question weighing down my tongue.

Victoria Browning's lips separate into a slow, malicious smile. She keeps her gun pointed at my face as she speaks. "Bogotá" is all she says.

"Bogotá?" I repeat, my mind going over my last year at CORE for any memory of something happening in Colombia's most populated city. But my mind is blank. I remember nothing about Bogotá. "I don't understand."

My eyes widen and I hope my curiosity will keep her talking. Browning takes in a breath and lowers my gun. She and I both know I'm not getting out of here alive. She takes a few steps toward us and Harper crushes my hand, terror manifested into a grasp.

"Yes, Bogotá," she says again, the gun at her side, her finger still near the trigger. "Your parents are the reason that Santino was thrown out of the Black Angels. He didn't leave on his own to run his business. That's the story the agency crafted. The story they want everyone to believe so that he is the enemy. Your parents and a failed mission in Bogotá were the catalyst for all this."

She waves her hands around the room, motioning toward Fernando, toward the guards with heavy artillery gripped in their meaty palms.

"I still don't understand," I say, narrowing my eyes at her.

"Just tell her, Vicki," Fernando insists, the familiarity in his nickname knocking me hard in my gut. They've known each other for years.

"What does it matter?" Browning scoffs. "We're going to kill her anyway."

"If I'm going to die, I'd like to die with answers," I say, my voice surprisingly calm. For the last twenty-four hours, my body has seesawed between all-consuming panic and deep determination. But now that I know there's no way out, that there's nothing I can do to save us, my limbs, my face, even my fingertips, have gone completely numb. My nausea has settled. The suffocating knot looped around my lungs has loosened. I feel unnervingly tranquil, settling into a paralyzing state of surrender.

Browning taps her foot on the concrete floors, its echo matching my staccato heartbeat. She stares at me, wondering what she should say, how much she should tell me. Finally, she shrugs, the corner of her mouth rising into a sick who-gives-a-shit smile. I'll be dead soon. Might as well spill it all before I go.

"Santino Torres and I came into the Black Angels at the same time," Browning begins, her voice almost wistful. "He was a foreign agent and I was an operative from the Special Activities Division in the CIA. We were stationed in South America together. On our way up the ranks. We were on a mission in Bogotá with your parents that got botched by them."

"How so?" I ask, and she glares at me, clearly annoyed by my interruption.

"They had intel that a diplomat here was committing treason. He was killed," she continues. "Murdered by your mother, in fact. But it turns out, their intel was wrong. Your parents wanted to be the big heroes and insisted on rushing this mission before we could do proper surveillance and find out if the intel was credible, which of course it was not."

I narrow my eyes as Browning paces. I just can't see my parents being so foolish, refusing to examine their intel with a fine-tooth comb. They were always overly cautious. But if this happened early in their career, perhaps that's why they became that way.

"It could have turned into a political nightmare," Browning continues, her pace slowing. "But it was out of our field office, so to help the State Department, Santino and I took the fall. Even though it was *your* parents who screwed up, they never ended up getting punished. We did. And we paid big. Santino was thrown out of the Black Angels. My dreams of becoming Secretary of Defense or the head of the CIA were over. Your parents, who were our friends, people we trusted, took no responsibility for their actions. They said nothing. They let us bury ourselves. So, we turned on everyone. Santino started his business. And I helped provide intel to keep him safe. That was until you came along. And killed him."

Browning's last three words rattle against her throat with restrained emotion. Her free hand clenches into an infuriated fist and I watch her gray eyes turn glassy. I never thought I'd ever see this glacial excuse of a human so emotional. Santino Torres was more than just her partner.

"You committed treason," I say quietly. I stare up at Browning, someone who I always respected and thought of as the consummate leader, and feel disgusted by my admiration. "You fed a drug cartel information for what? For love? For money?"

"For both," Browning answers, clearing the sudden sorrow from her throat. "And for revenge."

"I understand being pissed at my parents, but you took an oath when you became a Black Angel. You turned your back on the United States government."

"They turned their backs on us," Browning says, pointing to herself, her finger coming to rest on the hollow spot in her neck. "We gave them everything. Santino and I dedicated our entire lives to the government, and for what? To be stuck in middle management the rest of my life? For a crappy salary and a windowless bedroom at CORE? I can't take care of my ailing parents on what I make. So, yes. I helped Santino. I helped the people who were always loyal to me. Because the Black Angels were not."

You think you know me. But you don't know the half of it. You don't know everything about your beloved Black Angels.

Those were some of Santino's last words to me in the warehouse in Indonesia. I thought they were just the final manipulative plea of a desperate man. I had him pegged as a villain right from the start. Born with that rotten seed at his core. But perhaps I didn't know the whole story. Maybe some monsters are not born, but made. Casualties of circumstance.

As I look up into Browning's face, pained by memories of loss and betrayal, the pieces begin to fall into place. That's why Santino always came after my family. That's why he continued to come after the Black Angels. And Browning is how he knew how to get to us.

"That's a long time to deceive people, Browning," I finally say, nodding my head.

"Revenge is a long game," Browning answers, picking up the pistol from her side, turning it around in her hand, studying it. "I wasn't planning on killing you, you know. I don't think you were even born during that botched mission. But then you got yourself involved. You killed Santino and changed the game. So I guess it's time for me to put down my final chips. When you get to the other side, tell Santino I say hello."

With those words, Browning points her gun at my forehead. I close my eyes, my heart compressing painfully in my chest, my body bracing for the bullet. I hear Browning click off the safety and Harper begins to scream.

"No, no, no!" she shrieks.

Boom.

A gunshot. I feel something warm spray across my face. But I feel Harper's hand, clasping down on mine and I realize, I'm still alive.

My eyes fly open in time to watch Victoria Browning collapse to the ground.

Boom. Boom. Boom. Boom. Boom. Boom. Boom. Boom.

Bullets from several guns fly through the air, striking Fernando in the center of his chest, then all three guards in their foreheads.

Their bodies fall to the ground with a quartet of thuds, their blood pooling around each frame. And the warehouse falls silent.

Air enters my lungs in thin, shaky gasps. My entire body, from my lips to my toes, begins to tremble. I slowly turn around in my metal chair to see where the gunfire is coming from and who just saved our lives. And from a shadowy corner, two figures step forward and into the light. My father. And Sam.

I want to run to them, to hug them, to jump up and down, but can't. I tell my limbs to move but they refuse. I am frozen, cemented to this three-foot-by-three-foot spot in the middle-of-nowhere Colombia.

"Are you guys okay?" my father calls out as they rush toward us.

But before they can reach us, my muscles jolt, sliding my body from my chair, my knees slamming against the cement floor. My stomach heaves, folding my frame forward, my burning face settling against the freezing concrete. I feel my father's hands on my shoulder, pulling me off the ground and into his arms. I claw at his chest, making sure he is real.

"I'm here, Reagan," Dad says into my ear. "I'm here."

I wrap my arms around his neck, pulling him closer. And I cry. And I cry. And I cry.

TWENTY-EIGHT

MY FEET ALL BUT SPRINT DOWN THE BETHESDA NAVAL
Hospital hallway. My borrowed jeans slide down my hips and the
shirt Sam gave me on the plane itches at the collar. I have yet to
shower and still smell like dirt and sweat and blood. But I don't
care. As soon as we got off the plane, I begged them to bring me
here. I had to see it for myself to believe it was true.

Beep. Beep. Beep. Beep.

The first thing I hear when I enter the hospital room is the sound
of a steady heartbeat. The curtain around his bed is pulled. I have
yet to see his face. But just hearing that sound, knowing he's alive,
brings my hands to my warm cheeks and tears to my exhausted eyes.

I carefully pull back the curtain, and those tears begin to well
at the sight of him lying in bed asleep, his wounds wrapped in ban-
dages. He stirs at the sound of the curtains scraping against the metal
bar. His eyelids flutter and finally I'm greeted by his pale blue eyes.
They shine and smile before his lips do.

"Hey," Luke says, his voice scratchy, his dimples folding at the center of his cheeks as his mouth curls into a cockeyed grin.

"Hi," I answer quietly, taking a few guarded steps toward him, trying not to bump the bed or monitors or wires coming from his body. "Am I allowed to hug you?"

"Of course," he answers, opening up his uninjured right arm and pulling my body toward him. I carefully wrap my arms around his neck and bury my face in his shoulder. Even though he smells like a sterile hospital gown, I still get the faint smell of cinnamon.

"Are you real?" I ask, my words muffled against his shoulder.

"Yes," he says back, softly placing his right hand on the back of my head. "Are you real?"

"I am," I say and nuzzle my nose into the skin on his neck, just to make sure.

I'm alive. He's alive. We're safe.

Luke squeezes my body against his, providing the catalyst for more tears. This time, I don't try to force them down. The impossibility of all of this has made me a weepy mess and I just don't give a shit. I turn toward Luke, and as my brown eyes connect with his two pools of cornflower blue, a tear breaks free. He smiles at me, gently touching my cheek with the back of his hand before wiping the tear away with his thumb.

"I've missed those eyes," I say, realizing it's the first time I've seen him without colored contacts since we entered the Shadow Program.

"And I've missed yours," he whispers. "Why are you crying?"

"Because you're actually here," I whisper back, carefully placing my hand on his chest. Another tear falls and I shake my head. "I was certain you were dead. I saw you get shot. And then I saw the article in the *Columbus Dispatch*. You were dead and now . . . you're here. In front of me. I thought I'd never see you again."

"I know," he says, his thumb blotting away another rogue tear. "They got me good in the shoulder. Enough to draw a lot of blood, so I thought if I fell just right, maybe they'd think they killed me and leave me there. So I collapsed and played dead. It was absolute torture listening to them take you away. It took every ounce of strength in me to just lie there and not run after you. But I knew if they thought I was dead, it was the only way I could get to your father. The only way I could really save you."

"They wouldn't have let you leave those woods alive," I answer, confirming that he did the right thing. "Your parents know you're okay, right? They never saw the *Dispatch* article."

"Yes, they know I'm fine," Luke answers, nodding his head. "I had surgery in Iowa and then the Black Angels made sure I got taken by medical plane here so they could keep a watch on me. The article wasn't real so they never had a reason to be alarmed. We owe Cam like a big cake or something. He's the real hero in all this."

Dad and Sam explained to me on the plane that it was actually Cam who figured out that Browning was the mole. After months of hacking into confidential files using all of Browning's credentials, he was on her server the day we were taken and saw some weird activity. So he started tracking her and told Dad he suspected *she* might be the mole. Cam and my father were the only two Black Angels who knew that Luke was alive and Harper and I were kidnapped. So the two of them doctored up an article saying Luke was dead. With Cam's hacker magic, they put it on the server for Browning to find. And sure enough, she found it and sent it to an email address that Cam traced to Colombia. They started following her every movement on the server and around CORE. And when she made up some bullshit excuse about taking time off between Christmas and New Year's, Sam and Dad followed her to Colombia, certain it would lead them to us.

"I can't wait to see him," I say with a small smile. "I'm going to knock him to the ground I'm going to hug him so hard."

Luke stifles a laugh and pulls on my arm, drawing my body onto his bed.

"Lie with me," he says quietly. And so I do. I climb into an empty spot on the bed next to him, wrap my weary arms around his waist, and rest my head on his chest, his heart pounding against my ear.

Ba-bump. Ba-bump. Ba-bump. Ba-bump.

I close my eyes and feel suddenly sleepy, hypnotized by that sweet and steady sound, that metronome of life. Luminous warmth explodes at my core, rushing through me until it reaches every part of me, the top of my skull and the arches of my feet. The sensation almost startles me, but then I realize: this is what it feels like to be happy. I haven't felt it in so long.

As my mind begins to fade into that gray space, somewhere between asleep and awake, Luke rests his chin on the top of my head. I feel his chest rise against my cheek, taking in a heavy breath.

"What is it?" I whisper, opening my eyes and tilting my face up at him.

"I know it was horrible for you to think I was dead," Luke says, staring out onto the gray December day outside his hospital window. "But it was terrifying for me not to know if they'd reach you in time. I don't think I've ever been so scared in my entire life, hearing you scream as I lay on the ground. And then of course the hours that followed. Trying to figure out where you were, just hoping you were still alive."

"I'm here," I whisper, hugging him tighter across his waist, nestling my face against his chest, breathing in his scent.

"I know," he says, kissing the top of my forehead.

"You ran after me again, Luke," I whisper, realizing how many times this boy has put his life on the line for me. "And even though I'm happy right now, even though we're both safe and alive and together, I still can't help but wish you had gone to that AP bio class. I will always wish you were at West Point and not a part of this dark life."

"Well, I never will," Luke answers quickly, pulling me up from the warm cave of his arm and chest. He holds me by the shoulder with his good hand, his eyes both warm and serious. "Even with all that's happened, I don't regret a thing. Because it means that I'm with you."

"Really?" I ask.

"Really," Luke says. "I love you, Reagan. I've always loved you. And I never want to lose you."

My heart pounds spastic beats of joy, my body surprisingly light under the weight of the heavy words I both longed and feared to hear. Because loving me is so complicated and inconvenient and chaotic. And I only want Luke to be happy. But maybe this is his happy. Maybe this really is where he's supposed to be.

Luke wipes away a fresh tear that has fallen from my eye as my mouth begins to form the words I thought were lost forever, buried next to Luke in the snow.

"I love you too," I say, my voice trembling against my throat. I stare up into Luke's striking face, and the future that was shattered by Fernando begins to rise. Jagged, colorful edges find their missing puzzle piece and in all of those maybe memories, again and again, I see Luke.

Luke's full lips slowly rise into a smile as his fingertips brush gently against my cheek, comb through my hair, and find the back of my neck. My entire body buzzes as he pulls me toward him, resting his forehead against mine.

"I never thought I'd hear you say that," he whispers, his long eyelashes brushing against my own. "Will you say it again?"

"I love you, Luke," I whisper, pulling my mouth toward his. And just before our lips touch, I breathe in the familiar scent that we somehow create together. Milk and honey. He leans into me, his mouth brushing against mine, and I fall helpless and hopeful into his kiss.

TWENTY-NINE

"SLAY, GIRL! LOOK AT THAT SEXY NEW HAIRCUT," I hear a familiar female voice call out as I near the cafeteria at CORE. A long wolf whistle follows. I turn around and see Anusha and Cam rounding the corner by the intel center and coming toward me.

"Oh my God," I yell and take off running. I sprint past other trainees and senior leaders and trainers and once I reach them, it takes serious restraint not to tackle my friends to the ground. Instead, I throw my arms around both of their shoulders, bringing them in for a hug. I squeeze them hard against me, pulling their breaths from their bodies and sparking a round of laughter. "I have missed you guys so much."

"We've missed you so much," Anusha says, her dark ringlets tickling my chin as she enfolds me against her strong frame.

"PS: thanks for freaking saving our lives," I reply, pulling out of our shared embrace and patting Cam on his warm cheek.

"Hey, I learned from the best rule breaker out there," Cam answers with a small smile.

"Seriously," I say, letting go of Anusha and grabbing Cam by his shoulders. I look up into his teddy-bear-brown eyes so he knows that I'm serious. "If it wasn't for you figuring out that Browning was the mole, Harper and I would probably be in Fernando's incinerator right now. So thank you."

Cam's jovial smile falls and he pulls my body into his big frame for another hug. "You're welcome," he says quietly, squeezing me hard for an extra second and kissing the top of my head before letting me go.

"I always knew I hated that bitch," Anusha says after a heavy, emotional beat, causing Cam and me both to laugh. "No seriously. She was always a total see-you-next-Tuesday."

"A what?" Cam asks, arching a confused eyebrow up at Anusha. "What's a see-you-next-Tuesday?"

"Oh God," Anusha says and rolls her amber eyes. "You Black Angel kids are so sheltered. Must I teach you everything?"

"This is what happens when you spend every free moment of your life learning criminal psychology or how to knock someone out with just a metal pipe," I answer, linking my arm through Anusha's as we walk toward the cafeteria. "Which did happen to come in handy at the Torres compound."

"Well, thank God you're okay," Anusha says, pulling tighter on my arm and kissing me on the cheek. "And honestly, I'm really digging the blond." She runs her hands through my hair, playing with a thick strand.

"Seriously?" I ask, taken aback. "I hate it. I can't wait to go back to being a brunette."

"Are you allowed to go back to your old look?" Cam asks as we get in line for food. The lunch menu on the chalkboard reads, *Lemon Chicken, Herbed Risotto,* and *Fresh Vegetables*. Yum. Finally, some real food that isn't from a convenience store or possibly poisoned by a serial killer.

"I'm waiting to find out. They just released Luke from the hospital this morning and we have a meeting later with some of the senior leaders," I answer and grab a tray. "I had debriefings all day yesterday with Homeland Security and the State Department and the CIA. But from what I've been told, with Fernando dead, the cartel is starting to fall apart. All the Torres brothers are dead. A CIA and Black Angel task force just arrested the last remaining high-ranking officers in the cartel last night. They think it will just break up into a bunch of small cartels and we won't really be on their radar anymore. They're even letting Harper go home today."

"They don't think there's still a threat against her?" Anusha asks, carefully picking out a roll from the breadbasket with a pair of tongs.

"I mean, everyone with any power is either in jail or dead," I say, shrugging my shoulders. "They're going to have a watcher on her and her family for a couple months just as a precaution, but they're pretty sure she's in the clear."

"What about you and Luke?" Cam asks, accepting a full plate of food from one of the cooks behind the line. "What's going on? Are they keeping you in the Shadow Program? Are they going to let you guys back in here?"

"God, I hope they do!" Anusha practically screams, throwing her head back with frustration. "Lex Morgan has become even more of a monster without you here to shut her the hell up."

"Anusha, I can hear you, you know," Lex yells, a few people away in the lunch line.

"I know you can," Anusha yells back, leaning forward and looking past the other trainees. "Why do you think I said it?"

"Oh man, how I've missed you and your mouth," I chuckle and follow my friends to our old spot in the CORE cafeteria.

Over lunch, they catch me up on Qualifiers and how another round of cuts should be coming soon. They debate who is in and who is out. Who is being super annoying and sucking up to all the trainers (Lex) while making life completely miserable in the dorms (also Lex). We talk about their Christmas at CORE and how they wish we could all go out in DC for New Year's Eve.

"Are you okay, Reagan?" Cam says, finally asking me the question floating above both their heads like a cartoon thought bubble, while we've been talking about everything and nothing. I follow his eyes as they look over the cuts on my face and finally land on the deep purple bruises around my wrists. Part of me wants to take my hands off the table, tuck them away so people cannot see what has happened to me. I don't know why my first instinct is to hide these scars. But I fight it. I leave my hands on the table. I let the world see my bruises, my cuts, the trauma branded on my body.

"I've been scared to say something," Anusha says, her voice just as soft as Cam's. "But you're like a sister and we worry. You think you're going to be okay?"

I take in a breath, trying to suppress the terror that lingers just below my skin. Trauma is a hard thing to erase. Feeling like you're going to die is something that's impossible to forget. The cuts and bruises from the beatings at the hands of Fernando's assassins will eventually fade. The emotional scars? I don't know if those will ever go away. But I'm trying to be grateful for everything and every moment. Because if I don't, if I let myself wander back into the black like I did after Mom died, I'm not sure I'll make it back this time.

"I don't know," I answer, my voice shaky. "I think I will be. Or at least I'm going to try like hell to be okay."

Help me, Mom. Help me.

It's moments like this that I really wish she were here to put her arm around my shoulder and kiss my cheek. To tell me everything is going to be all right. I want so desperately for those words to be true. I want so badly to be okay. To be happy even.

"You're never going to forget what's happened, Reagan," Anusha says, reaching across the table and grabbing my hand. "But this doesn't have to be your story. And if there's anything we can do to help you make sure of that, we're here."

"I know," I say, squeezing her hand, pushing down the tears threatening in my throat. "I don't want to be the girl everyone here feels bad for. I don't want all this pain to destroy me."

"So don't let it," Cam says, touching me gently on the arm.

I nod my head and stare down at the table. It'd be so easy to become the victim. To be the girl everyone whispers about. I want to be the girl who walked through fire, who dove into the deepest, coldest ocean of grief, and fought her way up to the surface, fought to survive.

"Reagan," a voice from behind me says, causing my body to jump. I turn around and see Thomas Crane, one of the senior leaders at

CORE, standing behind me dressed in an official-looking suit and tie. "Sorry to interrupt your lunch. But we need to see you and Luke in the Tribunal. Can you come with me?"

"Of course," I answer, slowly standing up from my seat, my stomach forming a weighty knot at the thought of stepping in front of the Tribunal again.

"We'll see you later," Anusha says, her inflection forming almost a question rather than a statement.

"I hope," I say quietly before turning around and leaving my friends.

I follow Thomas out of the cafeteria and through the West Hall, where we pass a few trainees and Black Angel agents, each of whom greets me with a pat on the shoulder or a "Welcome back." I have no idea who really knows where I've been or what just happened to me. "Welcome back." It's just a friendly, go-to greeting. But as I walk around the intel center and down the East Hall, the insides of my palms begin to prick, my mind racing. Are we back? Or will we be put back out into the world, forced to take on yet another set of new identities? And if we are welcomed again into the Black Angels, do I even want to be here? Do I really want to live this life of darkness again?

As we approach the Tribunal Chamber, I see Luke seated on the steel bench outside, dressed in khakis and a light-blue button-down shirt, his injured arm in a sling, waiting for our turn behind those double doors.

"Wait here, please," Thomas says, pointing at the empty seat next to Luke. I slide next to him, the cool metal soaking into the yoga pants I borrowed from Sam this morning. (Oh, how I miss my clothes. But at least these were clean.) Thomas pulls at the handle and slips into the chamber, leaving us alone in the empty hallway. The door closes, its loud, metallic clank echoing through the cavernous underground bunker.

"I didn't think I'd ever hear that sound again," I answer, my stomach still folding into itself, like kneaded dough. Luke reads the worry on my face and slips his right hand through mine, squeezing it three times.

"Me too," he replies as I begin to count the familiar gobs of paint on the cinder-block walls.

One. Two. Three. Four.

The door opens again and I quickly stand, preparing myself to be ushered in. But instead, it's Harper who comes out from the other side.

"It's you," I squeal, throwing my arms around her. We were separated during debriefings and I haven't seen her in over twenty-four hours. "I didn't know if we were going to get a chance to say good-bye."

"Me either," Harper says, wrapping her arms around my rib cage and holding on to me like we've been separated for years instead of a day. She smells different. Like lavender. Not her normal sugar-and-lemon scent. Borrowed shampoo and body wash I'm sure.

"Oh, Luke," Harper says, finally letting me go and carefully wrapping her arms around Luke's neck. "I'm so, so glad you're okay. We were so worried."

"I'm okay," he answers, kissing Harper on the top of her forehead. "I'm just glad you guys are okay."

"Emotionally scarred, but that's what therapy's for, right?" Harper says with a small smile before letting go of her hold on Luke. "At least I'm alive. And I'll actually get to have a life and go back to school and stuff. If they weren't going to let me go back to New York, I was going to flip out on them."

"So, they're really letting you go home now?" I ask.

"Yes." Harper nods with an almost wistful grin. "They're going to have a watcher fly me home right now."

"What about security?" I ask, my hands gripping either side of her arms, suddenly panicked and protective.

"A watcher will be stationed at the house and on my family for a couple months. They'll have someone assigned to me once I go back to Manhattan. But everyone seems pretty confident I'm safe now."

"Thank God," I say with a heavy sigh. "I was certain I not only almost got you killed but also deprived the world of its next very important filmmaker."

"They just made me sign a lot of papers," Harper says, pointing over her shoulder at the chamber doors. "So when I get asked in future interviews how I came up with this crazy plot where a girl and her best friend get kidnapped from a motel in Iowa and held hostage in Colombia, I'm going to have to come up with a really good lie."

"Harper," a voice calls to her down the hallway and I turn to see a watcher, waiting to transport her home. "Sorry, but we've got a plane to catch."

"Okay," she calls to him before standing up on her tippy toes and wrapping her arms around Luke's neck. "Love you, buddy. Be good to my girl. Or I'll hunt you down and finish that assassin's job, okay?"

"Okay," Luke says with a laugh, giving her a tight squeeze with his good arm before letting her go.

"Bye, Harper," I say, my voice seizing up in my throat as I wrap my arms around my best friend. I pull her into me tight, not wanting to let her go, not ready to watch her walk out of my life once again. She puts her hand on the back of my head, pulling me closer to her.

"Thank you for keeping me alive," she whispers in my ear.

"Thank you for keeping *me* alive," I whisper back, holding on to her for one more second.

"Will I see you guys soon?" she asks, wiping a stray tear from her eye as I finally release her.

"Not sure," I answer with a shrug and point toward the door. "I guess we'll find out in there."

"I sure hope so," she says, running her hands down my arm until they lace with my hand. "And next time, let's not meet up because someone is trying to kidnap me, okay?"

"You got it," I answer with a laugh.

"Love you, Reagan," she says, letting go of my hand and taking a few steps down the hallway backward.

"Love you, Harper," I answer, giving her a wave, thankful that this is not good-bye. That I will one day see my beautiful friend again. "See you soon," I can't help but add.

Harper holds up her hand, her sluggish smile rising, turning around before it can reach its peak.

I keep my hand up, waving to the back of Harper's head, my heart suddenly full and maybe even happy.

Harper turns around for one second, just long enough to give me a wink, before reaching the waiting watcher. The two of them turn the corner and disappear.

Good-bye, my friend. Good-bye.

THIRTY

MY BODY IMMEDIATELY ACHES AS I SIT IN MY METAL chair.

Hello, old and sadistic friend, I think, tapping it on both sides, wondering why the Black Angels don't invest in some comfier seating in this room.

The senior leadership team sits two intimidating steps up from us on their little stage. Victoria Browning's seat is now occupied by someone new: my father. He nods at me as Luke gets settled in his matching, uncomfortable metal chair to my left.

"Thanks for joining us today," says the man I dubbed Stony Face during my first time in front of the Tribunal. He runs his large hands along the front of his suit, smoothing it out. "I'm relieved that the two of you are okay. I know you've both been through quite a harrowing last few days."

"Thank you for doing all you could to save us," I answer, hoping he can hear the genuine appreciation in my voice.

"You're welcome," he answers. "You did a lot to save yourself, to be honest. If it wasn't for Browning double-crossing you, I'm pretty sure you would have made it back here alive on your own."

One of the female senior leaders clears her throat and picks up where Stony Face left off.

"We are happy that you are both okay," she says, her hands running along a sheet of paper in front of her. "But while some of us on this council are celebrating your skills and talent, there are still senior leaders, myself included, that cannot ignore the fact that you both went rogue again. You left your safe house in Vermont to save your friend in Manhattan. You did the right thing in rescuing her, but again, you did it without the help or knowledge of the Black Angels."

"I know, ma'am," I answer, nodding my head. "I'm sorry. I just didn't see another way to reach her without tipping off the mole and in turn, tipping off Fernando and his team."

"Well, I think you did the right thing," Stony Face says, his hand over his chest. "Several of us do see why you felt the need to keep us in the dark. I commend you for putting another's life before your own. That is clearly the sign of a Black Angel."

His praise sends my body backward. I glance over at Luke and his eyes are wide, like he was expecting the same scolding I was.

"One of the main reasons we expelled you from Qualifiers after Indonesia was to protect you," he continues. "Not because we didn't think you could do this work. We know you can. And again you exhibited your abilities. All on your own. So, with that in mind . . . we've taken a vote and we'd like to give you both one last chance to prove yourselves in the Qualifiers. It was a very close vote, three to two, but I, for one, would be proud to see you two as full Black Angel agents."

My body tilts back again and it takes me a moment to realize that I've pushed my chair off its two front legs. I immediately pull myself forward, not wanting to answer Stony Face's offer with the sound of my body crashing to the floor.

My mind floods with conflicting emotions. Excitement and dread. Joy and sorrow. Pride and pain. I thought my life in the Black Angels was over. But now, here it is again. The chance to be a part of the most top secret, elite spy agency in the world. The chance to help people, to be a silent hero.

To whom much is given, much is expected.

The unofficial Black Angel mantra comes back to me. It was painted in black on the wall of our martial arts rooms in every home we ever had. Being a Black Angel gives me the power to do so much good. But it took so much away too. My face buzzes, edging toward numbness.

"What happens if we don't want to come back?" I ask quietly and watch four pairs of eyebrows rise around the room. I can tell everyone is surprised that I wouldn't jump at the chance to come back. Everyone but my father. He knows I'll struggle with this invitation.

"Then you can do what you want," my father answers, leaning forward in his chair and resting his hands on a pile of papers in front of him. "We'll keep a watcher on you both for a while just to be sure you're okay. But the threat from the Torres cartel is very weak now. So you can go to college. Move to Europe. Do whatever makes you happy."

Do whatever makes you happy.

I don't think those words have ever been said to me before. Certainly not when it came to my future. Growing up, I wasn't just encouraged to be a Black Angel. I was expected to follow the path my parents had laid out for me before I was even born. And now, here I am again, standing at the fork, completely unsure of which way to turn. Unsure of which path will make me truly happy.

"Why don't we give you both some time to think it over," Stony Face says with a nod, our cue to stand up. Our chairs scrape against the concrete floors, and if my body wasn't so weighed down right now, I'd probably shiver at the sound.

"Yes, try to have an answer to us by this time tomorrow though," my father says, then looks directly at me. "Whatever you choose, we know it will be the right decision."

He holds my gaze for a moment, a small, proud smile curling up his thin lips. It's the first time in my life I feel our relationship shifting. He's looking at me, talking to me, like I'm an adult, capable of making up my own mind. And no matter what I decide, I know he'll stand behind me.

"Thank you, everyone," I say, looking at the Tribunal and then back at my father. "It really means a lot."

With that, I turn on my heel and walk toward the double doors. I push them open and throw my body out into the hallway, my breath suddenly coming into my lungs in shallow gasps.

What do I do? What do I do?

Luke grabs my hand and pulls me down the hallway.

"Come on. Let's go talk," he says, his voice calm and even.

One of the smaller conference rooms is empty, so I follow Luke inside and flip on the light. As he closes the door behind him, I hop on the smooth wood table, my legs dangling, kicking back and forth with nervous energy.

"So," he says, turning back around and resting his right hand on the top of my left thigh. "What do you want to do?"

"Oh my God," I say, rubbing my face in my hands. "It's like you're asking me what I want to have for breakfast. This isn't an eggs or chocolate chip pancakes type of decision. How are we supposed to decide the rest of our lives in twenty-four hours?"

"Well, at least tell me what you're thinking," Luke says, standing back up straight. "What's your gut saying?"

"I don't know," I say, taking in a noisy, full breath. "It's like half of me wants to just run away. Go to college and become a doctor. Live a normal life where I can have a family and go on vacation and grab Starbucks every morning on the way to work."

"You can still do all that as a Black Angel," Luke answers.

"Well, live that life and not have to worry about having a gun pointed in my face."

"Okay. Got it. And the other half?" Luke asks.

"The other half . . ." I begin, a sudden flood of emotion momentarily stealing my voice. I clear my throat and try again. "The other half thinks about all the people who would have died without my mother. Without her being there to save them. When I fought my way into Qualifiers, that's one of the reasons I did it. It wasn't all about killing Santino. It was for all the people that I could save. That I could help. It seems like a waste to just throw all my training away. It's like I'm giving up on those people."

"There will still be Black Angels there to help them, Reagan,"

Luke answers, placing his hand on my rib cage and staring into my eyes. "I said this to you a long time ago. You can't live your life for other people. So what do *you* want to do? What will make *you* happy?"

"Being with you," I answer and Luke can't help but smile. He leans in and kisses me lightly before turning back to me, his face serious again.

"You've got me," he says. "But seriously, Reagan. What will make you happy? You only get one life. What do you want to do with it?"

Ba-bump. Ba-bump. Ba-bump.

My heart beats louder and louder in my ears, my blood racing through my body. I think about it. Its color. The pellets of red blood cells. The way it moves through me, warms me, keeps me alive.

You have Black Angel in your blood.

That was something my mother used to say to me. That I was *born* to do this. Born to be a Black Angel. But the question still remains: Do I really want to be?

———— ◆ ————

Light shines out of Dad's small office. The overhead fluorescent bulbs buzz, filling the silent hallway, as I make my way down to where I know he'll still be working. I pass one of the digital clocks. It reads 9:52. I've been roaming the halls or sitting by myself in empty conference rooms or dark martial arts spaces for hours, trying to process the chance that was given to us today. To rejoin Qualifiers, even with all I've done wrong. And as I make my way toward that light, I can't help but wonder which way my father voted: in or out.

After settling into our seats on the flight out of Colombia, I still had one more obstacle to face, one last apology to make.

"Thank you for saving us," I said quietly to him as the jet's nose tipped into the air, taking us far away from that nightmare. "I know I've done some things you haven't agreed with. And I'm very sorry. So thank you for helping me."

"Reagan," Dad said, turning in his seat and putting his hand on my forearm. "You are my daughter. There's nothing I wouldn't do for you."

"I know, but you were so angry with me during our last call," I said, staring down at the carpeting. "I'm so sorry that I screwed up and went rogue and disappointed you and . . ."

"Stop. I'd go to the ends of the earth to help you," my father said gently, his fingers tightening around my skin. "Even if I thought you were wrong. Which . . . honestly . . . I'm not quite sure you were."

"What? Really?" I say, looking up at him surprised.

"You've disobeyed rules," my father said, nodding his head. "You've broken plenty of Black Angel Directives. But those are all in place to protect you. And I guess that's why I've been so angry. Not because you were wrong. You won't really understand this until you have a child of your own, but all I've ever wanted to do is protect you. So I guess . . . it's been more the fear of losing the last thing I love. I understand why you killed Santino. I'm not saying I agree with you going rogue, but I understand it. Same with Harper. I get why you were too afraid to involve us and why you needed to rescue her on your own."

"You really mean that?"

"Yeah. You're so much like your mother. Maybe even more than you realize. Your heart is always in the right place. So I guess keep following that heart of yours."

And with that, my father took my cheeks into his hands and kissed my forehead. He told me to go to sleep. And so I did.

As I walk closer to his door, I hear a familiar voice. Sam. I smile and take the last few steps down the hall, appearing in front of his open doorway. My father sits behind his desk, a pair of glasses that he never used to need balanced on the tip of his nose. His tie and coat are gone, his shirt unbuttoned at the top and wrinkled. He leans his body toward Sam, who's sitting in a chair next to him, going over a file.

"Hey," she says, seeing me first, a smile parting her lips as she leans back in her seat. "Come on in."

"Are you sure?" I ask, taking a tenuous step backward. "I don't want to interrupt."

"No, it's fine," my father answers, closing the file and waving me in with the beige folder. "We were actually just talking about some of the upcoming testing for Qualifiers. Please. Take a seat."

"Testing, really?" I say, sliding into a metal chair next to Sam. "Want to tell me about it?"

"Well, that depends on whether or not you're staying," Dad says, taking off his glasses and tossing them on his desk.

"You still don't know, right?" Sam says, her voice quiet, her eyes examining me. "I can tell you've been wrestling with it all day."

"How?"

"Your eyes. They give you away when you're anxious."

I hate that I thought for even a single second that she could be the mole. I told her about my suspicions on the plane. At first, she was shocked and a little hurt. But she went through the timeline of the last couple years and said she understood how I could draw that conclusion. She was always near the trauma, but never directly impacted. I still feel slightly nauseous with guilt for ever thinking she could betray my family.

"So, have you made up your mind?" my father asks, pulling my attention back to the major life question at hand.

"Not entirely," I answer, leaning back in my chair and crossing my arms over my sore stomach, the agony of this decision sitting on my internal organs like a block of lead. "They're pretty much opposite choices. And it's not like I can change my mind. If I decide to leave, I'm gone. If I decide to stay, I'm fully committed. I'm a Black Angel for life. It's basically deciding between two totally different lives, two totally different worlds. Each life, there are elements I love. But then there are elements that I guess scare me too."

"It's a really big decision," Sam says, leaning forward in her chair and resting her forearms on her thighs. "I don't envy the position you're in. And I'm not going to try and sway you either way. Honestly, I've wanted both lives for you. We both have."

Sam looks over at my father and he nods.

"We all saw your talent and were desperate for you to be a Black Angel," Sam continues. "But we wanted to protect you from it too. I mean just a few months ago I all but begged you to turn your back on this place and be normal."

"But what part of me has ever been normal?" I answer, looking back and forth between the two people who have loved and guided me my entire life. "You guys said it. Mom said it. I'm just not normal. And part of me wonders if Mom was right. Maybe I wasn't meant to be happy. Maybe I was meant to help change the world."

"I don't think the two things are mutually exclusive," Dad says, staring directly into my eyes. My father has a nervous tic of glancing away mid-conversation. This time, he doesn't. He looks right at me while he speaks. "I think you can be a Black Angel and be both happy and change the world. And I think you can live a more normal life and do both of those things as well."

"They said today the vote was three-to-two," I reply, tilting my head at my father. "Which way did you vote?"

"You know I can't answer that, sweetie," he responds, but from the smile on his face, I know which way he cast. He voted me in. "I want you to choose for yourself. Not what I want for you. Not what your mother would have wanted or Sam wants or Luke wants. What *you* want. I've tried to push you down too many paths. This one you've got to decide on your own."

"Listen to your heart, Reagan," Sam adds, resting her hand on my arm. "What does it say?"

Ba-bump. Ba-bump. Ba-bump.

My heart beats loudly in my ears, my blood filling every part of me. I take a breath. I let it flow. And I listen.

EPILOGUE

THE NIGHT IS BLACK; THE MOON AND TINY PINPRICKS of stars are hidden by a blanket of clouds. The type of dark where you can barely see your hand in front of your face. I stare out the car window into nothingness.

I feel Luke's hand moving across the leather seat. Without even seeing it, I open my palm, welcoming his hand into mine. His fingers dance along my skin, sparking a wave of goose bumps, until our palms kiss and my body feels that rush of warmth, that feeling of home.

With all the places I've moved in my life, I longed for the feeling of home. It took my mother dying for me to realize that home never really was a place. Home was people. Home was once my mom. But now, home is this. Home is Luke's hand in mine.

He squeezes my hand three times. And I squeeze three times back. The darkness hides my slowly rising smile.

When I was seven years old, I asked my mother how she knew she wanted to marry my father. I remember the moment so well. I was watching a show on the Disney channel. She was folding laundry next to me. And I remember every word she said.

"I knew your father was 'the one' on our second date," she said, her voice almost dreamy at the memory as she folded his thinning white cotton undershirts into perfect squares. "We went to the movies together and I remember he grabbed my hand during the previews and didn't let go. I couldn't pay attention to the movie because I was so distracted by how perfectly our hands fit together. It was like our hands were two puzzle pieces, designed by God to fit only each other's. And that's when I knew."

Since that moment, I've been on the search for my puzzle piece, for my perfect hand. And every time I hold Luke's, I'm distracted by how perfect it feels. And I know I've found it. My hand. My person.

"Team two, you are three hundred yards from the target," a voice crackles, and I push my earpiece deeper into my ear canal to hear the commands. "Let's go the rest of the way on foot."

"Copy," I hear the driver and mission leader respond, slowing our SUV down and putting it into park.

"You ready?" Luke asks, reaching up with his free hand and double-checking the strap on his helmet.

I let go of Luke's hand and clutch the M4 carbine on my lap.

"I'm ready," I answer with a nod, my heart picking up speed. Adrenaline floods my bloodstream as I grab my gun, open the car door, and jump back into the darkness.

ACKNOWLEDGMENTS

To Jean Feiwel, Kat Brzozowski, Lauren Scobell, Kelsey Marrujo, Ashley Woodfolk, Brittany Pearlman, Emily Settle, Holly West, Rich Deas, Starr Baer, Raymond Colon, and the entire rock-star team at Macmillan: Working with all of you has been a dream. Thank you for changing my life. I will always be grateful.

To Merrilee Heifetz: Not quite sure what I'd do without you. Thank you for your boundless encouragement and valuable guidance. I am the luckiest author.

To the amazing authors I'm lucky to call friends: I'm so grateful for each and every one of you. Thank you for being a source of constant support. To Kayla Olson and Nadine Courtney: I wouldn't make it through a book without my accountability partners! Thank you for helping me march toward deadlines.

To Jen Meredith, Christopher Barcelona, Mila Goodman, Katie Logan, Rhonda Litton, Kate Watson, Tayce Hutta, and Kelsey Chapekis: Thank you so much for your valuable insights while writing this book. I'm so lucky to have access to all your brilliant brains.

To my friends: I'm so fortunate to have so many supportive people in my life. Whether you were at signings, helping me patch plot holes, or cheering me on, your love means the world to me.

To my readers: The fact that I get to write stories you want to read is a dream come true. I'm so grateful for each of you. Thank you, thank you, thank you!

To booksellers, librarians, and book bloggers: Thank you for putting my book into the hands of readers. I'm so thankful for your support.

To everyone at Muirfield: Thank you for keeping me caffeinated, hydrated, and well-fed while I wrote this book. I'm so appreciative!

To Mom: My biggest cheerleader by far. I feel your love and pride in all that I do. Thank you for shaping me into the person I am today.

To Dad: Thank you for reading every school paper, short story, and manuscript. And thank you for giving me the confidence to dream this big and see it through.

To Katie: My forever friend. Thanks for picking me up, cheering me on, and telling me the truth when I need it.

To Samantha: You are the sweetest thing and the light of my life. I am so in love with you and adore being your mom.

To Michael: I couldn't do any of this without you. Thank you for your endless encouragement and limitless love. You've given me the world and I'm so grateful. I love you so.

Check out more books
chosen for publication
by readers like you.

DID YOU KNOW...

readers like you helped to get this book published?

Join our book-obsessed community and help us discover awesome new writing talent.

1

Write it.

Share your original YA manuscript.

2

Read it.

Discover bright new bookish talent.

3

Share it.

Discuss, rate, and share your faves.

4

Love it.

Help us publish the books you love.

Share your own manuscript or dive between the pages at **swoonreads.com** or by downloading the **Swoon Reads app.**